RUNAWAY: AN ESCAPE NOVEL

CASEY COX

ISBN: 978-0-6451403-3-0

This book is a work of fiction. It has to be, otherwise the world really has gone mad. Any references to real people, organizations, media sites, types of alcohol, actors and locations are completely fictitious. Characters, names, plot points and dialogue are figments of the author's imagination.

SYNOPSIS

Ever woken up and realized your life is one big cliché?

Waking up married in Vegas? Been there, done that... Twice.
Base-jumping off Mount Fuji in Japan? That's, like, a chill
weekend.
Partying in France with supermodels? Meh, très overrated.

Despite being born into the most powerful family in the highly
prestigious cowbell industry (yeah, you read that right)—I'm feeling
more than just a little lost. So, partying and living it up has become
my default avoidance coping mechanism.

Until I spot him one night on vacation staring out into the dark
ocean, looking all sorts of Cali-cute.

When he speaks, he catches my interest.
When he serves me back my own sassiness with an added helping
of nerdy smarts, he burrows into my brain.

And when he peers up at me through sun-kissed lashes with those glittery eyes and smiles?
Damn, he captures my heart like no one ever has.

But how do you keep the one you want to be with forever from slipping through your fingers?

RUNAWAY is a woke-up-married, fake relationship (after insta-love) rom-com style MM romance. It features a loveable bad boy getting up to no good (for all the right reasons) who meets a boy with a bucket list.

You can expect plenty of gasps, giggles, and OMG moments including Fermi pickup lines, terrible...y good karaoke, cowbells, mystery midnight walks, a life-changing ATM glitch, one outrageous grandmother who intends to take full advantage of an all-male clothing optional resort, small townspeople that will melt your heart with their kindness, and a happily ever after that will make you feel like you've just returned from the best vacation ever. (Piña coladas and other creatively named cocktails not included.)

RUNAWAY is part of the super sweet, light and fluffy *ESCAPE* series. There are no cliffhangers (ew) and no cheating either (double ew). You can read the books in whatever order your heart desires!

PROLOGUE - JEDFIRE

12 MONTHS EARLIER...

Cricccck ka-duuuum!

Thunder rumbled loudly as lightning blistered across the night sky, the unexpected late summer downpour setting in. I tugged at the collar of my denim jacket, yanking the faux-fur-trimmed hood over my head.

Great, I'd show up dripping wet for a late-night hookup. Which, now that I thought about it, mightn't have been such a big deal, after all. It could actually help to considerably speed up the whole *clothes coming off* part of the initial proceedings. Because, yeah, speed and wanting to get things over with were always good omens for an impending fuck.

I sighed. Still, I could've thought of better things to be doing than getting drenched in a freak storm on a Saturday night. I glanced down at my watch. Only just still Saturday night. Almost Sunday, technically.

I cursed to myself as a drop of rain penetrated through my

hooded fortress, trickling its way down my neck. It slid down my back, its presence a slow, teasing, and prickly wet reminder that my life was on the wrong track. In so many ways.

Because of course the last thing my dumbass brain had considered doing was to look out the damn window before jumping into my truck. Had I done that, I might have noticed the clouds brewing over the horizon of the family ranch and, I don't know, maybe grabbed an umbrella to take with me.

Heck, if I'd been thinking with the head between my shoulders, I'd have seen 'em rolling in on the twenty-minute drive into town. In my defense, Southern California didn't get a lot of rain, so it wasn't like being on rain-alert was a common occurrence 'round here. On average, Cowbell Creek enjoyed sunshine three hundred days of the year. But still, you had to be in a special kind of way to have totally missed a slow rolling thunderstorm moving in.

So yeah, typical me at the moment. Blindsided and in a *very special kind of way.*

It wasn't until I'd parked my shadow-gray metallic Chevy Silverado outside of Mrs. Clover's Bread & Butter bakery on Main Street and heard the first crack of thunder that my senses were stirred by something other than the need pulling in my belly. A need fueling my senses. A desire dragging me out of my warm bed, longing to be fulfilled.

I tapped my fingers on the steering wheel as the first heavy drops began to land on the windshield. Not that tonight would go any way toward filling that emptiness or penetrating through that rim of searing pain that had encased my heart for the last five years. Ever since...

Nope. *Sooo* not going there. Not only because it was a boner killer—with a capital, bold and italicized ***BK***—but also because it was depressing as fuck.

Tonight was going to go like it had gone the previous handful of times Hayden and I had hooked up. Hayden was the pretty, blond bartender at one of Cowbell Creek's bars, of which there were two in total. For a town where the bovine population outnumbered human folk by a ten to one ratio, Cowbell Creek was surprisingly progressive.

Not that The Tipsy Cow was a gay bar. But it didn't need to be. Folks around here were cool like that. Surprising? Maybe. I'd give it maybe a five out of ten on the *bet-ya-didn't-see-that-one-coming* meter.

The fact that almost everyone in town could rap along to every Missy Elliot song ever, including sixty-eight-year-old bakery owner Mrs. Clover. Now, *that* was a ten out of ten surprise-bomb.

Cowbell Creek was a quintessential rural American town where everyone knew everyone else. And they all knew me—and my family. I was a seventh-generation Burns and enjoyed all the privileges, as well as the burdens, that the family name brought with it. Especially since my family owned the largest business in town, and I was the co-firstborn heir to said family business.

I shook my head, trying to snap myself out of my pre-fuck funk. This was why I avoided spending too much time back here. Thoughts of family business empires and the reason why I was in line to take it over in just over a year were inescapable. Insufferable.

Instead, I put as much space as I could between me and Cowbell Creek. Since I turned nineteen—well, eight days after to be precise, which was the day when my life was rocked by a tragedy that changed my trajectory forever—I'd been running.

I'd seen the world twice over. Yep, I'd bungee-jumped, skydived, mountain biked, hang-glided, heli-skied my way around the globe. I'd partied with supermodels during Paris Fashion Week, base-jumped off Mount Fuji in Japan, swum with dolphins on the east coast of Australia, and pretty much every other typical bucket list adventure item you could think of.

Because life was short, and you *gotta live every day as if it's your last*, right? Or something like that. I used to be able to convince myself that was why I was doing it, acting out in the ways I had been since eight days after I turned nineteen.

But lately, I hadn't been so good at being able to convince myself of that anymore. And you know you're in a special kind of way when you stop believing your own bullshit.

Which brought me neatly back to Main Street, Cowbell Creek, walking toward the ATM, my eyelids fluttering against the large raindrops that were drenching my face. I could barely see more than a few feet in front of me. I didn't need the cash right now, but since I was driving through town, I figured why not get it?

It was only as I ducked under the bank's awning that I noticed a figure standing at the ATM. "Mrs. McClusky, are you all right?"

I would have recognized her teetering frame, neatly tied back gray hair and signature white cardigan anywhere. She was my grandma's best friend. I'd known her my whole life.

I stepped up next to her. She was hunched over the keypad intently, her tongue slipping out the top corner of her mouth. I gently placed my hand on her shoulder, not wanting to startle the poor thing.

"Everything okay, Mrs. McClusky?"

She peered up at me, the furrow in her brow easing. "Oh, Jed, thank goodness you're here." She glanced back down at the machine. "I can't see these darn buttons. It's too dark for me. I think I'm pressing in the wrong pin number. Can you help me, dear?"

I reached for my cell phone in my back pocket. "Let me shine a light for you, Mrs. McClusky. It'll help you see better."

She waved my phone-holding hand away before I could find the flashlight app. "My pin number is 1933."

"Oh, Mrs. McClusky. You really shouldn't be telling people your—"

"It's the year I was born."

Her kind blue eyes met mine. I placed my hand over her soft fingers as she stepped to the side, giving me better access to the machine. "All right, I'll do this for you this one time, Mrs. McClusky. But you have to change your pin number, okay? It's not a good idea to let other people know what it is."

She gave a nod, but I had the feeling my words were falling on deaf ears. Not literally. Her hearing was fine. It's just that Mrs. McClusky didn't have a distrusting or dishonest bone in her body, and by her way of thinking, neither did anyone else in the world. Which meant like so many folk around here, she was a goodhearted, trusting person.

After typing in her pin number and withdrawing the amount she had asked for, I handed over the cash and her card. Before I could repeat my previous request for her to change her pin number, she spoke. "Thank you for your help, Jed."

"No problem, Mrs. McClusky."

She patted me on the back, opened her umbrella, and began to walk away. I turned back toward the machine. All right, let's do this. Despite the distractions of the rain and running into Mrs. McClusky, I still had a horny itch I needed to scratch.

I couldn't remember how much money I had left in my savings account. Grandpa had been tightening the reins lately, but I wanted to see if my monthly allowance had landed.

Yep, *allowance.*

I was a twenty-four-year-old who still had an allowance. And fuck if that wasn't fifty shades of depressing. Thunder vibrated loudly, and it sounded like the storm was getting closer. Rain continued pummeling down, hitting the sidewalk hard.

Hmm, that's weird. The display read, *Balance Unavailable.*

I shrugged, took the card out, and placed another one back in. My platinum credit card. I'd check my balance on that instead.

Ba-bowm. No luck there, either. The same message popped up on the screen again. It looked like there might have been some sort of glitch in the bank's system. I had an idea. I'd try transferring money between the accounts to see if that worked.

Just as I had finished entering my pin number for the third time, the sound of a semi blaring its horn rang out. With my finger still pressed on the keypad, I twisted around as a bolt of lightning ignited the night sky. Through the rain, I spotted Mrs. McClusky on the road...and in the direct path of the semi!

"Mrs. McClusky!" I yelled at the top of my lungs as I leaped out toward her. I raced out onto the road, pulling her to safety in my arms as the truck swerved, its blaring horn gradually fading into the background. I held onto her, my grip tight, until we were both back under the safety of the awning.

"Are you okay, Mrs. McClusky?"

"I'm fine, dear."

I eyed her up and down. She seemed fine. In fact, she hardly seemed rattled for someone who had almost met her fate.

"I was trying to find my car keys in my purse when I stopped in the middle of the road. I shouldn't have done that."

I breathed out a sigh of relief. "You have to be careful, Mrs. McClusky. You could have gotten—" Nope. I can't even say the word. "I'm going to walk you back to your car."

Before she could protest like I knew she would, I threaded my arm through hers, grabbed her umbrella (making sure it covered her entirely, I was fine to get a little wet), checked both ways for oncoming traffic, and led her back to her 1978 fern green Jaguar XJ Coupe.

Before getting in, she cupped my face between her soft fingers. "Thank you, Jed. You're good boys, all three of you. You're honest, hardworking—"

She paused, her eyes searching. Her love of triple alliteration was well known around here. I had a *H* word I could suggest —*horny as fuck*. But no, of course I wouldn't actually say that.

A tender smile glowed across her face. "Humble."

"Well, you're welcome, Mrs. McClusky." I handed her umbrella back. "Just please be careful and promise me you'll change your pin number." Hey, it was worth a shot.

She hooked a finger under my chin and smiled warmly. "Your parents would have been so proud of you, Jed."

She gave my arm a light squeeze, closed the umbrella, got into her car, and drove off.

And there it was. Not just in my thoughts, but in the people, too. Everywhere I went in Cowbell Creek, the memory of my parents and what had happened to them was constantly on the cusp of everyone else's thoughts, too, making their way into innocuous conversations in the most unexpected ways. It was enough to leave a guy more than a little on edge.

I checked both sides of the road and made my way back to the ATM. By this point, I was drenched to the bone. I saw the screen still flashing an error message. With a shrug, I withdrew my card and flicked it back into my wallet. No big deal. I'd deal with my financial situation later.

Little did I realize that what had just happened would change my life forever, leading me down a path so crazy, so outlandish, that if it were turned into a movie, people would think it was a made-up, fucked-up, twisted-to-the-core modern fairytale. A story too wild to ever be true.

But for now, I didn't care about any of that.

I had an itch I needed to scratch.

THURSDAY

Present Day

1

JEDFIRE

I rolled onto my front and immediately felt a familiar pain flooding my gut. Grumbling, I settled into a comfortable position on my left side, clutching onto the pillow like it wasn't a rectangular piece of cloth stuffed with feathers but a nice, warm body instead. I patted it down a few times, nestling it against my chest, the lower edge of it grazing my aching hard cock, otherwise known as the thing that caused me to wake up every day.

Morning wood.

Painful to lie on morning wood, to be precise. My very own internal alarm clock. Trying to lie front-first always woke me up since, well, it's kinda hard to lie down with a massive erection jutting out of your body.

Yep, even at almost twenty-five, it was an affliction that I grappled with on a daily basis. Sure, as far as afflictions went, it was a pretty good one to get. It always *came* with a *happy ending* (double double-entendre intended), but it also served as a bitter reminder of the loneliness in my life. I mean, jerking off in the shower by yourself first thing every morning didn't exactly scream *living your best life*, did it now?

My size fifteen feet, squished on top of one another, dangled off the side of the bed. *Wait.* Why the hell was I in a queen-sized bed, anyway? At six foot six, I always ensured hotel rooms I stayed in were equipped with a king. Ideally, a California king.

Which led neatly to—*whose* queen-sized bed was I in?

Shit.

Curiosity overrode my reluctance to get up. I cracked one eye open. The room was dark with a ray of light streaming in through a skinny gap in the curtains. A chair in the corner of the room was covered in clothes. Possibly mine. Possibly not all mine.

I flipped onto my back as my other eye fluttered open. I scrubbed my face with my hand. At least I wasn't too hungover; that was a good thing. Don't get me wrong. I'd probably downed a good farmer's dozen shots last night. I would have gone Jed-level overboard as was par for the course for me, just not *extra-extra* overboard.

I peered down the length of my body, palming my cock out of the way, holding it against my thigh, to get a better view of the hotel room. Except for... Wait... This didn't look like a hotel room. It looked more like someone's actual bedroom in someone's actual apartment.

And I'd be damned if I knew who that someone was.

Okay, *that* jolted me upright. Fuck, I hoped I was still in Vegas. I had a bad habit of waking up in new countries without the faintest recollection of how I'd gotten there. I strode over to the window and peeled the curtains apart.

After recovering from the initial *being blindsided by the annoyingly bright morning sun* moment, I was met with a view of the tops of hotels that lined the strip, as well as the rounded edge of the Linq Ferris wheel that looked like it was a few blocks from wherever I was. I drew the curtains back and gave a relieved nod. Okay, still in Vegas. That was a good thing.

I roamed around the room, my erect cock guiding me like those people you see at the beach, metal detector in hand, eyes zoomed in on the ground in front of them. I was a man on a mission, on the hunt for clues, to give me some idea of where I was...and what I had done the night before.

The room was on the small-ish side, decked out in heavy-handed shades of navy blue and brown. The pile of clothes on the chair was mainly mine. The pair of designer jeans and even more designer-y underwear on the floor next to it wasn't.

There wasn't a whole lot more to the stuffy bedroom. A mirrored wardrobe lined the length of one wall, and an open door led to a bathroom. I could see part of the shower from where I was standing.

I walked up to the full-length mirror, figuring a shot of reality would do the job until I could get a cup of joe into my hands. Like most people, I hated looking at myself, hated being confronted by my appearance, which was far from conventional.

I was a giant tower of messy, tangled hair, big ears that flopped around the side of my face, a long prominent nose, and a wide but crooked smile. But I worked with it, combining post-hipster chic with a larger-than-life attitude to distract people away from the weirdness of my appearance with...well, more weirdness. Somehow, it worked a treat. Oh, that, and buying copious amounts of alcohol for everyone. That never failed, either.

Besides, I had a killer lean body and a cock that brought all the boys to the yard, so it wasn't all bad.

Speaking of which, my cock finally got the hint and thankfully began its retreat to semi-chub territory. It still flapped around, slapping itself against my legs as I walked to remind me not so subtly of its presence, but it had gotten the hint. I was firmly in *no action, get the fuck outta here* mode.

I grabbed my clothes off the chair and began getting dressed. As I buttoned up my Italian-made short-sleeved, tiger print shirt, something shiny reflected off the tiny sliver of sunlight poking its way into the room. My eyes dropped, and that's when I spotted it: a thin line of gold on my second from the left finger on my left hand.

I lifted my hand in front of my face, my eyes scanning the band. I lowered my hand, covering it over my heart as I mourned the official death of my morning wood. And in most likelihood, my official legal status of non-married. Getting wasted and married in Vegas was so beyond cliché, even my own cock had now completely given up on me in disgust. Maybe I'd inadvertently stumbled upon a solution for my morning wood affliction?

I finished getting dressed, picking up my wallet and phone from the nightstand as I whistled out an uncomfortable breath. I'd have to call Tommy, our family's lawyer and my own go-to person for getting me out of prickly and messy situations such as this one.

He'd gotten me out of trouble in London when I was photographed stumbling out of a ritzy gentleman's club with a well-known member of the royal family. I wouldn't mention any names, of course, but let's just say there's a reason why the cheeky ginger decided to settle in California.

Helped me out when I accidentally stomped over a hobbit's house on a set tour of *The Lord of the Rings* in New Zealand (seriously, though, those things were tiny; I was just taking a shortcut, but apparently, it's a serious crime in NZ).

Deftly handled my *accidentally ended up on a cruise ship and I need to get off right now* situation.

And in just a few minutes, he'd be getting me out of this marriage to—

Speaking of...where was the other lucky groom?

I opened the door and walked down the narrow hallway guardedly. "Hello. Is—is anyone here?"

I stepped out into an eerily silent and empty open-plan kitchen and living room. I sat down on the sofa while I put my socks and black combat boots on.

I stood up and looked around, drawn to a wall of what looked to be family photos. Two smiling parents and three equally beaming children, at various ages from super-young kids right through to awkward teen years.

I noticed a framed photo of a group of five guys wearing beanies and sunglasses, smiling cheesily and posing in front of a giant Banff sign. Maybe one of them was my new husband?

Over on the bookshelf, I spied an old-school vintage brass antique armillary globe. It reminded me of the one Grandpa had given my adopted brother, Mitchell, for his thirteenth birthday. I tested it to see whether it actually did spin. Some of them didn't, they were purely for display only. This one did, which was a good thing.

Some people used the internet to plan their travels. All I needed was *this*.

I closed my eyes and gave it a twirl. After a few seconds, I pressed my finger against it. Opening my eyes, I groaned, not liking where it had landed. But, I knew the deal. No ifs, buts, or maybes. The finger had spoken, and for whatever fucking reason, fate had decided to send me off to Florida.

I double-checked to make sure I had my phone and wallet before leaving. In the elevator on the way down, I texted my driver to pick me up from...okay, I'd have to send him the GPS coordinates because I had no idea of the address.

A few minutes later, Jevon's car pulled up. I stepped out of the lobby and into the cool air-conditioned air of the hybrid.

"Thanks." I buckled up my seatbelt in the backseat as he sped off.

"No worries. It's what I'm here for. So, where to, Mr. Burns?"

"The airport. But first, can we make a pit stop?"

Jevon's eyes glanced up at me in the rearview mirror. "Sure. Where to?"

I drummed my fingers against my thigh. "Do you know of any charities in the area? Maybe, like, an LGBTQIA+ charity for homeless teens or something like that."

Jevon made a funny sound as he sucked air into his mouth, thinking about my question. "From memory, there's a place out on

Maryland Parkway. I saw their booth at Pride last year, but I can't remember what they do."

"That sounds perfect. Let's go there."

"Sure thing, boss."

As Jevon made a right turn, I glanced into my wallet. Dammit, no receipt. I mustn't have made it to an ATM last night. I grimaced, annoyed at myself that I'd missed it. I only had one sixty-second window every day at exactly 11:59pm to do it. I couldn't miss it. If I did, it wouldn't work, and I'd have to wait until the next day at exactly 11:59pm.

Believe me, I'd tried. It took me about three months after that night with Mrs. McClusky at the ATM to figure it all out. The timings, the amounts, the sequence. It only ever worked when everything lined up perfectly.

And even though I knew it was a million types of wrong, it was also the only thing that gave my otherwise empty, meaningless life any point. I had finally found a purpose, despite all the moral ambiguities it churned up.

The internal battle it produced allowed me to focus on something other than the thing I had been running away from, so that was good. Replacing one kind of heartbreaking loss and grief with the raging of an internal ethical war. Seemed about right.

Jevon pulled into a parking lot as pride flags reflected in the car's windows. "This is it," he announced over his shoulder.

"I'll be right back."

"Sure thing, Jed. You're, uh, not gonna rob the place, are ya?" His lips were suppressing a smile.

"No. Quite the opposite, in fact."

I got out of the car, and as I walked toward the entrance, my heartbeat ticked up a few notches. And no, not in a bad way. In the best possible way. In that exhilarating, *this is what I want to be doing for the rest of my life* way.

Fifteen minutes later, it was all done, and I was back in the car.

"Can you take me to Henderson, please? I don't have tickets, so I'll need to charter a private plane."

Jevon's eyes widened slightly and he cleared his throat. "Of course."

As Jevon took the exit for Henderson Executive Airport, I fished out my cell phone and called Tommy.

He answered on the first ring, like he always did. "What have you done now, Jedfire?"

"Tommy." I laughed nervously, running my fingers through my still-uncombed hair, his use of my full first name making the skin on my neck all itchy. "What makes you think I've done anything?"

Silence. A *long* silence.

"Fine. I do have a *slight* dill of a pickle situation on my hands." I pressed the phone against my ear as I slid the wedding ring—the stubbornly tight wedding ring—off my damn finger.

"Ahh, that's better."

"What's better?" His voice crackled with suspicion. A well-deserved tone, if I was being honest.

"Um, nothing." I wriggled the ring into that mini pocket that all jeans seemed to have at the top of the front pocket. Until now, I didn't know why they even bothered to make that pocket. Now I knew. It was designed for people escaping Vegas after a night of too much partying, desperately trying to forget about a wedding they could barely remember being a party to, much less the main attraction of.

"I'm in Vegas." I turned to face the window. "And I, uh, kinda got married last night."

"What?" He let out what I'd come to refer to as his signature sigh-slash-groan combo. "You mean...again?"

I blew out a noisy breath. "Well, uh, yeah. Again."

"Fine." I heard some rustling down the line, like Tommy was flicking open a new page on his *Times I've Had to Get Jedfire Out of Mega Shit* notepad. Third edition.

"Where did the ceremony take place?"

I scratched the back of my neck. "Uh, I can't remember."

"Okay. What's his name?"

"Hmm. I don't actually know that, either."

"*Fiiine.*" The tightness in Tommy's voice sounded anything but fine. "Do you know where he lives, at least?"

"I can send you the GPS coordinates of his apartment building?"

"Sure. It's a start, at least. When are you back in Cowbell Creek?"

"Uh...next week?"

"Are you asking me or telling me?"

"Well, at this stage," I said as Jevon drove through the airport gates, "I'm off to Florida for...I don't know...maybe a week. I can be back after that?"

"Fine. I'll be in touch in a few days with an update. Oh, and Jed, please try and stay out of trouble in Florida. The only reason you managed to escape getting in trouble there last time is because your grandpa is good friends with the governor."

I rolled my eyes. "Don't worry about me, Tommy. I'll be fine. I'm going to stay at the resort Mitchell stayed at when he visited last year. I'll just be lounging by the pool, chatting to hot guys, and sipping cock...tails. That is it."

"Practically a choirboy, then," I heard Tommy mutter under his breath.

I chuckled. "You won't hear a peep out of me, Tommy. I'll be good. I promise."

But like my grandma always said, you shouldn't make promises you won't be able to keep.

FRIDAY

2

CONRAD

It all started six months ago.

I gripped the white railing as I stared out into the black ocean, trying to stop my mind from replaying the events from exactly half a year ago to the day. The lights from the bar behind me lit up the water enough for me to see the foamy waves as they crashed on the shore. The sound of it, unfortunately, drowned out by the godawful karaoke taking place inside the bar.

I closed my eyes, jutting my nose into the salty night air. This was it. The last stop on my whirlwind five month around-the-world adventure. And what a fancy stop it was.

Elysian consistently made the top ten lists of most exclusive resorts in the world, and little wonder. I'd only arrived that afternoon, but the breathtaking location overlooking the Gulf of Mexico, not to mention the attentive, friendly staff made me feel like I was a movie star or something. A far cry from the youth hostel dorms I'd been trudging around in. Not that I minded. I still couldn't believe I'd gotten the chance to see the world before...

My eyes shot open. No. This was my last chance to not have to deal with *that*. It'd be waiting for me when I got home. I'd let the walls of my mental dam break then. For now, I wanted to enjoy the next five days as much as I could. I had no concrete plans, but spending time lying by the pool and going for long walks on the beach sounded like my idea of heaven. Okay, bad word choice.

In addition to being a tropical, luxurious hideaway, Elysian just so happened to be one of the most famous LGBTQIA+ resorts in the world. It was known for its inclusivity as much as it was for its stunning views and Michelin-star restaurant.

I'd never be able to afford it on my own. Heck, I wouldn't have been able to even leave San Clemente if it wasn't for my father raiding his 401K dry and taking on two extra jobs (as a Lyft driver and a night cleaner at the local college) in order for me to have this experience. Well, the giveaway he'd entered me into won me a stay here, but he'd paid for pretty much everything else.

I still remembered him waving me off at the airport. As he pulled me into his solid frame, he whispered into my ear, "Enjoy it, son. This is for all the times you gave up your life for me."

He wouldn't let me argue with him, but it wasn't true. Yes, I'd helped him deal with the PTSD he experienced when he got back from his second tour in Afghanistan, and I'd been there for him to pick up the pieces when Mom had left him for another man, and I'd foregone college to get him through his third—and so far, successful—attempt at sobriety.

But we were family. And that's what families did. They helped each other through thick and thin. And boy, had Dad and I been through some thin times. And now, it seemed, it was my turn.

I shook my head, determined to banish all negative thoughts out of there. *Good vibes only.* That was gonna be my mantra. At least, for the next five days.

"Conrad? Conrad McCallister?"

I turned around and found myself face to face with a man smiling warmly at me, his sparkling white teeth catching in the light. "I'm Leo Carter. I'm the owner of Elysian." His timbre was smooth and deep.

"Oh, pleased to meet you, Leo."

We shook hands. He was an older guy, maybe in his early forties. He had an all-American look with big eyes and a strong jaw. "I'm sorry I didn't get to meet you when you arrived."

"Oh, that's fine." I swiped my hand in the air while wondering if all owners of fancy resorts greeted their guests. Maybe that was a thing? This whole world of luxury travel was totally foreign to me. At a youth hostel, you'd be lucky if reception staff bothered to look up and make eye contact and you didn't end up catching bed bugs during your stay.

"Do you mind if I join you for a moment?"

"No, of course not," I replied. "I was actually going to ask to see you tomorrow."

"You were?"

"Yeah. I wanted to"—I dropped my head lower, suddenly feeling overcome with emotion—"I wanted to thank you, Leo. I could never afford to stay here, and because of your generosity, I can."

I felt his firm hand patting me across the shoulder. "You're more than welcome. I was incredibly moved by your story, Conrad."

Our eyes met. I tried to match his smile, but couldn't. I sensed a pity party coming on, and boy, that was the last thing I wanted.

"I'm just going to say this once because I get the feeling you're not the kind of guy who likes for others to feel sorry for him."

I blushed. "Sorry. Was I that obvious?"

"Don't worry"—he leaned into me and gave a friendly smile—"I'm the same. Excuse my French, but I fucking hate pity with everything I have in me."

I kicked my head back and laughed. I could tell Leo was a good guy. He reminded me of my dad in a lot of ways.

"So, I'm just going to say this once, Conrad. You're a very special person. I'm thrilled you won the giveaway, even if it was due to less-than-ideal circumstances. And please know that my staff and I are here to cater to your every whim this weekend."

I shook my head, hoping to brush away some of the emotion bubbling its way up my throat. "Thank you, Leo. That's incredibly kind of you."

That was the understatement of the year. The guy had not only gifted me an all-expenses-paid stay in an amazing suite with sweeping ocean views, but now, he was extending even more generosity my way. It was all way too much. I really didn't deserve it.

"My only whims are to take it easy and relax over the next five days."

"Well, if there is anything we can do, just holler."

"Thanks, Leo. I will."

A loud whooping sound rose up from the bar, like someone had just announced a free round of shots. Leo and I turned around at the same time.

"You should come in." He tipped his head in the direction of the bar. "It's Friday night, so we're having a meet and greet."

"Oh, what's that?"

"It's a chance to socialize, a way for the guests staying here for the weekend to get to know each other, with a little karaoke thrown in for fun. Totally casual," he added as if sensing my hesitation.

"I—I might come in a bit later."

I wasn't shy and had no problem meeting people. I just needed some time to myself, to clear my head a bit.

"No problem. Come in whenever you like, or stay out here and take in this amazing view." A kind smile graced his lips. "I'm sure I'll see you around, Conrad. Have a great stay and welcome to Elysian."

I watched as Leo headed inside until he disappeared into the heaving crowd, before I turned around to face the waves again.

I tapped my fingers against the cold railing, breathing in the salt-spritzed air. This was just what I needed. A few quiet days where nothing exciting or crazy would happen. Some time alone, gathering my thoughts, preparing myself for what was to come, while enjoying what I had.

I gripped the railing tighter, allowing my body to fall back. I lifted my head to the starry sky as I let out a deep sigh...

I wouldn't have it for long.

3

JEDFIRE

"Woot woot," someone in the crowd near the front of the packed bar yelled out.

"Thanks, man," another voice sang out.

"It's all good, my party people," I yelled back over the boozy cheers and someone's mauling of the Spice Girls' *Wannabe* (seriously, some songs should be declared musical-non-grata and *this* should have been one of them).

"You get a sloppy hole, and you get a sloppy hole..." I lifted the naughtily named alcoholic shots off the bar and began doling them out to the crowd, sounding like an X-rated Oprah in the process. About a dozen bodies had gathered around me like drunken moths to a flame.

Once all the drinks had found a set of hands, I raised my shot to the ceiling. "To the most epicest fucking weekend ever!" I bellowed.

Woo-hoo!

Shouts of happiness rang out in the air as we collectively threw back our drinks. The raspberry flavor tempered the throat burn of the vodka, but damn, that was one strong fatherfucking shot.

I spun my head around and shook my shoulders to loosen them. Okay, I was getting my buzz on. Vegas was still feeling like a nightmare, but one that was fading further and further into the background with each passing day. So far, the *each passing day* count numbered just one. But that was a good enough start for me.

I had arrived at Elysian late last night. My younger brother Mitchell had won a stay here a few months back courtesy of his super considerate older brother—*that would be me*—entering him into a radio contest.

Cowbell Creek's local station, KRLX92, was running a giveaway called *Happily Ever After*, where callers had to dial in and share their worst dating story. The prize was an all-expenses-paid weekend right here at Elysian.

Long story short, I called in on Mitch's behalf and won him the prize. The bonus was Mitchell actually finding his forever guy during his stay. I couldn't have predicted that, but I was so happy for both of them. Mitch was still floating on air eight months later, and Cayman was a good guy, one of the few who was actually worthy of my brother.

I twisted around, taking in the packed bar. That was one of the best things about being six foot six—unobstructed views.

Mitchell might have found his happily ever after here, but lightning didn't strike twice. And frankly, I didn't want it to, either. Both Mitchell and my other younger brother, Cooper, knew my well-worn mantra off by heart.

No strings. No repeats. No feelings.

Yep, I was the epitome of carefree, casual fun, and boy, was I up for it tonight. I kept scanning the scene, but nothing—or rather, *no one*—caught my eye.

My cock had been on high alert all day. Oh, did I mention that Elysian was a clothing optional resort? Meaning that a day spent sipping margaritas by the pool ensured I saw more dick than if I had a Premium Pornhub subscription.

So, yeah, I was pumped and primed.

And right at that moment, as my head craned slightly to the right looking over the tops of a sea of heads and baseball caps, my eyes landed on him. My pulse kicked up a notch.

Target acquired.

He was standing outside on the balcony, away from all the noise and chaos that swirled around me—that was in large part *because* of me and my offer to shout my newly acquired crew round after round of beverages—staring out into the dark ocean.

His hair and profile shimmered in the moonglow, giving him an ethereal, out-of-this-world feel. My feet started moving on their own, taking me past a blur of faces, bodies, eyes, and hands as I made my way closer to him.

He spun around just as I reached the terrace doors, and fuck, he looked all sorts of Cali-cute. He had the whole surfer look down pat, all blond hair and blue eyes, but there was something else about him, too. Something intoxicatingly innocent about his appearance that kept pulling me into his sphere.

I felt my jaw twitch, but I breathed through it, expelling the air out of my nose forcefully. I tapped my fingers against the side of my leg, my mind racing, searching for the perfect opening line. It needed to be something good, something memorable. You only ever got one chance to make a first impression, and I wanted this guy to remember me.

I did the math and calculated the probability of success. Sure, I had to make a few assumptions, but anything to increase my likelihood of getting this guy to notice me would be worth it.

There was a high chance the guy was a surfer. He was out here, standing alone, and not getting his drink—or his karaoke—on inside. And something about the seriousness of his gaze made me think there was a brain inside that pretty head of his. I couldn't just wing it on charm and instinct alone.

I needed something...more. Then it hit me.

I took a deep breath as I strode up and stood next to him by the railing. His head flicked in my direction. This was it, my opening. I grabbed it with both hands.

I smiled, licked my lips and leaned over, pressing my shoulder against his ever so slightly. "So"—I started as his eyes locked on mine—"how many waves do you think crash onto the shore around the world each day?"

I had almost a good foot of height on the guy. He tilted his head up, studying me like he was trying to solve a puzzle. "That's a good question." His voice was silvery and sweet, and fuck, if it didn't send a jolt of yumminess straight to my half-primed cock.

His gaze traveled back out into the black sea in front of us. I could hear the waves lapping the shore, in the short gaps of space whenever there was a lull in the music butchering going on from inside the bar. I copied his stance, holding onto the white handrail and leaning back slightly.

"I guess..." He continued talking, which totally caught me off guard.

My question was designed to stump and disarm. Then, in the inevitable silence that would follow as he'd be unable to answer the question, that's when I'd planned on making my move. A smile. A casual touch. Some chitchat. And then...an invitation back to my Presidential Apartment. But this guy wasn't stumped or disarmed—and for some reason, I really fucking loved that.

"...you'd have to start by considering what we know and going from there."

"So, what do we know?" I leaned forward and lower, lining up my eyes with his. He flicked me a quick glance, enough for me to feel a jolt of heat pummel my chest, before looking away again.

"We know a lot. How much shoreline there is in the world, the average duration of a wave, the frequency with which they break, the tide patterns."

Holy shit.

Time for a quick recap here of all the things I knew about the guy, despite having only met him less than sixty seconds ago.

He wasn't just Cali-cute; he was nerdy-smart as well.

Up close, his scent was clean with a hint of something cinnamony-sweet.

And now over to you, Mr. Cock, for the latest update—how are you finding this interaction so far? Great, I'll take that burgeoning semi-hard-on as a positive sign you're enjoying how things are going. Back to you in the studio, Mr. Brain.

He looked up at the quarter moon that hung in the sky above us.

I looked up, too. "Funny how that thing up there controls the water down here, right?"

He looked thoughtful for a moment. "Yeah, it is."

"But anyway..." I cleared my throat, hoping it would also have a similar effect on my mind which had gotten a little foggy in the time I'd been standing here with him. I didn't even know his name and he was already getting me off balance. How was he able to do that?

"...back to my original question."

His brows tilted in curiosity. "Have you heard of Enrico Fermi?"

I shook my head, lost in the wonder of this guy's moonlit eyes.

"He was a physicist. I think he even might have won a Nobel Peace Prize back in, like, the 1930s. Anyway, he developed an estimation process, which is now known as the Fermi problem. So, when someone asks a super big and hard-to-answer question like, say, 'How many waves do you think crash onto the shore each day all around the world?' there's actually a way to try and estimate an answer."

"Huh." I licked my bottom lip which had suddenly become drier than the desert. "Well, there you go, then. You learn something new every day."

The corner of his mouth twitched. "I guess you do."

"And what I'd really like to learn next"—yeah, I did the casual accidentally-on-purpose gentle shoulder bump thing again—"is your name."

His sparkly blue eyes roved across my face. I had no idea how he was doing it, but he was making me feel like he wasn't just looking at me; he was actually *seeing* me. It left me feeling exposed and alive in an intriguing way I'd never experienced before.

"I'm Conrad. Conrad McCallister."

"Pleasure to meet you, Conrad. I'm Jedfire Burns. But you can call me Jed."

4

CONRAD

Jedfire Burns was one of the most unusual looking people I had ever seen.

He towered over me and looked to be almost seven foot. His auburn hair was a scorched, tangled mess, mirrored by rich mocha brown eyes that were crazily fascinating, large, and expressive. His ears were big and protruded out wildly at the sides of his face and when he smiled, it was wide and lopsided. He also had tantalizingly full lips and a slight dimple in his chin. His sizeable frame bulged with an intoxicating mixture of muscles and flesh.

And his outfit. *Holy shit!* What was Jedfire Burns thinking when he put it on? Was he even thinking, or had he purposely closed his eyes and simply grabbed the first thing that landed in his hands? His *massive* tennis-racket-sized hands.

He wore a denim jacket with a faux-fur-trimmed hood. *Just* an open-buttoned jacket. Nothing underneath it. No shirt, no tank top, just skin. Lots and lots of skin. And a light smattering of hair across his chest. Oh, and abs. Lots and lots of lean, rock hard abs.

Further down, I was treated to a pair of black shorts so tiny, I had boxer briefs that covered more leg. For a tall dude, he had wonderfully muscled thighs, still lean but with plenty of meat on the bones. And he finished the outfit with a pair of black leather military boots and white socks drawn up halfway to his knees.

I realized I'd been pretty preoccupied over the past six months with other, more important things, but had fashion really changed this much? Or was it Jedfire Burns' one-of-a-kind uniqueness that meant he could pull this look off? Something told me it was option B. Yeah, definitely option B. It left me feeling a little plain in my boring ol' jeans and white T-shirt.

I eyed him up and down and despite the funniness of it all, the guy had an allure, an appeal. The moon wasn't the only thing exerting a strong pull. Jed's body must've contained a whole bunch of magnets, drawing me into him. Not that I could let anything come of this. No. It wouldn't be fair to him.

"Let me guess..." Jed's loud and confident voice crashed into my visual daydreaming of him. And judging by the gleam in his eye, he'd caught me checking him out, too.

"So, I guess you can see I've got big hands..." He raised his huge palms up for me to see.

"...big feet..." He lifted his right leg. I glanced down and holy shit, the guy had basketball-player-sized feet to match.

I lifted my gaze back to meet his.

"So, you're probably wondering if I have a big..."

Why was my heart clanging against my ribcage all of a sudden?

Jed tapped his long fingers against his chest. "...heart?"

Our eyes locked as he shot me a lopsided smile.

I blinked rapidly a few times and cleared my throat. "Actually, I was wondering about the size of your cock," I deadpanned.

Jed burst out laughing, and when I said *burst*, that's exactly what it looked like—a volcano exploding. His facial features contorting madly, eyebrows waggling, his shoulders bouncing around unevenly. Even his ears wiggled...*adorably*? What made me think of that word?

"So, you surf?" he asked once he'd settled down.

I nodded. "Yeah. Do you?"

Jed rested his forearms on the railing in front of us, matching my height. "No." There was an air of melancholy in his voice.

"Why not?"

He turned to face me, his pupils filling his chestnut eyes, making them seem even darker. "I don't think they make surfboards for people of my height."

I smiled. "Oh, I think *they* do."

He noticed the emphasis I had added and probed me with his eyes. Hey, Jed might have scored killer points for one of the most original pick-up lines of all time, but just because I looked all sweet and innocent didn't mean I wasn't going to keep the guy on his toes.

After a few moments of silence, Jed banged his huge hands against the railing with a loud thud. "Do you like karaoke?"

"I fucking hate it and think it should be outlawed in all fifty states."

His lips twitched at my strong response. "Aw, come on." He grazed against my body again for the third time. Not that I was counting, or anything. "You only live once. You're no fun."

I tipped my head up. "I'm plenty fun, I can assure you."

"Do you like Janet Jackson?"

My mouth fell open. "Uh, no. I don't like Janet Jackson... I fucking *love* Janet Jackson."

Jed turned immediately and took a few steps away from me. Where was he going? When he spun back around, he was clutching one hand over his sexy chest, I meant, heart. The other hand was balled into a fist near his mouth.

"Girls may have been easy," he sang into his fist-slash-air microphone.

He sashayed a step toward me in a move that would have made any one of the Backstreet Boys proud.

"But you..." He dipped his heavy hooded eyes to meet mine, a searing heat scorching through them. "...you have to please me."

His finger landed on my cheek, and I suddenly felt like a

groupie who had been plucked from the crowd and ended up on stage with the singer. The gorgeous, outrageous, impromptu singer…

He kept singing. His voice was actually pretty damn good. "What makes me think that I can say this to you?"

Ah, okay, *now* I got it. I smiled all wide and stupid-like, melting into the swirl of emotions this weird-looking goofball of a guy was stirring inside of me.

"I know"—he pressed his nose against the tip of mine, his breathy singing dancing across my face—"how bad you want this."

I recognized the mid-'90s jam. It was Janet's *You Want This*. Just as I opened my mouth to say something, Jedfire smiled all crooked at me, backed away, and ran inside the bar. I followed after him and reached the entrance.

A few heartbeats later, Jedfire Burns was on the stage, singing the same words he had sung to me on the balcony, now to the entire packed bar. He didn't need the words on the karaoke machine, he knew them by heart. Which was a good thing, because it meant that he could keep his focus on me. Which he did. For the entire song, his eyes never strayed too far from me.

Once the song ended and the thunderous applause had died down, Jed made his way back over to me out on the balcony. I leaned against the wall. Sweat glistened on his chest and he carried even more of a rock star swagger now.

"What did you think?" His scent was thick with superciliousness, but after that ballsy performance, he'd earned the right.

"I'm impressed," I answered, grateful to have the support of the wall holding me upright. That was the understatement of the decade. But I had to play it cool. I couldn't let him know—heck, he couldn't even get a whiff—of the insane attraction coursing through my veins for him.

If I so much as smiled, or looked at him a certain way, or reached out and ran my fingers down his chest like I so badly wanted to, he'd take it as a green light. Permission to continue down a road that, despite not wanting it to be like that, came to a dead end. Okay, again, bad choice of words.

Jed struck me as the kind of guy who—when he knew what he wanted—went for it. I had to play it safe and make sure that he didn't set his sights on me. It wouldn't end well for either one of us.

"So, uh"—I felt the warmth of his fingers on my cheek—"did I impress you enough to get a kiss?"

"You wish, jellyfish." I kept my eyes glued to the bottom of his throat, which was eye-level for me. I glanced up, just an inch, noticing how his Adam's apple bobbed against the skin of his neck.

"Well, then, can I see you again?"

I knew it. This guy was determined, and as much as I didn't want to admit it, part of me liked that. I'd never had anyone so focused on me before. I'd never given anyone the opportunity. Should I give this eccentric, never-met-someone-like-him-before guy standing in front of me a chance?

"I'm—I'm going for a hike tomorrow." I'd read a brochure in my suite about all the great hikes in the area. There was a courtesy bus leaving from the hotel at ten the next day. I thought I might do it. Alone. But some company *would* be nice.

Jed didn't say anything, letting a silence fall over my unspoken invitation. Well, not so much an invitation as me simply telling him what I was doing. Oh, right, he probably *was* waiting for me to invite him. *Duh.*

"Would you, uh, like to join me?"

He swept his fingers through his messy hair and nodded. "Yeah, I'd really like that."

He leaned back against the wall, cocking his head to the side as he took me in. "So, this Fermi friend of yours—"

"World-famous physicist. Not a personal friend," I pointed out.

Jed tossed me a smile. "Well, since he's so good at solving big problems, what do you think the chances are of you ending up in my bed by the time your vacation is over?"

My throat produced a weird, gurgle-y sound. I was half exasperated, half something a whole lot more pleasant. I pushed myself off the wall and stepped in front of Jed, stretching my arms out on either side of his face. Trapping him with my palms pressed into the wall, I leaned in and extended my chin. "I'd say you've got your work cut out for you, buddy."

Our eyes two-stepped with each other. It was a dance peppered with a thousand soft movements and slight shifts of focus. There was so much of Jed to take in. Close up wasn't anywhere near close enough.

Unexpectedly, he released a jittery giggle. "So...not a *no*, then?"

Before I could come out with some carefully worded, polite yet firm response, he glanced down at his watch and his eyes widened. "Dammit. I gotta go, Conrad. It's almost midnight."

I could feel both of my eyebrows lifting. "So? Are you Cinderella or something? Afraid you'll turn into a pumpkin at the stroke of midnight?"

I was stunned to see him taking my lighthearted joke so seriously, his eyes revealing a depth I hadn't noticed before.

He swallowed hard. "Yeah, something like that."

"Okay, then." I moved out of his way, clearing the path for him to leave.

"I'm glad I met you tonight, Conrad." He said it softly and in a way that made me know he meant it. "And I'm looking forward to our da—to hanging out with you tomorrow."

We exchanged a brief smile before he disappeared. I went back to the railing and stared out into the water again.

What an eventful night it had been. I was glad I'd met Jed, too. He was engaging and vibrant. He had a spirited air about him, and in all honesty, I found it more than just a little intriguing.

I slipped my fingers into my pocket and reached for my cell phone. It was just after midnight. A new day had just started.

I let out a hefty sigh. Great. *Less* than six months to go now...

SATURDAY

5

JEDFIRE

Our knees clanked against each other, knocking about as the bus took a turn off the main road and into the gravelly parking lot of the Key West Wildlife Center. I peeked over at Conrad and felt my tummy doing cartwheels as I saw the smile on his face. Just like me, he seemed to be enjoying the casual way our bodies rocked against each other.

He'd worn that same happy expression for the entire bus ride over here from the resort, along with a perfect hiking outfit of a green athletic shirt, black shorts and hiking boots. Me, on the other hand...hmmm, why did I think flip-flops were an appropriate shoe choice?

The bus hit a bump in the road, bringing our thighs into contact with each other. Still all innocent-like, but if I had my way, our bodies would be rocking against each other in a whole lot less casual, more *balls to the wall* ferocious kind of way by the end of his vacation.

We didn't talk much during the twenty-minute bus ride. Conrad made some light conversation, but I was still flustered. The events of Vegas were catching up with me. Then meeting this exquisite creature. And on top of that, I still had my one-minute-to-midnight schedule to attend to.

The resort had an ATM in the lobby, and I had only barely made it on time last night after I left Conrad and bolted from the bar. Somehow, though, I managed to and got what needed to be done right on time.

I'd be lying if I tried to pretend that it wasn't getting to me. The stress was snowballing. What had started off as this fun, *there's no way in the world this could possibly be true* thing had turned into quicksand that I couldn't get out of. The more I struggled against it, the further I sank. I was in deep and getting deeper into it by the day.

"Jed, we're here." Conrad's voice was a light murmur, as if he were carefully waking me up from a deep sleep.

I blinked and noticed we were the last remaining guests on the bus.

"You were daydreaming. I didn't want to disturb you."

"That's a good thing," I whipped back, getting up. Conrad followed. "I was daydreaming about you, so I would've been mighty pissed for the interruption."

His laugh echoed through the empty bus. As he jumped off the last step, the resort guide came up to us. "There are a number of trails you can walk here. Maps are free and inside the center. We're meeting back here in two hours. I'll see you boys then."

"Sounds good," Conrad replied brightly.

I so badly wanted to put my arm around Conrad or even just walk hand in hand with him, but it was too soon. He'd said I'd have my work cut out for me, which believe me, I didn't mind in the slightest. He did something to me that made me know he'd be worth it.

And in the meantime, I was going to be the most gentlemanly gentleman in the history of gentlemen.

Case in point: I'd pre-wanked twice. Once, after returning from my ATM run last night. Once again this morning in the shower.

Conrad was special, and I didn't want my little head messing with my big head by saying, or doing, something to ruin things.

Not that I wouldn't be serving up my signature brand of cocky confidence—because, hey, anyone could have seen just how much Conrad enjoyed it...almost as much as he seemed to delight in giving it right back to me.

I got a sense that something was holding him back, though, and it wasn't shyness. Something else was at play here, and if taking my time was the way to get him to open up and trust me, then I'd take all the time in the world.

"Hey, I didn't ask you last night," I began as we made our way toward the wildlife center. "How long are you staying here for?"

His eyebrows jiggled. "I leave Wednesday."

"Wednesday, huh?" I began counting out the days between today and then on my left hand. "So, I've got five days to make you fall madly in love with me, then?"

He smiled sunnily. "Fall in love with you? Last night, you were just trying to get me into your bed."

I shrugged. "I'll take love over sex."

Whoa... Why did I just blurt that out? I was such an idiot. My mind scrambled, trying to find something—*anything*—to not only fill the deafening silence that had fallen between us but, ideally, also erase the words I'd just vomited out.

Before my brain could formulate a sentence, or at least throw a few words together, I felt a set of soft fingers give my hand a squeeze. "That's good to know."

The automatic door to the center opened and the cool rush of air-conditioned air hit me in the face. But it didn't compare to the feeling Conrad's gentle touch had unleashed in me.

What on earth was going on with me?

I'd fucked a supermodel, a Golden Globe winning actor, and a world-famous kite surfer...all on the same night. How was it that this guy—this delicious looking, sun-tanned morsel—was playing hard to get, making me work for it, and yet here I was, blurting out crazy shit to him and getting all giddy from his fingers grazing mine?

Part of me wanted to resist it, to fight against the feeling that was crashing over me like a waterfall. I chased thrills for fun all around the world. Heck, according to Grandpa, I practically made a living out of it. But this was a feeling unlike any I'd known before. It was like standing at the gates of a whole new world, peering in with no idea what lay beyond.

"I'll grab us some maps."

As Conrad sauntered over to the counter to get the maps, I noticed a sign in the front window. The center was building a new enclosure to house endangered sea turtles. Their fundraising target was fifty thousand dollars. I smiled as I gave the sign a gentle tap with my fingers.

"All right." Conrad had returned with a map in his hands. "There are a couple of walks we can do, but given we need to be back by twelve, the lady suggested we stick to *Walk A*. We should be able to do it comfortably in about an hour and a half, and we get to see a lot of cool things, too."

"Sounds good. Lead the way."

I waved my hand in front of us, giving Conrad the right of way. He pointed a finger at my face and grinned. "Yeah, right. You're just going to check out my ass if I walk in front of you."

"You got me." I raised my hands by the sides of my face. "Guilty as charged."

"Well, I can't say I blame you." He leaned in closer, his lips lingering with a sweet happiness. "My ass is totally callipygian."

Calli-pygia-whaaaa? It sounded like something you'd put on a taco.

We exited the wildlife center and stepped down a flight of stairs—side by side. Ass viewing would have to wait, it seemed. As would consulting Dictionary.com the second I was able to.

A wide, paved trail covered by a dense canopy began to our

right. "This is the one," Conrad announced as we walked past the wooden *Walk A* post.

Most of the other guests from the resort were already ahead of us or had chosen a different trail, so it felt like it was just me and Conrad alone in the world—I meant, on the hiking trail.

I liked the guy. Like, I *really* liked him. He wasn't like the kind of guys I'd normally meet. For starters, usually alcohol was involved. Lots of it. And me buying all of it. That hadn't happened with Conrad. It wasn't how we started, which filled me with a sweet tingly rush.

"You actually have a pretty decent voice." He shot me a friendly smile. "I didn't get a chance to tell you that last night."

"Thanks." I felt my cheeks burning up. I think Conrad noticed, but he was pretending like he hadn't.

He strode over to a numbered post and gazed back down at the map. He began rattling off some information about trees or birds or plants. I tried to listen, I did. But the way his lips moved so sexily was distracting and, quite frankly, completely unfair. How could I take in anything he was saying when all I could think about was how pretty they'd look wrapped around my cock?

Dammit. If I hadn't slept in, I could have gone for a triple pre-not-a-date wank trifecta.

I nodded and put on my best *totally listened to every word you just said* face. Conrad nodded happily. We continued walking down the trail until we reached a gap between the native trees.

"I've heard about this." I pointed to the small, blink-and-you'd-miss-it unpaved pathway that peeked through the side of the trail. "Some guys were telling me about it last night at the bar, before I met you."

"Oh, yeah?" Conrad pulled up next to me and offered me his water bottle. "Want some?"

God, I wished he wasn't talking about a drink. "Sure. Thanks."

I drained half the bottle. I must've been thirstier than I'd realized. I handed the bottle back to him and he took a swig.

"See through there?" I pointed at a narrow gap between the trees. "I heard that pathway leads to a place affectionately known as Fuck Mountain."

I saw Conrad's head fall forward as he almost choked on his drink. "What did you just say?" he sputtered, wiping his mouth with the back of his hand.

"I think it's kind of implied in the name."

His blue eyes beamed in the sunlight and fuck, if it didn't make me want to wrap my hand around the back of his neck and pull him in for a fierce as fire kiss. "I'd be happy to show you. I'll even throw in a demonstration, if you're a visual learner."

He slapped my arm playfully. "Dream on, Pokémon."

A giggle escaped me. Shit. Since when did Jedfire Burns giggle like a schoolkid?

"What does actually happen there?"

"I'm not too sure about the exact details." I brushed a loose strand off my forehead. "The guys last night were saying that it's a private spot out in the woods, and so, you know, some gay dudes enjoy getting one with nature."

"You mean, getting *off* in nature," Conrad murmured, letting out a lighthearted snicker.

"Let's keep walking."

Conrad seemed slightly taken aback. Maybe he'd been expecting me to keep continuing down Innuendo Boulevard, but I had other plans. A detour down Innocent-Like Flirt Lane being the first.

"So, what do you do for a living?" I asked, taking a left into Getting To Know You Chitchat Drive.

His eyes softened. "I make surfboards with my dad."

"Oh, wow. That's really cool," I shot back enthusiastically. "Wait, so *that's* why you said they do make surfboards for people my height last night."

"You picked up on that, huh? I'm impressed."

"That seems to be a running theme."

Conrad furled his eyebrows at me. "What do you mean?"

"Me impressing you. I seem to be doing a lot of it."

His eyes found mine and I could see something twinkling in them. Something was happening between us. He had to be feeling this, too... I hoped.

"So, how did you and your dad get into surfboard making?"

The smile died on his lips, and the energy shifted immediately. "Sorry, I don't mean to pry." I thought it'd be an innocent question. I hadn't meant for it to tighten his jaw and draw a series of sharp breaths out of him.

"It's okay." His eyes scanned around us. He pointed to a bench. "Mind if we sit down? I'm a little tired."

"Not at all."

We walked over to the bench as Conrad explained, "It's kind of a loaded question, what you just asked me."

"I'm sorry," I repeated, sitting down. "I didn't know, and I don't want to make you feel uncomfortable."

Conrad's forehead broke out into a cavalcade of fine lines. When he looked up at me again, the softness in his face made me want to reach out, pull him into me, and never let go.

"It's a long, sad story. Are you sure you want to hear it?"

I nodded. "I do. But only if you want to tell me. No pressure."

He blew out a breath. "All right, here goes."

I felt the side of his hand brush against mine. Instinctively, I cupped it in mine as he began sharing his story with me.

"My dad is a veteran. He completed two tours. One in Iraq and then in Afghanistan. My mom cheated on him while he was away."

"Oh, no... Sorry, keep going. I didn't mean to interrupt."

"It's okay," Conrad said in a voice that sounded anything but okay. "Cheating sucks."

"It's the *fucking* worst," I concurred.

"So, yeah, my dad had a messy divorce to deal with, on top of PTSD. So..." Conrad's eyes went glossy as he looked out ahead of us.

"It's okay. Take your time, Conrad."

I hoped the warmth of his fingers nestled in mine was comforting him a little.

"He started drinking. Badly. It was out of control for most of my high school years. He went to rehab, came back and relapsed"—he squinted at the sky—"three times in total."

"Whoa, that's heavy."

Our eyes met briefly; his were filled with sadness. "It was. I showed a lot of promise in high school. I had gotten all straight A's and it looked like I had a good chance of getting a scholarship into college."

"But you never went?" I guessed by the bleakness in his voice.

"Nope." He played with a loose strand of material on his shorts. "Looking after Dad took up all of my time. My grades suffered and by graduation, there was no way I'd be getting a scholarship anywhere."

"Shit, that really sucks," I muttered under my breath.

"One day, in my last year in high school, my surfboard snapped. We didn't have money to buy a new one, so that Saturday afternoon, Dad and I went to the store. We bought supplies—and a six pack of non-alcoholic ciders—scoured YouTube, and learned how to make a surfboard by hand."

"No way. That's so cool."

Some of the shimmer returned to Conrad's eyes. "Yeah, it is. Dad really took to it. He loved it and so, he started to make surfboards. It turned out to be really good for his PTSD, too."

"Oh?"

"Yeah. There's no way Dad would ever do yoga, or meditation, or anything hippy like that. His words, not mine." We shared a smile before Conrad kept talking. "But making boards did something really good to him. I think it's because it gave him something to focus on, and at the end of it, he'd created something real. Tangible. Something he could hold in his hands and be proud of. Does that make sense? You can stop me if I'm babbling."

"It makes total sense, and you're not babbling. I'm enjoying listening to you."

I was in awe of Conrad. He'd given up so much of his life for his dad. A bitter residue of guilt formed in my gut. Here he was doing so much for his family, while I was doing everything I could to run away from my own responsibilities back home.

"When I graduated, I decided to help him out, and now we're using the shed in the backyard as our surfboard manufacturing headquarters." He let out a small chuckle. "We make enough of a living to get by. We'll never be millionaires, but it's enough and...and we get to do it together."

"Wow. That's amazing you looked after your dad like that." I squeezed tightly around his fingers.

Conrad shrugged. "I don't think so. Anyone else would've done the same in my position."

"Uh, no," I pointed out. "In fact, I think very few people, especially teenagers, would have put their dad's needs before their own."

One of his shoulders lifted. "It's family, you know. You do what you gotta do."

The guilt in my gut had crawled up to my throat.

Conrad was such a good guy. A decent son. Someone who put others before himself. In other words, he was everything I wasn't.

And wasn't that the most depressing thought ever?

6

CONRAD

Jed remained quiet for most of our walk back.

I guessed my story had bummed him out a bit. I knew it wasn't all sunshine and rainbows, but it wasn't all bad, either. I really loved my dad. He was the closest person in the world to me. And sure, missing out on going to college or having time to do high school stuff like hanging out with friends and having a boyfriend had eluded me, but I didn't feel that I'd missed out on all that much, really. I managed to maintain some friendships and sex was only ever a hookup app away. Not exactly romantic, sure, but it fulfilled my needs. Sort of... But I'd do it all again in a heartbeat if it meant my dad would live clean and sober, like he had been for almost seven years now.

I knew that Dad felt super guilty about what happened during those years. But what was done was done. Nothing could change that. I had learned a lot over these past six months; one thing being that unless it spurred you to action, guilt was a useless emotion.

"Have I depressed you?" I asked as the wildlife center came back into view.

"What? No." Jed's eyes lit up intensely. "Sorry, I was just thinking. And I need quiet to do that, apparently."

We shared another comfortable, almost familiar smile.

"Actually, Conrad. You've really impressed me."

"Ah, so now the shoe is on the other foot. *I* get to impress *you*."

He laughed, his shoulders bouncing around. "It sure is. I think you're incredible."

I looked away, trying to escape the heat emanating from him. But it was no use. Despite my best attempts to keep him at a distance—for his own good—Jedfire Burns had a way of making me melt into him. Worse, I didn't want to stop myself from doing it. That explained why I couldn't help but return his cheeky flirting with equal measure.

I scanned the parking lot. Some of the guests were already getting back on the bus, while a few folks milled around it, chatting away amongst themselves.

"Hey, listen, Conrad." Jed's long fingers landed on my shoulder, his fingertips teasing the base of my neck. "I just need to go inside real quick."

"Great. Me, too." My response seemed to unsettle him for some reason, but he tried to cover it with a smile. "I might get some postcards. Send one back to Dad and some friends back home, although—"

"You'll probably get home before they arrive," Jed finished my thought for me. Something about him being able to do that set off a fluttering of butterflies in my belly.

Our eyes locked, and I didn't know why, but I felt a pull, an urge to reach out and grab his fingers. He responded in kind, intertwining our fingers delicately together. We stepped into the center, hand in hand, and it felt all sorts of right.

"Okay, postcards." I pointed to a stand by the counter.

"Cool. I'll meet you out front." Our fingers drifted apart slowly and Jed headed toward the back.

After a few minutes, I'd picked out and paid for six postcards. I surveyed the center. There was no sign of Jed. He hadn't walked out, as I'd had a clear view of the entrance the whole time I'd been in here. And at his height, I could see he definitely wasn't around the front, either.

I noticed a half-open door along the back wall. I glanced at the time on my cell phone. We had to be back on that bus in less than five minutes.

I walked over to the door and heard Jed's unmissable voice as I approached.

"It's fine, it's fine. I'm more than happy to do this."

I peered in through the crack and saw Jed sitting at a desk. An older man dressed in the center's khaki colors was sitting opposite him, looking very happy.

"This is such a generous and very unexpected gesture. I can't even begin to express my gratitude, Mr. Burns."

"Call me Jed. Please."

I slid over to the right so that neither one of them would see me. I knew it was wrong to eavesdrop, but what was Jed doing? Curiosity got the better of me, and I pressed my ear toward the office.

"Last year, we didn't even reach half of our fundraising total. And for you to so kindly offer to donate the entire fifty thousand dollars—"

Whoa. I snapped my head back. Jed was donating money to the center? A whole bucket load of money. I hadn't seen that one coming.

I peered through the gap in the door. The other man was busy scribbling down a whole lot of information. I propped my head against the wall, listening intently.

"The only thing I ask"—Jed's voice carried a seriousness that seemed so out of character to the guy I was getting to know—"is that no one can know about this. Absolutely no one. I'd like—no, I *need* this donation to be completely anonymous."

I chewed down on my fingernail. Okay, that was a bit...odd.

"Are you sure, Mister—Jed? We would be more than happy to do a media release to let people know about your very kind—"

"No," Jed snapped back, his voice even firmer than before. "No media. No mentions of me. Nothing. Complete anonymity."

"Well, of course. We'll respect your wishes."

I stepped away from the door and made my way back to the bus, my brain buzzing with what I'd just overheard. I found two empty seats near the back. I rested my forehead against the window just as Jed came into view, bouncing down the steps of the center.

He got on the bus and I waved him over. He had to bend forward quite a lot to keep from banging his head against the ceiling. He slid into the empty seat next to me and nudged into me with a big smile covering the lower half of his face.

"All good?" I asked.

"Uh, yeah." He looked straight ahead. "I was trying on a T-shirt, but you know, they didn't have one in my size."

I eyed him curiously. "Uh-huh."

In addition to donating fifty thousand dollars, I was discovering another interesting thing about Jedfire Burns—he was a terrible liar. He couldn't even look at me when he'd said it.

Maybe he was shy? That could possibly explain why he wanted the donation to remain anonymous and why he wasn't telling me about it now. And, yeah, maybe I would've believed that was the reason if I hadn't, I don't know, spent more than two minutes with the guy.

No. Jedfire Burns was loud and loved attention. He was the type of guy who bought rounds of drinks at the bar for strangers. He got up and sang the shit out of a Janet track at karaoke. His fashion sense alone indicated that he was anything but shy. For our hike today, he wore a Tiger King tank top (I was hoping ironically; I was too afraid to ask) and ripped denim shorts. His hair was tied up in a red and black bandana, and he wore flip-flops (yes, flip-flops for a hike).

Jed was a lot of things, but the shy and retiring type he was not. It didn't make sense for him to be keeping something like this to himself.

With everyone on board, the bus pulled out of the parking lot and our knees began bumping against each other like they had when we'd arrived. This time, though, I felt something else on my knee. Jed's hand.

He glanced over at me with those rebellious eyes of his. "Is this all right?"

I clasped my hand over his. "Yes."

"Did you have a good time?"

I nodded. "Yeah, I did."

Jed shot up and pointed a finger right at my face. "You said yes twice in a row. That means you have to say yes to whatever question I ask you next."

"Oh, really." I smiled, taking his finger out of my face and placing it back down onto my lap. "Is that the rule?"

He put on a mock-serious expression. "It totally is. And you don't want to be a rule breaker now, do you, Conrad?"

I couldn't help but laugh. Rich, coming from him, but okay...I'd go along with this. "So what's your question, then? The one that I have to"—I rolled my eyes—"say yes to."

He was wearing an unfamiliar expression. It wasn't until I heard the shakiness in his voice and saw a gentle twitch permeating across his jaw that I guessed it was probably...nerves?

"Will you have dinner with me tonight?"

I swallowed hard, looking into those deep brown eyes of his. The sunshine illuminated his whole face, bringing out the reddish tinge in his hair.

Who was Jedfire Burns?

There were layers to the guy, layers that I wanted to peel open and peek under. I'd only ever met the guy twice but he'd made more of an impression on me than any other guy I had ever been interested—that I had met. I meant any other guy that I had ever met.

Oh, who was I kidding? Yes, Jed sparked my interest. Why deny it?

I wiggled my fingers against the warmth of his palm. "All right, Jed. Yes, I'll have dinner with you tonight."

7

JEDFIRE

"Cowbell Creek?" Conrad's golden-tinged eyebrows pulled together adorably as he cocked his head to the side.

"Mhmm." I nodded, raising the glass of the 2009 Château Margaux to my lips. I took a sip, closing my eyes briefly as I savored the slightly peppery, full-bodied red. "What? You've never heard of it?"

Conrad shook his head. Fuck, he made earnestness look so damn good. His choice of a button-up white linen shirt for dinner was a good one, too. It accentuated the glow of his tanned face, as well as the tops of his hands. I'd been wanting to reach out across the table and hold them, like he'd summoned my fingers at the wildlife center.

But I was holding back. The night was young. We had all the time in the world. And, in a very *unusual-for-me* move, I actually wanted to get to know the guy. With clothes *on*. At least, during the early portion of the evening. Later was a whole other story.

"It's about two hours southwest of L.A.," I explained.

"That's crazy. San Clemente is an hour south of the city. We live in the same state, and yet, I've never heard of Cowbell County."

"Creek," I corrected. "Although County would probably make more sense since there actually isn't a creek in Cowbell Creek."

More adorable earnestness and confused face pulling met me. "There isn't?"

"Nope."

Conrad tipped his head forward and peered up at me through his sun-kissed lashes. "But there are cowbells, right?"

"Oh, fuck yeah, there are cowbells." I downed the remaining wine in one giant swill. Almost immediately, the server returned to refill my glass.

The service at Elysian's on-site restaurant—like everything else about the resort—was exceptional. I'd asked for the best table and boy, did we get it. We were sitting at an open window, the sun flirting with the horizon as the Gulf of Mexico stretched out in front of us.

"My family runs a cowbell plant."

Conrad let out a light, airy laugh, but when he looked at me and could see I wasn't laughing along with him, his mouth snapped shut. "Wait. You're being serious?"

I smiled, cocking an eyebrow. "Yes, I am. We're the largest manufacturer of cowbells and other bovine-related products in the country, the second biggest in the world behind a German company."

"Okaaay."

"The bovine industry is a pretty closed-circuit thing. The outside world doesn't really know we exist. And in some ways, we like to keep it that way. But it's a hugely profitable sector—"

"And your family runs the plant?" Conrad interjected.

"Yeah. Been in my family for seven generations. Although, technically, my grandpa runs it. At least for one more month."

"What happens in a month?"

I sighed, letting my shoulders sag. "I turn twenty-five."

"Uh-huh." Conrad took a sip of his water, his electric blue eyes superglued to my face.

"That's when I'm due to take over."

Our eyes met. His were curious, almost like they were excited by the prospect. Mine were... I had no idea. How did the eyes of a person who felt trapped, depressed, and like they were being forced into a life they didn't want for themselves look to someone else?

"I'm sensing you're not happy about that?" Conrad's carefully chosen and softly spoken words hung heavy in the air.

And then it happened. Shit, it had been a good few months at least since the last time. And damn, after all this time, and even though I could sense it coming on, I was as powerless as ever to prevent it. I guess that's why it was called an involuntary twitch.

It started, like it always did with a funny bubbling sensation brewing at the back of my throat. That would send my heart rate ticking up and my back teeth gnawing against each other. My jaw would clench and then, with me witnessing it but being absolutely powerless to stop it, my tongue would flick up into the roof of my mouth and make a not-too-loud, yet *totally audible to anyone within a few feet of me* popping sound.

I looked down at the table, unable to bring myself to see the reaction on Conrad's face. A sneer. Pity. Disgust. Whatever it would be, I'd experienced it all from guys over the years. Hence the need for my *keep it casual* mantra. Okay, that, and the fact that I was completely emotionally unavailable and incapable of getting anything right in my life. Including love.

I felt warm fingers brushing the top of my hand. Exhaling, I stole a quick glance up at Conrad. He smiled sweetly, his eyes exuding nothing but kindness. My jaw slackened and I could feel my tongue relaxing, too.

"We don't have to talk about anything you don't want to, Jed."

I took another sip of wine. "Thanks. But, you opened up to me during our hike. I want to be able to share some stuff with you, too."

"I'd like that." Conrad tilted his head as his smile disappeared. "Permission to hurl a million questions about cowbelling at you?"

I smiled as the server arrived with our appetizers, grateful for both the food arriving since I was famished and what I sensed was Conrad's attempt at a detour into some lighthearted conversation. "Permission granted."

Over the course of our mouthwatering five-course meal, Conrad peppered me with more questions about my family business than anyone ever had.

He started off by wanting to find out what a cowbell actually was.

I explained to him that cowbells were simply a bell and clapper hung around the neck of free-roaming livestock so herders could keep track of their animals via the sound of the bell.

He wanted to know how we made cowbells.

I didn't know all of the exact ins and outs of that since my family ran the plant and hired workers who actually made the cowbells. But that plant had been like a second home to me since I was a kid, so I knew enough to tell him that bell and clapper parts were mainly made out of iron, bronze, brass, copper, or wood. We used thin, flat pieces of plated sheet metal. The collar, used to hold the bell, was traditionally made with leather and wood fibers. Up until about thirty years ago, everything was made by hand, but these days, machines had taken over. We still employed over forty people, though.

He was curious about the industry as well. So I told him about the two fabled peaks of the cowbell industry—the California Gold Rush in the 1800s and the rise of hip-hop and R&B from the late '80s into the early 2000s.

"Really? You're being serious?" We were onto dessert and I'd lost count by now, but it had to have been at least the seventh time Conrad had asked me that same question—in that precious slightly higher register—that evening.

I got it. It was a lot to take in.

As usual, I nodded and filled him in with all the details. "It's one of the reasons everyone in Cowbell Creek loves hip-hop so much. You hear it in all the stores, blaring out of people's cars as they drive by. Almost every cowbell sound in hip-hop was from Cowbell Creek. It gave us a much-needed economic boost."

"Wow, that is...just...wow." Conrad's spoon was suspended in mid-air, the vanilla ice cream beginning to drip over the side.

"It's funny. Most kids have clowns or magicians at their birthday parties. My brother, Cooper, and I, we had The Beastie Boys."

"Anything else I should know?" Conrad's lips tipped upward in a captivating smirk.

"I think we've covered pretty much everything. Wait, there is one more thing."

He leaned closer, the spoon dangling casually from his mouth. "Tell me."

"Nah, forget it. It's dumb."

"Well, now you have to tell me. You can't leave me hanging like that."

Why did I even open my mouth? "There's a magazine called *Cowbell People*."

Conrad covered his mouth but didn't quite manage to suppress the giggle before it escaped.

I went on. "It's just like the real *People* magazine, except it's for the Cowbell Industry."

"Do they have a Sexiest Man Alive edition?" Conrad teased and was grinning widely, until I gave him an answer he clearly wasn't expecting.

"Yeah, they do."

"Oh. Okay..." He angled his chin up, brushing his tongue against his lower lip. "And let me guess, you're the current title holder?"

I shook my head. "Nope. Runner up. Three years running now...to my younger fucking brother."

"Wow."

After enjoying a few scoops of ice cream in silence, a heaviness returned to my chest. I should have just pushed through it and said nothing, but talking to Conrad made me feel good, lighter. Besides, he was interested so I figured, why not?

"The good times are well and truly behind us now. The cowbell industry is in serious decline. It's facing some serious challenges."

Conrad's eyes softened. "Like what?"

"Where do I start? Technology, for one. There are new tracking devices available to farmers these days, making cowbells obsolete. Then there are concerns by animal rights groups about the impact of cowbells to the animal's wellbeing."

"Are those concerns founded?"

I bit down on my lip. "Jury's out on that one. Some research indicates that sounds over one hundred and thirteen decibels may cause the animals pain or deafness. Which is why we've spearheaded an initiative to develop leading-edge technology that not only reduces the volume of the sound, but also stimulates happy responses in cows."

"Wow." There it was again, the word of the evening.

"But cows are having a bad moment, too." I reached for my fourth, now almost empty glass of wine. "Everyone blames their methane emissions for contributing to climate change... So, as you can see, it's a lot. And I inherit this lovely shitshow in a month. Yay for me."

Conrad's lips tapered into a thin line. "And you're worried you won't be able to meet the challenge?"

I shook my head. "No. I'm worried I don't even *want* to meet the challenge. This—this isn't what I want to be doing with my life. I'm not passionate about fucking cowbells."

"Well..." Conrad pushed his dessert bowl away and shot me a look as if he were mulling something over in his head.

"Well, what?" I prompted after a few moments of him saying nothing else. "Don't leave me hanging here, Conrad."

"This is just an observation..."

I narrowed my eyes. "Uh-huh."

"But for someone who says they have zero interest, you sure do know a lot about it."

More silence. This time due to me as I let his words sink in.

"And"—his voice was tender, like he was verbally carrying something precious and didn't want to drop it—"the way you spoke about the initiative you're developing to make cowbells better for animals...well, your whole face lit up as you were talking."

"It—it did?"

He nodded firmly and smiled.

I shrugged. "I guess I am proud of that. I like being able to do things that help other people. Or animals, in this case."

"You're a good person, Jed."

My pulse quickened. No, I wasn't. I was a deeply flawed person who was getting into more and more trouble with each passing day.

I wiped my mouth with the napkin. "I'll get the bill."

Conrad's eyes widened. "Oh, no. Please. Let's at least—"

"No." My voice easily overrode his. "I insist. Please let me get this. It's my way of saying thank you for a wonderful day."

Conrad looked uncomfortable, and I noticed a rosy hue had filled his cheeks. "Um, okay. Thank you, Jed. For dinner. And for today, too. I had a really good time with you as well."

"Hey, Conrad." Slowly, he lifted his head and our eyes met. "The night is still young. Whaddya say we have a drink back in my suite?"

8

CONRAD

"One drink, and one drink only," I announced as I scooted in behind Jed as he opened the door to his suite. Except, holy shit, this wasn't a suite like mine. This was a full-on apartment. He started turning on the lights, revealing the true size of the place. It was like one of those ginormous penthouses you'd see in movies or magazines.

"Wow."

"A drink?" Jed asked as he flicked on the fireplace because, of course, the place had a gas-light fireplace that could be turned on with the press of a single button.

"Sure."

"What can I get you?"

"Water will be fine. Thanks."

I took the place in. To my left was a kitchen practically the size of the bungalow Dad and I lived in. It led out to a massive combined living and dining area. To my right, there was a white curved staircase. *A freaking staircase!* In an apartment. I had never seen anything like it before.

"That leads up to the bedrooms, in case you're wondering."

I set my eyes onto Jed, his lips fixed in a cheeky smirk. "I wasn't wondering, but thanks for letting me know."

"Hey"—he came over and handed me a glass of water—"let's just be open and see where this night takes us."

He lifted his glass and we *clinked.*

I took a sip and looked over at the light brown liquid in his glass. "Bourbon?"

Jed nodded. "Woodford Reserve. The best thing to come out of Kentucky since fried chicken."

I giggled and headed over to the floor-to-ceiling windows designed to perfectly capture the magnificent view of the ocean.

"Wanna sit outside on the terrace?" Jed asked, pulling up beside me.

"Yeah. It might be nice."

He opened the sliding door and motioned for me to go out first. "Eyes at eye level, please," I ribbed. Although would Jed checking me out really be such a bad thing?

Yes. Yes it would. You're here for one drink. And one drink only.

Despite my initial reservations, Jed turned out to be a perfect gentleman as we sat and talked... and talked...and talked. Okay, so maybe one drink had turned into three. For him at least, I was sticking to water. All we were doing was chatting. Clothes remained on, and we even had a little distance between the two armchairs we were each snuggled up in.

When the wind picked up, Jed went inside and brought out two blankets, carefully placing one over me. His spicy cologne mixed with the salty breeze and infiltrated my senses.

"So, tell me about your love life," Jed said, kicking off his socks and shoes and stretching his legs out onto the coffee table in front of us. Freed from shoes, even flip-flops, his feet looked even huger.

"We've reached that part of the evening, have we?" I shot him a speculative look.

He returned my smile, and there was something else I was

picking up from him. A kindness, a genuine interest in me. "We have."

"There's not much to tell, really." I pulled the blanket up a little higher, bringing it across my chest. "Looking after Dad didn't just affect my grades—it kinda killed any hope I had of dating, too."

"Does your dad know you're gay?"

"Oh yeah." I smiled. "I came out to him when I was fifteen. He just hugged me and said he loved me and wanted me to be happy."

"You can't ask for a better reaction than that."

"No, you can't. What about you? Are you out?"

"Oh, yeah." He waved his hand in the air. "Everyone knows I'm gay. Both of my brothers, Cooper and Mitchell, are gay, too."

"Really? The trifecta."

Jed barked out a laugh. "Yep. Family's cool. Cowbell Creek townsfolk are cool. I'm super lucky it's never been a big deal."

"So, yeah." I returned to his original question. "I've never actually had a boyfriend."

"Oh, so does that mean..."

I twisted to face Jed, his face uncharacteristically flustered.

"I mean, have you..."

I settled back in my seat, enjoying this display way more than I should have. But he was just so freaking cute.

"You're not a..."

"Virgin?" I finished his question for him as relief flooded his face. "No, I'm not a virgin, Jed. Why? Are you?"

He tipped his head back, his Adam's apple protruding from his throat. "No, not a virgin. But also never had a boyfriend, either."

"Why not?"

He froze, his face suspended, looking up at the night sky. For a minute, I thought that maybe he hadn't heard my question. But when he brought his head down and kept his stare fixed on the onyx black ocean in front of us, I knew he'd heard. For some reason, though, he couldn't put an answer into words.

I decided not to push it. "It's getting late." I placed my glass on the coffee table, shrugged the blanket off me, and stood up. "I should get going."

"Stay, please. Let's keep talking." Jed scrambled to his feet as well. "I'm enjoying it...and I'm on my best behavior."

My lips edged up at his earnestness. Plus, he was right. He had been displaying nothing but exemplary behavior. "I'm enjoying it, too." I pulled back slightly to get a better look at his face. "This isn't some ploy to keep me here until my resolve weakens?"

Jed closed the distance between us. "Why? Is it weakening?"

I held my ground, looking straight into those expressive, puppy dog eyes of his. "No."

He took half a step back. "Well, this isn't a ploy, I swear. I'm respecting your wishes, Conrad. In fact, I think I deserve a fucking medal given how much I want you in my bed."

"Ha! Not likely." The words tumbled out of my mouth with way more force than I had intended. More than that, I hated the jilted look that met me in response.

Before I could say anything to try and recover, he dropped his head, staring at the tiled terrace floor, his left leg swaying loosely. "You—you don't think I'm attractive?"

I stepped in closer, hooking my fingers underneath his chin. Our eyes met. "Is that a trick question?"

"No." His voice came out low, laced with vulnerability. "I'm probably not your type, anyway. Right? You're probably into surfer dudes. And I—I don't look like a surfer boy."

"You look all right."

He arched an eyebrow. "I do?"

"Yeah, I like your face." My fingers gently flickered over his exposed forearm. "Especially when you smile. Everything lights up and your eyes get this mischievous glow to them."

He let out a soft chuckle. "What about my big floppy ears?"

"Yeah, they're adorable."

He let out a rapid-fire round of blinks. "Did you just call me adorable?"

Dammit. I knew this would happen. He'd gotten me to drop my defenses, succumbing to his intoxicating charm. I'd touched his arm, and now I'd inadvertently complimented him, too.

I scratched the back of my neck. "I guess I did."

His eyes searched mine, and it felt like he was burrowing into my brain. "I'll give you three seconds to take it back if you didn't mean it."

I didn't know how he was doing it, but Jedfire was making my skin tingle in ways I'd never felt before.

"Three..."

Should I say something? What? What would I even say? *Yes, I called you adorable, but I didn't really mean it.* But I *did* mean it. So what sense did it make to cover up the truth with a lie?

"Two..."

Fuck. Okay. *Think, brain, think.* What's the best way out of this? *Was* there a way out of this? Did I want to save face? Maybe... Kinda... Actually, now that I gave it some thought, no, not really.

"One."

Silence. My lips stayed snapped shut and...that wasn't the worst thing in the world.

A smile slowly broke out across Jed's face and it was the most beautiful thing I'd ever seen. It reminded me of a sunrise, the way the rays of the sun would peek over the horizon line, giving the first indication of the new day.

As his lips stretched wider and wider, consuming the lower half of his face, his eyes shimmering, a realization dawned on me: I needed him. I needed those lips on me like night needed morning. Even if nothing more could ever come of it.

"Can I—"

"Yes," I breathed back, instinctively knowing he was going to ask if he could kiss me.

His smile took over his whole face now. "Geez, this whole 'being a gentleman' thing is really paying off. I should do it mo—"

I grabbed the back of his neck and pulled him into me, our lips smooshing together. He let out a surprised gasp. I opened my mouth to take him in. I wanted his lips, his taste, inside of me. It was at that moment that I realized due to our height difference, I was basically bending Jed forward in order to match my height. I pulled back a moment. "Is this comfortable for you?"

"I'll take your lips any way I can get 'em."

I pulled back even more, my palms resting against his chest. "I'm serious, Jed."

"So am I."

And with that he scooped me up into his lengthy arms and pressed his lips to mine again. He was holding me up and kissing me at the same time. I looped my hands around his neck, praying I wasn't too heavy for him, while losing myself more and more with each passing second into the deepest, most passionate kiss of my life.

Jed's kisses—much like everything else about him—were like nothing I'd ever experienced before. His tongue was strong, dominating my mouth with a sweet, probing force that somehow, encouraged me to sink even deeper into the kiss. His strong hands housed my body protectively against his warm flesh. I felt safe and lifted and so wondrously happy.

When he finally lowered me to the ground, he kept his hands around my waist, which as it turned out, was a good thing. I needed a moment to get my balance back.

"Wow."

He shot me a withering look. "Yeah. Wow."

I ran my tongue over my swollen lips. "That really happened?"

He smiled and gave a nod. "It really did."

"I—I don't know what to say."

"I think *wow* covers it pretty well." He ran his hand across his chest. "Stay the night. And before you say what I know you're going to say, hear me out."

I clamped my half-open mouth shut.

It had all started with the promise of one drink. Which led to three. That in turn led to God only knew how many hours of talking and laughing. Capped off by a pretty fucking terrific kiss. And now *this* latest proposition.

All right. Let's see how Jedfire Burns was going to convince me to spend the night with him.

9

JEDFIRE

"Do you like puppies?"

Conrad blinked and shook his head. "Sorry, what?"

I curled my hand on his shoulder. "Just answer the question—do you like puppies?"

"Yes."

He was looking confused and a little disorientated. Perfect. Onto question number two.

"What about Janet Jackson's *The Velvet Rope* album?"

"What about it?" he whipped back.

"Do you like it?"

"Yes. Of course. It's my favorite album of hers."

My pulse quickened. Cute guy. Super smart. Hot body. And not only a Janet fan, but a *correct-era* Janet fan. (Her sound in the '80s was too poppy and Michael Jackson-lite, while anything from her 2003 post-wardrobe malfunction era was, well, an aural malfunction. Her '90s jams were her creative zenith.)

I turned on my heel and headed over to the edge of the terrace.

"I don't understand what you're doing, Jed. Aren't you meant to be trying to convince me to stay?"

I looked over my shoulder and licked my lips. "You just answered *yes* to two questions in a row."

A knowing look hit him as he shook his head.

"And you thought that would work?"

I nodded. "Yeah."

He placed a hand on his hip. "What if it doesn't?"

"Well if it's not working, then why are you smiling?" I shot back, resting my chin on my shoulder. Was I trying to look all coy and seductive, hoping that would help lure him in? Yes. Yes, I was.

The guy had said I was adorable for fuck's sake. That statement alone had my heart doing cartwheels inside my chest. No one had ever called me that before. Or anything even remotely in that ballpark. Compliments I'd received for my physical appearance were limited to words like *tall* and *big* and *interesting-looking*. Never adorable.

Until tonight.

"I'm not trying to trip you up or get you to stay on a technicality, Conrad." I spun around, leaning against the brick wall that reached halfway up my body.

"Oh, yeah." He moved toward me, slowly. I could see he was conflicted by the way his eyes darted about, unsure whether he could trust me. But...he *was* inching closer to me.

"Have I been the perfect gentleman all night?"

"Yes." His lips tipped upward. "And technically, that yes is the third *yes* in a row."

"Good," I responded. "Because I want you to stay here because you want to be here. With me."

He swallowed hard and I could tell that he didn't know what to do with himself. His arms hung awkwardly by the sides of his body, his fingers fidgeting.

"You can either stay in one of the spare rooms..." I waited, giving him a moment.

"Or?" he prodded.

"Or you can sleep in my bed. But, Conrad, and I know this is going to be very hard for you to hear"—his eyebrows furled—"you will not be able to have sex with me tonight."

The confused look he'd worn a number of times during the evening made its grand reappearance.

"Snuggles, yes," I went on. "But sex, no. And butt sex with two *T*'s, also no."

A cackle flew out of his mouth as he shook his head. Yeah, I was a lot. But I could tell he was diggin' it.

I returned to my faux-serious routine. "Those are my terms and conditions. I'm sorry, but you'll just have to put all your primal lust and desire for me to the side. I am not your sex toy." Rant over, arms crossed over chest. Now...waiting for a reaction.

Conrad glanced past me into the distance, grinning. "You're"—he shook his head before his eyes landed on me—"the most unique person I have ever met, Jedfire Burns."

I raised a finger. "And adorable, too. Don't forget you said that before."

"I have a feeling you won't let me live it down."

He reached where I was standing and it took everything I had in me not to loop my arms around him. This gentleman business was a hard gig. No wonder it had died in the modern age.

But I still hadn't gotten my *yes* from him. And as someone who too often thought with his cock, I wanted Conrad's response to come from the heart. Not because I was touching him, and not on any silly technicality, either. I needed to know he meant it.

He stared at me with glittery eyes. I felt my pulse beating out of my neck. He was so fucking beautiful he made breathing difficult.

"Yes. I'll stay." His warm breath danced across my cheeks and lit me up inside.

I resisted the urge to break out into a happy dance, fearing my flailing arms and terrible attempts at doing the running man would ruin the tender moment. Instead, I summoned all my self-control and asked in a measured tone, "And will you be going with option A or option B for your preferred sleeping arrangement?"

He looked at me with eyes the color of ripe blueberries. "Option B. What can I say? I'm a sucker for snuggles."

My heart stuttered in my chest. "Very well, then."

We both smiled at my attempt at faux maturity, before his expression turned serious. "Now, I have a question for you. Are you a—"

"Small spoon," I replied, hoping I'd guessed what he was about to ask me. Judging by the way he nodded approvingly, I had.

"I was hoping you'd say that."

"You were?" Because of my size, most guys presumed I was a big spoon. But nothing felt better than having a set of arms wrapped around me as I drifted off to sleep. Or, at least, I assumed it felt good. I'd never actually fallen asleep like that with anyone before. I always gave in and assumed the big spoon role. At least until the guy had fallen asleep and I could resume *Operation Get the Fuck Outta There.*

Conrad smoothed his hand across my chest. "You draw me in, Jed. I've—I've been fighting with myself, trying to resist the pull you seem to have over me since the moment we met."

Heat crawled up my neck as I grazed his jawline with the back of my fingers. "Stop trying to fight this. I won't hurt you."

His lower lip quivered. "You promise?"

"I promise."

We stood in silence for a moment, an undeniable energy swirling around us. He had a vulnerability that made me want to care for and protect him. But he was no weakling or pushover, either. And I needed to feel his arms around me so fucking much.

"Time for bed?" I suggested, and he nodded.

Ten minutes later, we'd both showered—I was sticking to my gentleman promise and used one of the spare bathrooms—brushed our teeth, and were ready to hop into bed. I'd already snuck in under the covers when Conrad turned off the bathroom light in the en suite and padded barefoot into the bedroom.

My eyes traveled down his body. He only wore a pair of tight clinging black boxer briefs. His skin was tanned all over, light hairs only smattering his lithe arms and surprisingly muscular legs.

"I'm keeping these on." He tugged at the top of his briefs, which only drew my attention to the massive bulge they contained.

I pulled down the comforter, revealing my own yellow-and-brown striped pajama bottoms. "Same here. See, total gentleman."

That drew a sweet giggle out of him as he got into bed. I propped myself up, elbow on pillow, watching him as he lay down. A yawn escaped his mouth and he didn't catch it in time to cover it.

"Sorry. I'm a little worn out."

"It's been a big day."

He turned his head to look at me. "Yeah, it has been. Fun, though."

"Heaps of fun," I agreed.

And with that, I shuffled down the bed and flipped onto my right side. Seconds later, Conrad's fingers glided over my hips and wrapped themselves around me. We both moved in closer, pressing our bodies as close as we could against each other.

"Lock your arms around me." I trembled as I said those words. I didn't know why. I'd said way more explicit things to guys before, but there was something about telling Conrad that I wanted his touch that made me feel so vulnerable.

His lean arms did just that. They locked me firmly into position against his body. I held onto his forearm as I settled into the delicious feeling of just being held.

"I'm going to get a boner," Conrad announced suddenly. "I need you to know that it's just a bodily reaction because we're lying together. It has nothing to do with you."

I flicked my head back, catching only the top corner of his face. "Nothing?"

He nuzzled his chin into the crook of my neck. "Okay. Maybe a little."

A warm feeling settled in the center of my chest and my eyelids grew heavier. I'd looked at the time before I jumped into the shower. It was ten past midnight. I'd lost my ATM window for the day, but I honestly didn't care.

I wouldn't have missed this for anything in the world. Conrad's breathing got deeper and heavier. His chest pressed against my back, his lips resting against my shoulder—it felt divine. I folded my knees so that our feet could tangle together at the bottom of the bed.

This was what I'd craved for so long but had never been able to find.

Sure, a fuck was nice. But a snuggle? I felt like I had been shrunk down to Lego size—*Honey, I Shrunk The Kids* style—and gotten wrapped up in a lightly toasted cinnamon roll. I wiggled my bottom into his body. Yep, he was hard. And by the feel of it, big, too.

Not tonight, though.

Funny. At the start of the evening, having sex with Conrad was all that I had wanted. But lying here, falling asleep in his arms, I couldn't have imagined a better ending to the day.

For the first time in a very long time, all was right in my world. Or at least, I let myself believe that for a few blissful moments as my eyelids grew heavier. I nestled deeper into Conrad's warmth and drifted off into a peaceful sleep.

SUNDAY

10

CONRAD

I rolled over into still-warm sheets and patted my hands around, searching for him. He fell asleep in my arms, and there was a very good likelihood neither one of us moved an inch last night.

But now, he was gone.

I let out a yawn, rubbing my eyes as I opened them. The room was light and a freshly showered scent lingered in the air, a gentle reminder he'd been here. As if I could ever forget.

"Jed," I called out. The door to the bathroom had been left open. No response. Maybe he'd gone downstairs and was making me breakfast? A smile spread across my lips at the thought.

I folded the pillow in half and propped it behind my head, the smile in no hurry to leave my face. What was happening here? Was it possible to fall for someone this quick? Not that Jedfire Burns was just anyone, but still, didn't this kind of thing only happen in Hallmark movies and fairytales? An image of Jed riding a horse shirtless on the beach at sunset entered my mind and for some reason, filled my chest with bubbles of happiness.

I rubbed the sleep out of my eyes and propped myself up onto my elbows. Okay, this little fantasy I'd concocted was just that—a fantasy. I needed to remember that. Today was a new day. One that might hopefully include breakfast with Jed, but which would, in all likelihood, then be followed by a, *see ya, might catch ya 'round the pool sometime* goodbye.

Oh, and maybe just one more kiss. A more subdued, morning kiss because I didn't think my heart could take another kiss like last night. Although, feeling Jed's tongue roaming in my mouth one more time wouldn't be the worst thing in the world.

I drew the sheet off me and got dressed in last night's clothes. I glanced over at the closet, tempted to take a peek and see if Jed had anything I could wear. But given his size, not to mention his, er, eclectic fashion taste, I didn't think I'd find anything. Besides, it didn't feel right to be going through his stuff.

I splashed some water on my face and patted down the wayward strands of hair that were sticking up stubbornly at the top of my head. The thought of having a quick shower crossed my mind, but then I'd lose Jed's smell which had latched itself onto my skin. I didn't want to wash that away. Not just yet.

As I made my way down the stairs, I heard voices. I glanced over at the million-inch TV screen taking up the entire wall in the living area, but it wasn't on. I headed toward the kitchen, the voices getting louder with each step I took.

I snuck my head in around the door frame and could see Jed leaning against the counter, an unhappy, deer-caught-in-headlights look on his face. An elderly lady dressed in three-quarter-length white linen pants and an intricately patterned blouse was elegantly perched on one of the bar stools. She may have been older, but as I squinted, I couldn't see a single wrinkle on her face.

While an older guy, dressed in brown slacks and a faded yellow button-up shirt, paced up and down the kitchen. It was his voice I'd heard. His loud and very *angry* voice.

I backed up against the wall, realizing I was doing it again. Eavesdropping. But what would be ruder—listening or barging in?

"I just don't understand, Jedfire..." The man's voice carried an authoritative air, underpinned by exasperation. He was holding up some papers, flicking them in front of himself as he strode back and forth in the kitchen, Jed's sunken eyes following the man's every movement.

"Your legal fees are astronomical. Twenty-seven thousand dollars in one month! How is it possible that your personal fees are bigger than what we spend for the entire plant?"

Jed's shoulders slumped, but it seemed like a rhetorical question since the man sucked in a breath as if he were about to keep going, when the woman raised a well-manicured hand into the air. "Walter. Don't be so mean to him."

The man—Walter, I presumed—turned on his heel and approached the woman. His demeanor changed immediately, softening as she grazed long fingers down his back. "It's for his own good, Catherine—"

"Katie." She flicked her index finger up, meeting the tip of his nose. "We're on vacation, remember? Katie sounds younger and less *grandmother-ish*." She screwed her nose up at that last word, but yep, still hardly any lines. The woman looked unbelievable for her age.

She nuzzled up against his shoulder and Walter's face melted like butter, a crooked smile tugging at his lips. Wait, I recognized that slightly off-kilter grin. It reminded me of Jed's. The people seemed a little too old to be Jed's parents. I guessed they were his grandparents.

"Speaking of which, do we really need to be talking shop? I want to get down to the pool and have some fun. I spotted some hotties in there already as we walked over."

"Grandma." Jed stood up tall, his index finger pointing straight at his grandmother. "Behave."

I suppressed a scoff. Since when was Jed the responsible one, telling his grandmother of all people to rein in her behavior? As if she could be any wilder than her grandson.

"Well, I'm heading out. This body ain't gonna tan itself. Play nice, you two." She grabbed a coffee mug and made her way to a door at the other end of the kitchen.

Once she left, Walter's gaze returned to Jed. They were having some sort of mini standoff. Why on earth was Jed spending so much money on legal fees? Was he in some sort of trouble?

I could see Jed's prominent nose and full lips on his grandfather's face. Despite yelling at Jed, I could feel a strong bond between them. Jed, seemingly, was in the process of getting caught doing something bad, but the affection between them was palpable.

"Want to tell me about Vegas?"

Jed's jaw twitched, and then I heard it. A loud *clank* sound. It was the same sound he'd made at dinner last night when I'd asked him about his work. It sounded like a tongue pop or something.

"You heard about that?" Jed muttered.

Walter nodded, sitting himself down on the empty stool left by Catherine. He remained rigid, his spine completely straight, but he lowered his voice. "Tommy called. Jed, you know how much I love you. I'm worried. Tell me, please, what is going on? Why are you behaving like this?"

Melancholy inched its way up Jed's face until it reached his eyes. "I don't know, Grandpa. I don't know why I do any of the stupid sh—stuff that I do."

"We both know that's not true. You're a bright boy with lots of potential. You need to harness it, Jed."

"Why?" Jed's eyes shot up at his grandfather, defiance suddenly glaring in them. "What's the point? What's the point of anything?"

Walter propped his elbows up on the counter, tapping his fingertips together and let out a heavy sigh. "What happened wasn't fair, Jed."

"Understatement of the century," Jed scoffed, turning away from Walter.

I winced. Okay, I definitely shouldn't have been listening to this, but it was too late. I had been sucked into it, and now, I needed to know the source of Jed's pain.

Then I would walk away.

"And how exactly does getting married in Vegas help?" Irritation returned to Walter's voice. "Once, I could forgive. We've all done stupid things. But twice? Come on, Jed. This is just ridiculous."

"No, what's ridiculous, Grandpa, is that in less than a month, my life is over."

"Come on, Jed. You're exaggerating."

"No, I'm not. What else would you call it? Having to take over a business I don't want to. Living in Cowbell Creek where everywhere I go, everyone I meet, reminds me of what I've lost."

Walter slammed his hands down on the counter. "You're not the only one who's lost something. Need I remind you that you have two younger brothers? I don't see Mitchell and Cooper squandering their lives away like this."

"Grandpa, I'm not squandering anything, I'm living my life to the fullest. I'm traveling. I'm meeting people. I'm 'finding myself.'" He used his fingers to indicate air quotes for that last part.

My heart was beating in my throat. It had been for a few minutes now. I banged the back of my head against the wall. Were Jed's parents dead? Was that what he meant by being reminded of what he'd lost?

Something was stirring in my gut. An urge. An urge to do something, anything, to help Jed out. I couldn't un-hear all the things I'd heard spoken between them, and I sure as heck couldn't stand by and not do anything to try and help him.

"And how exactly is marrying a stranger finding yourself, Jed?" Walter demanded.

"He didn't marry a stranger." I turned the corner and entered the kitchen. Both men's heads snapped in my direction. Jed looked like he'd seen a ghost as my feet carried me forward. "He married me."

Jed's eyes blew out to the size of balloons. My pulse was racing, but for some reason that I couldn't put into words, this felt like the right thing to do.

"And who"—Walter spun around to face me—"might you be, young man?"

I extended my hand as I approached the man, suppressing the nerves that rose in my throat with each step I took. "I'm Conrad McCallister, sir."

Damn, the man had a grip on him. He almost crushed my fingers. I did my best not to let it show, as he eyed me up and down.

"And you and my grandson are...married?" Walter's head darted between me and Jed.

"Sure are." I mustered up all my perkiness as I walked over to stand next to Jed. "Got married in Vegas and decided to come here for our honeymoon. Florida's a peach this time of year."

A freakin' *peach*. Okay, time to stop babbling. I couldn't pull it off any more than Jed could tell a lie. Which, shit, I had now forced him to do. To his grandfather, of all people. Okay, so maybe it would have helped if I'd taken five seconds and actually attempted to think this through. But nope, no time for that.

I looked up at Jed's face and smiled. "Hey...baby."

I could see his chest heaving with every breath he took. After a few moments, he caught his composure. I felt his arm slide around my waist as he placed a peck to my forehead.

"Sleep well...baby?"

"Like a log...baby."

Okay, we'd need to have a chat to refine our overuse of the word *baby*. Also, maybe find other cute pet names that were less nauseating.

Walter narrowed his eyes at us. "How long have you two known each other?"

Oh, crap! Questions. I hadn't been expecting that. What sort of grandfather had the audacity to ask questions when his grandson got married in Vegas for a second time to a guy he's never talked about? The man was clearly a monster.

"We met a few months ago," Jed replied, staring at the wall behind his grandfather. That's right; he couldn't make eye contact when he lied. I wasn't much better either. Keeping a secret? That I could do, and I'd been doing it well for the last six months. But outright lie? Not so much. Maybe this wasn't such a good idea, after all.

Worse, now I'd roped Jed into this mess, too. Would he be mad at me? Sure, his hand had nestled into the small of my back, and it seemed perfectly content there. I was fine with it as well. But an incidental touch didn't mean he would be okay with the clusterfuck of a lie I'd trapped us both in.

Walter pushed back from the counter, getting to his feet. "We need to find your grandmother, Jed. She was eyeing the pool when we arrived this morning and something tells me she plans on getting into trouble."

Trouble? Jed's grandmother. She seemed like such a nice, normal lady. Well dressed. Classy. Looked thirty years younger than what I assumed her actual age was. What kind of trouble could she possibly get into?

Walter gave us both a clipped nod. "We're not done talking about this, Jed. Now, come on, boys. Help me find that feisty wife of mine."

11

JEDFIRE

"Are you mad? Oh my God! I'm so sorry. You're mad, aren't you? You have every right to be. I shouldn't have done it. I don't know what got—"

I planted the back of my hand against Conrad's chest. "I'm not mad." I tipped my head at Grandpa who was walking only a few feet in front of us. "Just keep it down, okay?"

Conrad nodded, but then he twisted his neck forward right in front of me and peered up, blinking at me through those sunlight-tinged lashes of his. "Are you sure you're not mad at me?" He whispered it so sweetly that I couldn't help but giggle...and feel giddy.

This was so not the morning I had planned when I'd gotten out of the warm bed I'd shared with Conrad. No. My plan involved making him a delicious breakfast, serving it to him in bed, and, if I played my gentlemanly cards right, maybe serving something *else* to him in bed, too.

So, imagine my surprise when the doorbell rang. Firstly, because I didn't know the apartment had a doorbell and then, because I was met with both of my grandparents. Luggage in tow, accompanied by the fiercest frown I had seen on my grandfather, since, well, my last misadventure.

"Surprise!" Grandma yelled out as she threw her arms around my shocked body. Yeah, you could say that, all right.

When I asked—keeping my tone as polite as possible—what they were doing here, I was met with one of Grandpa's infamous steely glares. There was a reason why the man was known as the *Cowbell King* in the industry.

So, yeah, it was pretty obvious I was in trouble. The only question I had was—which one of my misdeeds had they cottoned on to? Yes, there was a list. Although in my meek defense, it wasn't a particularly long one at the moment, just one that was escalating in seriousness with each passing day.

And then, just as Grandpa was digging into me for my stupid Vegas mistake, a certain ray of Californian sunshine announced his presence by sauntering into the kitchen and introducing himself...as my husband.

I really wasn't mad at him for that. Astonished? Bewildered? Dazed? Yes, yes and yes. Also, strangely, a little turned on. But that's what I got for not cranking one out in the shower this morning. I was saving myself for him... I still was.

"This pool is huge." Grandpa stopped and waited for us to catch up to him. "I'll go left. You boys go right."

"Sure, Grandpa." I tugged at Conrad to follow me.

"Jed, are you sure you're not m—"

I stopped and placed both hands square on Conrad's shoulders. I scooped my eyes lower to meet his. "I promise you, Conrad, I'm not mad."

"Really?"

"Yes, really." I let go of him and started walking, slower this time, with my eyes scanning the pool area on high Grandma-alert. "Why did you do it?"

Conrad scratched the side of his face. "I didn't like hearing your grandpa yelling at you like that."

My chest oozed with a warm, gooey lava at his words. Conrad cared about me, and that was the coolest thing in the fucking world. "Believe me"—I threaded my fingers through Conrad's—"Grandpa doesn't know the half of it."

Before Conrad could ask me the question I saw forming on his lips, we heard the sounds of a female shrieking in the middle of the pool.

"Woohoo, I'm riding a fatherfucking cowboy!"

We spun around, following the voice coming from the middle of the pool. My mouth fell open when I saw who it was.

Conrad stood next to me, his shoulder delicately brushing against my arm. "Hey, isn't that your—"

"Grandma." I nodded. Grandma was on the shoulders of a tanned, brawny, muscled guy, cocktail in one hand, her other lassoing around like she was...*shit*, riding a cowboy.

I crashed my hands into my face. "Oh, god."

"Is she, uh..." Conrad's voice trailed, but I couldn't bring myself to finish the question for him. He'd have to say the word because I just couldn't.

"Topless?"

I peered warily through the cracks in my fingers. Yep, Grandma was topless in the middle of the pool and drawing quite the crowd. She'd caught the attention of the other people who until now, had been relaxing, sunbathing, or reading on the deckchairs. Not anymore. Now everyone had stopped whatever they were doing and were taking it all in—just like Grandma would've wanted.

"So, that's where you get it from."

I dropped my hands and stared at Conrad. He was smiling— *smiling!*—like he was enjoying the spectacle.

"What do you mean, 'that's where I get it from'?"

He ignored my question and took a few steps closer toward the edge of the pool. The chorus of cheers only getting louder.

"Go, sexy grandma," someone yelled out. Why? Why were these people encouraging her? Cheers and applause would only egg the woman on and embarrass me more than I had ever been in my entire life.

"Call me a MILF! I'm too sexy to be a granny, right?" Grandma yelled back, drawing even more hand clapping and cheering from the ever increasingly large crowd. Where were all these people coming from? Had someone sent out a distress-slash-let's-embarrass-the-fuck-out-of-Jed beacon to attract all these folks down to the sideshow unfolding in the pool?

Conrad looked at me. "I never thought these words would ever come out of my mouth, and I say this with nothing but mad props to the woman, but—your grandmother has got some seriously great breasts."

I groaned. "She got them last year, right before Christmas."

Conrad snickered and as much as I wanted to curl up and die, standing next to him made the embarrassment unfolding in front of us a little more bearable, somehow.

"Let's just say that was the first year our family Christmas cards were taken with a beach backdrop and a *Down Under* theme."

More sweet giggles escaped Conrad's lips. He nudged into me, and I placed my arm around his shoulder. "Hey, if you've got it, flaunt it. Good for her."

I turned away and thankfully, Conrad followed my lead. As much as I loved Grandma, there was only so much of seeing her breasts I could take in one morning. "I need to get outta here."

Conrad nodded knowingly. His face had retreated back into semi-seriousness. "Sure."

"I need to find Grandpa, deal with *that* situation"—I stuck my hand out in the direction of the pool—"but we also need to talk about this whole marriage situation."

"Oh, yeah, that. Geez, there's never a dull moment with you, is there, Jed?"

"No, there isn't." I smirked before licking my lower lip. "But I believe *you're* the one who told my grandfather we were married."

RUNAWAY: AN ESCAPE NOVEL

He blushed, and I fastened my hands around his narrow waist, pulling him in for a soft kiss.

"Thank you for doing that. I'm honestly not mad. It means a lot to me, that you...care."

Two blueberry eyes sparkled as he peered up at me. He looked like he was about to say something, but then stopped.

"How about dinner again, tonight?" I suggested. "You know, to go over all of this fake marriage stuff?"

"Yes."

He palmed my chest, sending a fierce heat right to the tip of my cock. Dammit. No pre-wank and now, I wouldn't be seeing him until dinner either...if I survived it that long without dying from a case of the world's worst blue balls first.

He exhaled. "But let me do dinner this time?"

"Sure."

"Great. It's a date, then."

Conrad's mouth gaped open as he realized what he'd just said. He let out a nervous chuckle and I could have sworn a gymnastics team burrowed its way into my chest and started doing cartwheel drills because just seeing the expression on his face right now was making me woozy... in the best way possible.

"It's a date," I confirmed, and the sweet heat that infused my face was the best feeling in the world.

12

CONRAD

"You're eating well?"

"I am."

"What about sleep? How are you sleeping?"

"Fine."

"And you're not doing too much? You're resting and taking it easy, I hope."

Okay, I was beginning to see where I got my incessant question-nagging from. This conversation was reminding me of checking in with Jed about him not being mad at me for blurting out that I was his husband to his grandpa. I guess when we McCallisters wanted to know someone was okay, we *really* wanted to find out for sure.

"Conrad, are you there?"

I swept my fingers through my hair. "I'm here, Dad. You can stop worrying about me. Everything is fine. I love it here. It's beautiful. I'll send you some photos of the room. The view is amazing. I even went for a hike yesterday—"

"A hike?" His voice prickled with concern.

"A short one," I quickly assured him.

I took the phone away from my ear and pressed the speaker

button. I placed the phone onto the table as my feet landed in the spare chair on the balcony, giving my legs a nice stretch. Not that I'd been doing anything more strenuous than reading a book by the pool all day. Still, I was on vacation, and being comfortable was the name of the game.

"You can stop worrying about me, Dad. I'm fine."

"I'm never going to stop worrying about you, son. And *just* fine?"

I chuckled. "Actually, more than fine."

Should I tell Dad about Jed? What was there to say? How would I even begin to capture Jedfire Burns with something so limiting and restrictive as words?

I'd never had a boyfriend before, not that that's what Jed was. But my love life up until this point had been pretty bleak. More like nonexistent, actually. Otherwise, I probably would have talked to Dad about it, if there was anything to tell.

"How are you feeling about coming home?"

I cast my eyes out over the water, shimmering in the late afternoon sun. "Good," I replied after a pause. "I think I'm at that point you get to on a vacation where you've had a good time, but you're also ready to get back and sleep in your own bed. But..."

But then I'd met Jed.

And suddenly, everything in my world felt...different. He was a force of nature. Like no one I'd ever met before. And the more I kept trying to shake him out of my thoughts—the harder he seemed to lodge himself in there.

"But, yeah, things are going to be pretty heavy when I get back."

"They don't need to be, son. We will get through this together. I promise you."

I picked at a piece of loose skin underneath my thumbnail. "I know, Dad."

"In the meantime, Conrad, you've still got three days there. Enjoy them. Carefully, of course. Make the most of it. Whatever life throws at you, go for it and have some fun. Lord knows you deserve it."

"Dad."

"It's true. You've given up so much for me. And now, you won't even get a chance to—"

"Dad! Stop. Please."

"I'm sorry, I'm sorry, I'm sorry." I heard him clear his throat and I could picture what he'd be doing so vividly in my mind— straightening his shoulders, resetting his look to the usual calm and collected man I knew him to be...before the tours, before Mom walking out on us, before I'd come home one day six months ago and dropped the bombshell to end all bombshells.

"I miss you, Dad."

It had been over five months since I'd left to go travel the world and I really did miss him. But he wanted me to do this. He had to practically push me out the door, but I was beyond grateful that he did. Otherwise, I wouldn't have gotten the chance to see and experience the world like I had.

"I miss you too, son. So, what are you doing for the rest of the day?"

"I've actually got dinner plans." A smile infiltrated my voice and Dad picked up on it straight away.

"Dinner plans, hey. With anyone...special?"

Oh, yeah. With someone extraordinarily special. "Just someone I met." I tried to keep my tone light, but I wasn't sure if I was doing a good job of it.

"Does he have a name?"

Oh, yeah. He has an extraordinarily special name. "Jedfire."

"Jedfire?" Dad exclaimed. "Seriously? That's his actual name."

I giggled as it dawned on me that until this conversation, I didn't even blink twice at the uniqueness of his name. "Yes, it is. And Dad, he's..." My breath caught in my throat. "...He's wonderful."

"He'd better be if he's to deserve you."

"Thanks, Dad." It warmed me up inside, knowing that Dad never had any issues with my sexuality. I had friends who weren't as lucky and it sucked big time.

"And what does this Jedfire do for a living?"

Eep! "Uh, he, uh, works in his family business. Kinda like you and me."

"What does his family do?"

I took a deep breath. "They—they manufacture cowbells."

"Cowbells?"

"That, *and* other bovine-related products. They're the largest manufacturer in the US," I hastened to add.

"Conrad." I heard a deep sigh infiltrate through the speaker. "Are you sure you're all right?"

I could tell by his dry tone that he was only half kidding.

"He's a real person, Dad. I'm not making it up." Still, I did pinch myself on my arm, *juuuust* to make certain. Nope. Definitely awake. This was happening. Jedfire wasn't a figment of some beautiful dream I was having.

"All right, then. Enjoy your dinner. And I look forward to hearing all about this cowbell-making Jedfire when you get back. I love you, son."

"I love you, too, Dad."

13

JEDFIRE

"I hope this is okay." Conrad glanced up at me, his cerulean eyes crinkled in the corners. "I know it's no fancy five-star restaurant like you took me out to last night, but I couldn't afford that. So, I hope—"

I pressed the top of my index finger against his soft lips. I noticed that Conrad rambled when he was nervous. Or when he needed to make sure I really wasn't mad at him for becoming my fake husband. And fuck, if that didn't do something crazy to my insides. It meant he cared about me. I knew I was repeating myself, but that meant the world to me. Apart from my family, no one cared about me. Not like this.

"This is perfect, Conrad."

I inhaled deeply, taking in a good dose of salty air. The beach was empty, the sun was falling in the sky, and Conrad had spread out a blanket and was reaching into the picnic basket he had brought with him.

"More than perfect, actually. It's quite romantic."

"I'm glad you like it." He started taking out small Tupperware containers and placing them on the blanket. "I thought you might have expensive taste or something."

"Expensive taste? Who, me?"

Our eyes met and he gave a cheeky shrug. "You are staying here. This place is super fancy and costs a mint."

"You're staying here, too," I pointed out.

He scratched the back of his neck. "Yeah, but I, uh...never mind."

Okay, that was weird. What was he avoiding saying? I didn't want the moment to get uncomfortable so instead, I decided to prove to the guy just how inexpensive my tastes were.

"Thrift store," I said, tugging at my faded Guns N' Roses shirt. I patted the black-and-blue polka-dot shorts I was wearing. "These belonged to a friend, but somehow found their way into my luggage during a week in Greece."

Conrad smiled as sunlight hit his gorgeous face, lighting him up so beautifully.

"And these"—I lifted both my legs into the air and wriggled my feet, drawing attention to the black sneakers I had on—"were on sale at *H&M* in London. Got them for less than ten bucks."

The bottom hem of my shorts had slipped down my thigh, revealing the green boxer briefs I was wearing underneath. I only realized it had happened after following where Conrad's gaze had fallen to.

"Can I help you with anything?" I murmured softly.

Conrad's eyes stayed glued to my still suspended in the air legs for a moment longer. "Huh?"

I glanced over at the spread he had been preparing, lowering my legs—and the cause of his distraction—down onto the blanket.

"Nope, all done." He shook his head and produced two plates from the basket, handing one to me. Because, yeah, *that's* what I'd been talking about.

As he began to open the lids—revealing an assortment of

cheeses, olives, and tomatoes—I couldn't resist teasing him...just a little.

"It's okay to look, you know."

He tipped his head up. "Look at what?"

"My legs." I wet my top lip, brushing it with my tongue. "After all, you are my husband. You have every right to enjoy my body."

Conrad swallowed hard and suddenly, the air around us got a whole lot hotter.

"That is," I continued, lowering my head so I could get a proper view of his face, "if you like my body."

Conrad reached for a bottle of water, bringing it to his lips with a shaky grip. "You have a nice body."

"I don't believe you."

"Huh?"

"You need to work on your believability, Conrad. I mean, if we're going to try to convince my grandparents that we're in love and happily married, you need to make *me* believe it first."

A knowing grin spanned his lips. He'd caught on to what I was doing. Clever guy.

"Oh, is that so?"

I nodded, mustering up all the earnestness I could find.

His eyes sparkled with an inviting effervescence. "And how would you suggest I do that?"

I tapped my fingers on my chin. "Look, I don't know you well enough to gauge what your acting chops are like. So, I'm willing—for your sake, of course—to let you...sample the goods. That way, you won't have to act and risk the possibility of embarrassing yourself if it turns out you're no Leo DiCaprio."

A hearty laugh bubbled out of his throat. He rested his plate on the blanket and started to crawl over. Fuck, if the sight of him on his hands and knees, making his way closer to me, didn't turn me on like crazy.

With a few graceful, panther-like moves, his face leveled off inches away from mine. "And how do you know"—his breath tingled its way across my face—"that if I sample the goods, I'll be happy with them?"

I grabbed him by the shirt and pulled him into me. He lost his balance and his body weight landed on top of me as we fell to the sandy ground. His body landing on top of mine felt incredible.

"Oh, I'm pretty confident you'll like what you get."

He nuzzled his lips into my neck as he lowered himself onto his elbows. I felt his hardness pressing against my thigh.

"And what is it that you'll give me, Jedfire Burns?"

How did he manage to make my name sound so damn sexy?

I caressed the side of his face, drawing my fingers along the ridge of his jaw. "I'll give you whatever you want, Conrad McCallister. I know I don't have expensive taste—"

He let out a deep laugh, his body rumbling against mine. "But I can buy you anything in the world."

"And what if I'm not interested in things you can buy?" He dipped his head, getting a good measure of me. "What if what I want can't be bought?"

"Then tell me what it is and I'll give it to you."

Conrad shook his head, blowing out a jittery breath.

"Are you okay?" I asked. I could see he was lost in his own head.

"This—this feels real, Jed. A little too real, if I'm being honest."

"It *is* real."

His expression tightened. "Aren't we meant to be pretending?"

Oh, right, *that* whole thing.

"I'm not. Are you?"

Lines etched their way across his forehead as he studied me carefully. "No."

"Good, then."

I cupped his upper arms in my hands and gently repositioned us so that we were sitting, cross-legged, facing each other.

"We can figure out a game plan for the whole *we got married in*

Vegas thing in a minute. But for now, Conrad"—I lifted his fingers to my lips, savoring his taste—"let's just enjoy this."

And so that's how we sat—still, with the waves crashing and the sun setting, as we stared into each other's eyes. If you'd told me a few days ago that *this* was what I'd be doing in Florida, I would've rolled my eyes at the sheer cheesiness of it all. All that was missing was a Celine Dion backing track and one of those Lifetime camera filters where everything was shaded rosy and soft around the edges.

But being here in this moment with him, *man*, it was better than any thrill-seeking, adventure high I'd ever chased.

After nowhere near long enough, Conrad finally reached for a plate and handed it to me. "We should probably eat."

I let out a breath and nodded. "How did you manage all of this?"

Conrad's eyes twinkled. "Oh, I have my ways."

And with that, we dug in, enjoying the food and settling into an easy banter.

"So"—Conrad wiped his mouth with a napkin and handed me one as well—"wanna tell me how you ended up married in Vegas?"

I blushed at the sheer stupidity of my actions, but I was honest with him. A not too debaucherous night that somehow ended up with me getting married to someone I didn't know or couldn't remember. Cliché Central, right?

But, amazingly, Conrad took it all in. No judgment. No comments. Just a series of soft, understanding nods. A sudden gust of wind ruffled his hair and I wanted nothing more than to reach out and run my fingers through it.

"So, how do we convince your grandparents we're happily married?"

I finished chewing. "It would make sense if we lived together. I mean, that tends to be what newly married couples do."

"True." Conrad shot me an expectant look.

"What? Why are you looking at me like that?"

"Urgh, do I have to spell it out for you?"

Clearly, he did.

His knee rocked up and down. "I'm waiting for an invitation."

"Oh, right." I chuckled. "Conrad McCallister, would you like to move in with me?"

He pushed his plate away and sat with his knees tucked under his chin. After a few more moments of silence, he murmured, "Yes. I would."

I scooted across the blanket, nudging my body against his. "So, then, it looks like I'm ahead of my game plan, then."

His brows pinched. "What do you mean?"

"Well, the first night we met, I said I'd have you in my bed by the end of your vacation." My lips twitched. "Now, you're my fake husband *and* I've got you moving in with me."

His eyes roamed up and down my body before shrugging. "That's not the worst thing in the world."

Laughter floated in the air between us as I grabbed his hand. I never wanted to let Conrad McCallister slip through my fingers.

14

CONRAD

"No, no, no. We are *not* doing this."

"Oh, come on. Please."

Dammit, Jed had the most puppiest of puppy dog eyes I'd ever seen. He'd just helped me pack and move my suitcases into his apartment. His grandparents had sent a text earlier saying they were catching up with friends in Key West, so we knew we had a window to move me in without them finding out.

But, now, of course, Jed wanted to take things to the next level. The Jed-level.

"Fine, then." He puffed his chest out and crossed his arms. "I'll just do it, anyway."

"I don't think so, mister. I do get a say in the matter and I'm saying—*woooo!*"

Jed's arms swooped down around the backs of my legs and before I knew what was happening, he had lifted me off the ground and was carrying me in his arms.

"There. Not so bad, is it?"

I wanted to protest, to demand he put me down this very instant. But he was right; it wasn't so bad. It was even kinda nice having the side of my body jouncing rhythmically against the front of his. His strong hands gripped me firmly and *shit*...I was starting to get a hard-on.

"All right, let's do this. But hurry up, please."

"If I had a quarter for every time a cute boy I was carrying in my arms said that to me."

My head fell back and I barked out laughing. I also reached around his body to give his backside a firm slap. His surprisingly solid backside.

"Just so you know," he informed me as he kicked the front door farther open, "if that's my punishment for saying stupid shit, then prepare yourself for a torrent of even stupider shit coming out of me."

I giggled, shaking my head, as Jed turned around and took me back in through the front door, carrying me proudly over the threshold as fake husband and fake husband, like he'd been wanting to do—and pestering me about—for the last fifteen minutes.

"Feel better?" I asked as he gently brought me down.

He nodded sharply. "I do, actually. It felt right. Fitting."

"Hmm..." I walked around him, tracing my finger along his back.

He twirled around to face me. "*Hmm*, what?"

I was pretty sure my dad didn't have the human tornado that was Jedfire Burns in mind when he'd told me to go for it, but here I was, fake married to the guy for at least the next three days. It'd all be over once I left, so maybe I should do what I had never done in my life up until this moment and just...go for it?

I felt my pulse ticking in my neck. "So, if we're going for this whole believability thing"—I motioned at the stairs that led up to the bedrooms—"what else is it that two honeymooning grooms would do that we haven't done yet?"

Jed's jaw dropped to the floor. "Are you—are you being serious right now?"

I gulped but somehow managed to find the strength to nod my head at the same time.

Jed stepped up next to me, grazing his mammoth fingers down the side of my arm. I couldn't read his expression. "Do you *really* want to do this, Conrad?"

"I do." I let out a chuckle as I realized the double meaning of my answer.

Jed's face stayed tight for a moment longer as he examined me carefully. Then lightness exploded as he let out an almighty roar, scooping me up in his arms again and striding over to the stairs.

He bound up the stairs, taking them two at a time, his giant legs making light work of them. This was by far the craziest thing I had ever done in my life, but as my body rattled and rocked against his, I felt so...free.

He galloped down the hallway, turning his back to the door to push it open and to take me through the second threshold in as many minutes. My mind was spinning, my heart racing, but I knew deep down what I was doing. And that this was right.

I slid my fingers around Jed's waist as my gaze wandered up his body, to his lips, and landing on his lust-filled eyes. He was blinking heavily, as if the reality of what we were doing—and about to do—dawned on him.

For all his outward bravado and exuberance, I was discovering there were plenty more layers to the guy. Softer ones. Deeper ones. Parts of Jed that I didn't think he showed to many other people. I didn't know why he kept these parts of himself hidden. They were some of my most favorite things about him.

I stood up onto my tippy toes. "What are you thinking?"

"How good my cock will look sliding in and out of your ass," he deadpanned.

My lips met the dimple in his chin and I took my first nibble. "What are you *really* thinking?"

His top teeth bit into his lower lip. "How much I like you."

"Then we're in agreement"—I licked along his jawline—"because I like you, too."

"Why?"

His question surprised me and I landed on my heels with a heavy thud.

"Lots of reasons..." I traced my finger along his collarbone. "Because you're good at karaoke."

I skimmed my fingers along the skin just under his shirt sleeve. "You have exquisite fashion sense."

Jed grabbed both of my wrists and pulled me into him forcefully. "I'm serious, Conrad."

My eyes shot up and I could see that he was. I'd misread his question, thinking he was being flirty and fun. The dark depth to his eyes showed me he wasn't. Looking him straight in the eyes, I told him the truth. Plain and simple. "I like you because you're a good person, Jedfire."

"And what if I'm not?" he replied straight away.

"Then you can *become* a good person. You have goodness and decency in you. I know you do, Jed."

"How can you be so sure?"

"Because I feel it in here." I moved my still-held hands to the center of my chest.

He let go of them, cupped the sides of my face and pulled me into a deep, passionate kiss. His tongue parted my lips and he dove in, claiming my mouth.

It was as if my words had given him what he needed. Not just permission. No, it was more than that. Validation, perhaps? For some reason, Jed didn't see himself the same way I did.

Was he carrying around guilt? Had he made a mistake and was now punishing himself for it?

All the signs I'd seen—and overheard—pointed to the opposite. His generosity at the wildlife center and his insistence to keep his donation anonymous showed me who he really was. Sure, maybe he wasn't perfect. Who was? But deep down, I just knew in my heart of hearts that Jedfire Burns was a good person.

I broke the kiss and pointed to the bed. "Shall we?"

With his lips swollen and cheeks flushed, he panted out a quiet, "Yes."

I grabbed his hand and led him to the bed. Jed's energy had changed. I guess I'd expected him to be the kind of guy who took charge in the bedroom. But all the signs were pointing to something else.

He preferred being the little spoon. Did that mean that he was also a—? Okay, this moment called for me to do something else with my mouth: talk.

We sat down on the edge of the bed. "Do you want to fuck me?" I moved my face in front of his and looked up to meet his gaze. "Or would you like me to fuck you?"

He kept looking at me. The only part of his body that was moving was his chest, heaving slowly with every deep breath he was taking. "I'd like to fuck you...please."

Something in the gentleness of his words, the politeness of his demeanor, tugged at my heart. Every time I thought I'd expanded my awareness to encompass who Jedfire truly was, he'd do something new to show me there was still so much I hadn't the faintest clue about.

"In that case"—I rose to my feet—"let's get out of these." And with that, I shrugged my shirt off over my head. Jed's eyes traveled across my torso, a small smile peeking through his fragile expression.

Remaining seated on the bed, he took his shirt off. For a tall guy, he was ripped. Lean and long biceps, broad shoulders with a pronounced collarbone and a drizzling of auburn chest hairs that yummily covered his delicious abs *and* trailed down ever further.

My eye caught our reflection in a mirror in the corner of the room. It revealed Jed from another angle. His strong back was a moonscape of muscles. Tight, hard, and sinewy muscles that stretched from his wide shoulders, tapering down into his slim waist.

Jed looked at me expectantly, rubbing his thumbs against his fingers. Was he...nervous? If he was, then it made it even more important for me not to be. All his confidence and cockiness had left the building. What I was seeing now was something rare and precious, and I wanted to treat him with the reverence he deserved.

I stepped in, dropped to my knees, and began to unbutton his pants. I could feel the heat radiating off his body, even as I looked up and saw the dazed expression on his face. "You okay?" I checked in with him.

"So good."

I smiled and returned to the task at hand, which, as expected, was pretty fucking monumental. I pulled his pants down so they bunched up around his ankles. I was one piece of thin material away from the monster that was wanting to free itself.

I grabbed Jed's cock forcefully, right as he speared his fingers through my hair. He let out a dirty moan that swirled around us as I tugged the material closer to me and opened my mouth, licking his thickening bulge through the material.

"No more teasing."

I giggled and glanced up. "Are you capable of saying more than three words in a row?"

Jed looked down, his eyes the color of just-made coffee. "Computer says no."

I grinned and yanked his briefs down to his thighs. His cock sprang out in front of me. It was thick and veiny and as big as his other, equally big body parts hinted it would be. But it wasn't his impressive heft that made me gasp and let out a sharp, "Wow."

Jed shuffled back and sprawled out on the bed. "You've never seen..."

I shook my head as his question trailed off. I kept staring as my initial surprise was overtaken by a more pleasant sensation.

"Pubic hair," I muttered as I ran my fingers through the thick tuft of ginger-tinged hair at the base of his cock. It was all perfectly groomed and manscaped, but the thick patch was something no other guy I'd ever been with had. Californian guys, and especially Californian surfer guys, tended to be smooth all over.

"Whaddya think?"

"I like it," I replied. "Now let's get these pants and briefs off your legs so that I can get in closer."

And with that, we worked together to peel Jed's remaining clothes off him and I resumed the task I had started earlier, this time, sans any pesky material standing between me and his glorious cock.

I began by giving it a sloppy wet lick up, then down, his entire length. I wasn't tremendously experienced when it came to giving head, but strangely, I wasn't worried. What I felt more than anything else as I knelt in front of Jed was that I wanted to feel him, be close to him. Yes, there was a sexual attraction between us, but there was something more too, something even more exciting.

"That feels so good," he hissed as I took the tip of his cock between my lips, my tongue flicking around the underside. I held him in my mouth, while I ran my fingers through his thick pubic hair.

I glanced up and was a little surprised, borderline unnerved, really, to see Jed propped up on his elbows with his eyes fixed on me. I felt a tremor of vulnerability roll through me. As if sensing the shift, Jed eased his hand onto my shoulder and said, "You're so beautiful, Conrad."

His words thrummed in my chest and ignited a fire within me. In one big swallow, I engulfed his cock in my throat, taking it as far as I could. I peered up again. I was met with those same focused eyes staring at me, and this time, he didn't have to say a word. I *felt* beautiful.

With my mouth working his shaft, I freed my own cock and began to jerk myself off. The sensation at both ends of my body felt incredible. There was nothing cheap or smutty or rushed about the moment; everything felt like it was happening just as it should.

Jed grabbed his cock with one hand as I focused my mouth on his inflamed cockhead. I timed stroking myself to his movements. I cupped his balls with my free hand and instantly felt them tighten and lift. He was close. So was I.

After a few more strokes, he arched his back. "I'm getting close."

I nodded, my mouth not wanting to leave his dick for even a second. He looked down at me, as if he were giving me an out, a last chance to escape the impending explosion. I nodded again, indicating I was ready—and not budging an inch.

His whole body rocked and he let out a wild groan as his cock flooded my mouth. I came at the same time, my release spilling onto the floor. I closed my eyes, the loud thundering of my heart catching me unaware.

My eyelids fluttered open as I swallowed around his softening cock, tilting my head back to savor his taste. His fingers hooked under my armpits and I used his momentum to launch myself onto the bed. He looked tentative for a moment, like what had happened wasn't just a physical thing. It certainly wasn't that for me.

I had tasted Jedfire Burns. I had a part of him inside of me forever.

However long forever was.

MONDAY

15

JEDFIRE

I didn't normally do this part. You know, the whole *waking up with the person you had spent the night with* thing. Staying after sex? Yeah, not my scene at all. Normally, I'd be tiptoeing around the room, gathering my clothes and getting the fuck outta there before <insert name here> cracked open an eye, if I even got so far as falling asleep with someone.

But there were a few things that were different here.

Number one, technically, Conrad and I were married. Or, at least, fake married. That alone lent itself to sharing a bed for the sake of believability.

Number two, I'd never known that having someone's arms wrapped around you was the secret recipe for the best sleep of your life. Seriously, whoever bottled that shit would become a trillionaire.

And number three, Conrad didn't just give me head last night. Spoiler alert: I was stepping aboard the train to Cheeseville Central with stops at Lovesick Lane and Sappy Avenue. What Conrad and I did, the connection we explored with each other last night, was special. It meant something to me. A whole lotta something, to be honest.

And, yes, despite what it may have looked like, I was there and fully present for it. Even if I had handed him the reins to take the lead. I guess I just never recovered from what had preceded us being together. Specifically, Conrad informing me that he thought I was a good person. That sent me spiraling down the most unexpected of tunnels, and I guess I never recovered from that.

How did he do that? How did he see so deep into me, into who I really was, and not the image I projected out to the world?

The fact that he'd been able to see past all the bullshit and bravado I put on to who I really was had moved me in a way that— as I lay next to him the next morning, his warm breath hitting my shoulder—I *still* couldn't wrap my poor brain around.

Because the thing was, deep down, I *was* a good person. But I'd closed that part of myself off exactly eight days after my nineteenth birthday when my family's lives came crashing down. I'd gone down a similar path to Grandma, which was code for "we both lost our shit and started acting out."

Until that point, she'd been the epitome of everything you expected a 'traditional' and 'normal' grandmother to be. She and Mrs. McClusky weren't just best friends, they were practically twins. Same style of clothes, hair, and makeup. Same grandmotherly vibes and outlook on life. Everything you'd expect a doting grandma to be, that was her to a tee.

Not anymore.

Not only did she have no problems taking her top off in public and riding gay men like a cowboy, she now boozed it up, changed up her fashion to whatever the latest looks were, and even by her own estimation, had maybe gone a little too far with all of the Botox and plastic surgery.

Despite all the changes, she and Mrs. McClusky were still best friends, and she was still the best grandma in the world, but she was different.

Grandpa went the opposite way. He'd had to, as the weight of responsibility of the plant fell onto his shoulders again.

My younger brothers, Cooper and Mitchell, became my support system even though I was technically the oldest. Mitchell, my youngest brother, he really stepped up. Even though he was adopted, he became the rock that helped Cooper and me through the heartbreaking loss. I guessed having gone through something similar himself helped him to recognize our pain.

I heard Conrad's head rustling on the pillow behind me. I wiggled back even closer to him, sealing any gaps created between our skin until there were none. God, this felt so good. Being this close to him was perfection. But the non-gentlemanly part of me wouldn't be satisfied until I was even closer to Conrad. Or *in* Conrad, to be precise.

"Morning," he murmured into my shoulder, his fingers gracefully smoothing down the skin of my belly. I felt his cock twitch and smiled. Seemed that I wasn't the only person in this bed who woke up with wood in the...

"Morning," I breathed back, holding still and hoping his hands would never let go of me. But as he stirred, letting out a massive yawn, oblivious to the steel rod jutting out of me—and him—he rolled onto his back and released me from the viselike grip he'd kept me in all night.

I missed the warmth of his body instantly. And how stupid was that? A week ago—no, wait, three days ago, Conrad and I were complete strangers. Yes, we lived in the same state, but with a population nearing forty million, our paths had never crossed. He'd never even heard of Cowbell Creek.

And now, less than seventy-two hours after I had first laid my eyes on the striking figure he cut outside on the terrace of the bar, staring out into the waves, I was missing his touch. How strange and funny this thing called life was, huh?

I twisted around to face him, hoping for a dose of reality to hit me in the face. Because nothing screamed *get the fuck outta here* like a severe case of morning breath. And maybe that's what I needed: a cold-shower realization moment that this sappy little bubble we found ourselves in needed to pop right open and ground us to the fact that this was...just too unreal, too good to be true. It had to be, right?

But, no, any hopes of that kind of reality continued to elude me as I drank in his early-morning softness. He was all fluttering eyelids and slight head nods as he tried to get comfortable on the pillow. The only scent in the air was the gentle residue of his cinnamony sweetness.

Come on. Burp. Spit. Fart. Do something gross to wake me out of this trance you've put me under. But no, Conrad had to choose that moment to let out a contented sigh, didn't he? And my heart, of course, had to respond in kind by fluttering throughout my chest, leaving me feeling lightheaded and giddy and stroking Conrad's silky-smooth hair through my fingers. *Damn.*

Reality was playing hard to get, fate was pointing at me and laughing...and I was perfectly fine with that if it meant this beautiful boy would never leave my sight. Watching Conrad come to was like witnessing the unfolding of something special because when someone wasn't fully awake yet, their true being shone through. And his being was gentle and gracious and so exquisitely delicate that it brought out every protective instinct in me.

Yep, I got all that from the few everyday, completely normal movements Conrad made as he woke up in front of me. The train had officially arrived at Lovesick Lane. *All aboard!*

"How did you sleep?" I asked, my fingers gently tousling his wispy hair.

"Good. So good."

"Are you hungry?"

"Pancakes," he replied, his voice still groggy.

I planted a kiss on his forehead. "Now who's the one who can't say more than three words in a row?"

He blinked his eyes open, staring at me with a wanderlust that made something feel-goody shoot up my spine, unleashing a torrent of dopamine to my brain.

I took the small curve that had settled in his lips as a sign to keep talking. I wanted to explain my behavior from last night, why I went to jelly and how if I ever got the chance to be with him again, I'd show him that I could take the lead or, at the very least, reciprocate.

"So, about last night..." I began.

"Shhh." He pressed his index finger to my lips. "It's all good."

"It is?"

He nodded.

A lump formed in my throat. "But you don't even know what I was going to say."

Conrad wiped his eyes and sat up to face me. He cleared his throat. "Was it something along the lines of 'I floored you with my comment about you being a good, decent person, and you never really recovered from that moment?'"

Holy crap! "How did—how did you know?"

Our eyes stayed connected, and it felt like he was answering my question just by looking at me. No words needed. And as he opened his mouth to speak, he lifted his fingers up to my cheek and thumbed away the tear that was rolling down. "Because I have eyes. I see you, Jed. I can read you."

The banks of the lump in my throat broke and another tear streamed down my face. He deftly wiped that one away, too.

I had to shake myself out of this. I was not about to lose my shit in front of Conrad. I hadn't cried since... And boy, did I fucking cry that day. And night. And well into the next day, too. But not a single drop since that day. Until today.

I scooted up on the bed and sat with my back pressed against the headboard. Unexpected emotional baggage on the train tracks called for a detour to Let's Keep It Light station.

"So, any plans for today, Mr. Husband?"

Conrad joined me at the top of the bed. "First thing we need to do is figure out cute pet names for each other. Baby and Mr. Husband won't cut it, I'm afraid."

"Totally agree, snuggle-pie?"

"Oooh," Conrad's cheekbones lifted cheerily. "That's so bad that it's almost good, ya little tasty-peach."

"Oh, god," I scratched the side of my face, shooting him a concerned look. "We're terrible at this."

"The worst," Conrad agreed, setting off into a fit of contagious hysterical giggles that had me laughing along with him, too.

"So, what *is* on the agenda for today, Jed?"

"Agenda?"

He bobbed his shoulders. "What? I feel like *agenda* is a word married people say."

I chuckled. "The only thing on the official agenda for the day is lunch with my grandparents. They want to meet you. Properly. Is that okay?"

Conrad's jaw bunched up. Oh shit, this was too much for him, too soon. We hadn't even really gone over how this whole fake marriage thing would work, what we'd tell them about us, how we met, how we ended up at a chapel in Vegas.

Conrad opened his mouth and I braced for some sort of rejection. Instead, I was met with a cheeky, "Will your grandmother be wearing a top?"

"You asshole!" I reached around, grabbed the pillow I'd been leaning against and aimed it straight at Conrad's head. He somehow managed to not only deflect the incoming assault, but returned fire with much more precision than I'd demonstrated, his pillow landing with a soft thud right at the front of my face.

Next thing I knew, Conrad was on top of me, all glittery eyes and wide smiles. And, I was happy to report, the train had taken a surprise (but very welcome) stop at Morning Wood Is Back Again station.

His warm body might have been on top of mine, but I managed

to get hold of his wrists, holding them out to the side. He cocked his head. "What time is lunch?"

"I don't know. Midday, I guess."

He flicked his eyes to the clock on the bedside table. "Good. Plenty of time to work up an appetite, then."

And with that, Conrad's lips—and entire body weight—crashed into me. As we rolled and tumbled on the bed in a whirlwind of kisses, I never wanted the train to reach its destination. The journey alone was more than worth it.

16

CONRAD

"Here, wear this." Jed threw a striped black-and-white turtleneck in my direction.

I held my hand out but missed it, too busy checking out the hickeys—uh-huh, *hickeys*—that lined my neck. When I turned briefly to see the material he had flung at me, I couldn't help but chuckle. "Of course you would own a turtleneck, and of course, it would be black and white."

"Hey, I can't help it if I have exquisite fashion sense—no, wait, that's the wrong word. Vision. I have exceptional fashion vision."

"You are a vision," I said as I felt two warm hands massaging their way around my hips. Jed pulled himself in behind me and began nibbling the back of my neck.

I pulled away sharply. "No, no, no, no, no." I wagged a finger at him in the reflection. "This is how we got into this mess in the first place."

Jed stopped nibbling, but his warm breath kept caressing my neck as our eyes met in the mirror. "I didn't hear you complaining."

"That's because my mouth was otherwise occupied." I twisted around to face him and plant another kiss on those amazingly talented lips of his that I'd spent all morning kissing. I reminded myself of what I had been doing and pulled back. "I can't believe I'm going to show up for lunch to meet your grandparents with hickeys."

"Stop saying hickeys. It sounds so clinical."

"What should I call them, then?"

A devilish smile twisted its way onto Jed's lips. "Call 'em love bites. Because I love biting you."

I gave him a slap and spun back around, patting down the...love bites...that seemed to be growing more pronounced with each passing second. "I'm googling how to get rid of them. Surely, in the twenty-first century there's gotta be a YouTube video with a hickey removal hack."

"Urgh, so clinical." Jed flung himself onto the bed, while my fingers tapped madly across the screen of my cell phone.

Sure, maybe I should've seen it coming. Spending all morning in bed with Jed, kissing—that's right, nothing more; he was on his very best gentlemanly behavior—and what did I expect? The guy had practically mauled me...and I had totally let him.

"Banana peels," I said, looking up from my phone at Jed who was sprawled on the bed, all long legs and abs and skin.

He quirked his head in my direction. "Banana peels?"

I nodded. "Yeah. You got any?"

"Oh, yeah, sure," Jed sprang to his feet with an exaggerated enthusiasm. "Let me just find my secret banana stash." He dashed over to the wardrobe and flung the doors open. "Now, where did I put them?"

"All right, all right. No banana peels. I thought that was being a little too optimistic. What about a quarter?"

Jed made his way back to the bed. "Sorry, I'm a card-only kinda guy."

I rolled my eyes. "Okay, toothpaste. You gotta have toothpaste, right?"

"Uh-uh," he said with a firm head shake. "The fine folk of

Cowbell Creek don't believe in toothpaste or the evil dental industry in general. It's fake teeth all the way, baby." He flashed a toothy grin and tapped at his sparkly pearly whites.

For the life of me, I couldn't tell if he was kidding or not. "Are you being serious, Jed?"

He paused, looked at me, before erupting into that volcano-esque rapturous laughter of his. "Oh my gosh, you should have seen your face, Conrad. I totally had you there."

I placed a hand on my hip and enjoyed watching Jed bouncing around. Even if he was laughing at me, I could still appreciate the view, especially since the only clothing he had on were his briefs, and they weren't exactly doing a great job of covering his ever-present erection.

"You did not have me, at all."

Jed leaped off the bed and strode over to me, cupping my face in his hands. My eyes had no choice but to look up and meet his. "But I want to have you, Conrad. So badly."

I swallowed. Hard. Then, again. The fierceness blazing behind his eyes was unmistakable. It sent a rumble of adrenaline coursing through my entire body. Hearing how much he wanted me, seeing the response it was producing in his body, feeling it in the penetrating way he was boring into me with his eyes—the intensity of it was like nothing I'd ever experienced before.

It shook me to my very core and, evidently, melted my brain and capacity to utter a single word back. I stared up at him, lost in his eyes and the heat of his hands on my face. The best-slash-worst throwaway phrase I could come up with was 'Whatever, Trevor,' but it felt so out of place, and he didn't deserve that. No. Jed was being vulnerable with me, revealing his desires in this way. The very least I could do was match his honesty.

"I want you, too, Jed."

A gentle tremor swept across Jed's expressive face. He blinked heavily a few times, as if he'd misheard me or something. "You do?"

"Of course," I shot back instantly, placing my hands over his.

Why did he doubt himself like this? Whenever I paid him a compliment or when I'd said I thought he was a good, decent guy, he always replied in the same way. With a question, asking for confirmation that I'd meant what I said. Why? Why was he so down on himself? Why didn't he see himself the way I did?

Jed broke my gaze and headed toward the en suite. "Let me get you that toothpaste."

We spent the next few minutes applying, and then washing off, the toothpaste. It achieved nothing, except for making me smell like the inside of a dentist's office, forcing me to have a shower to wash the smell off.

As the warm water cascaded down my back, my thoughts wandered ahead to lunch with Jed's grandparents. Was I worried about meeting them? Uh, hell to the yeah. Between my ill-advised and out-of-the-blue announcement and Jed's total inability to lie, we were completely up shit's creek without a canoe, much less a paddle.

And then it hit me. A simple idea, really, but one that could possibly work. I cut the water and dried myself off in record time.

I stepped out into the bedroom. Jed was lying on the bed, staring up at the ceiling.

"Penny for your thoughts." I eyed him as I picked up the hideous striped turtleneck and shrugged it on. Unfortunately, at the same time I did that, the towel I'd wrapped around my waist slid *off*.

Jed's head perked up. "Well, I was stressing about lunch with my grandparents, but, uh, you've done a terrific job of distracting me, Conrad."

I laughed, picking the towel up from the floor and covering myself with it. "Glad I could be of assistance."

"I like the first part of that word." I looked over at Jed, smacking his lips like crazy. "*Ass*-istant."

"Focus, Jedfire Burns." I disappeared into the walk-in closet and found a pair of clean underwear. Reemerging into the room with it on, I was met with a sullen look and a thumbs-down gesture from Jed. "Boo! Give the audience what it wants."

"And what might that be?" I bounced onto the bed, sitting cross-legged and facing Jed.

"You. Naked. Pretty simple, really."

"You're a pretty simple man, aren't ya?" I teased back.

Jed nodded wholeheartedly. "A simple man with cheap taste, but a good eye for spotting physical perfection."

His fingers crawled up past my knee. "And you, Mr. McCallister, are the very definition of perfection."

His fingers tracked up my thigh, and it wouldn't be long until they reached my—

"Ooh, looks like someone's happy." His palm landed at my bulge and the wet mess that was pooling there.

"I've only just come out of the shower and you're making me dirty again."

"So don't shower and just stay dirty all day long."

Tempting. Thankfully, there were still a few active brain cells bouncing around the walls of my skull. "We have to meet your grandparents in less than fifteen minutes," I reminded him. "And I think I have an idea."

Jed let go of my still-hard cock and sat up in front of me. "I'm all ears."

I reached out and gently gripped his earlobes. "You sure are." I pressed a kiss to his lower lip. "And it suits you."

When I pulled back, Jed's cheekbones were stained with a rosy hue. "No one's ever liked my ears before." His voice was layered with insecurity.

I cupped his chin and looked straight into his muddied eyes as I told him, "That says more about the people you've met, than it does about you, Jed. Your ears are awesome."

"Really?"

There it was again. Responding to praise with doubt. Self-inflicted, but it had to be coming from somewhere. And dammit, I wanted to find out what that place was so that I could cut it off right at the source.

"Yes, really," I replied, keeping my frustration at bay. It wasn't aimed at him, but at whatever had caused him to be unable to process a simple compliment.

Jed looked away for a moment, exhaled, and then turned back to face me. "You said you had an idea?"

"Yes." I clapped my hands excitedly. "I'm assuming your grandparents are going to ask a few questions?"

Jed's head fell back as he let out a wild howl. "That's like saying the Kardashians have had a few plastic surgeries. Conrad"—he sat up a little straighter—"expect to be hit by a game show-style lightning round of questions. Especially from Grandpa. That man is tough as nails."

I gave a determined nod. "Perfect."

"Perfect?"

"Yes. This is a crazy situation and you're not the best liar in the world, Jed."

"Uh, neither are you, Conrad," he pointed out, a smirk stretching his lips.

"That's true," I admitted. So what I'm proposing is that we don't lie."

Jed's long lashes fluttered a few times. "What—what do you mean?"

"I mean, we don't lie about this." I wagged my hand between our bodies. "You like me. I like you."

Jed opened his mouth, but before he could get out the question I knew he would ask, I interjected, "Yes, I *really* do."

His eyes gleamed and it made me smile stupidly at him. "So that part we don't have to lie about. All we have to lie about is the timing."

"The timing?"

I got up off the bed in search of pants to complete my outfit while I kept talking. "Yeah. So, instead of saying we met... Hang on, what day is it today?"

"I've got no fucking idea. Saturday? Thursday? June?"

I snickered. "June's not a day, and I think it's Monday. We met on Friday."

"Really?" Jed ran his fingers through his hair. "It feels like so much longer."

"I'm going to assume you mean that in a good way. Ah, found 'em." I reached for my favorite pair of dark denims hidden away at the bottom of the drawer.

"Of course in the good way." I could feel the heat of Jed's eyes on me, even as I had my back turned to him as I pulled the jeans up my legs.

Once I'd zipped up, I spun around to face him. "Right, so instead of telling your grandparents we met three days ago, we tell them we met, I don't know, three months ago."

"Okay."

"We met here, at Elysian and we don't have to lie about anything other than the timing. We talked. You sang karaoke. We went for a hike together. And then, on a whim, flew to Vegas and got married. Technically, that part's a lie, but it's a small one. What do you think, Jed?"

Jed continued playing with a strand of hair. "I think it could work. Good job, Mr. McCallister."

"I just think we have a better chance of success if we try to stick to the truth as much as possible. Your grandparents don't know me, but they'll be able to spot your lies from a mile away."

"Hey." Jed rose to his feet. "I'm not that bad a liar, am I?"

"You're the worst."

"Really? Why?"

"Uh-huh. You break eye contact and look straight ahead." I noticed Jed seemed a little crestfallen by my revelation.

"Don't worry." I stepped closer to him. "It's not a bad thing to be a bad liar. It's actually a very good thing."

His worry dissipated and he pulled me in for a tight hug. Meanwhile, I felt like my own words were choking me. Here I was congratulating Jed on his inability to lie, when I'd been keeping something from him this whole time. Something big.

I pushed that thought away as I nuzzled into his neck, his strong arms stroking my back. "Thank you for doing this for me, Conrad. You have no idea how much it means to me."

I squeezed Jed even tighter. Anything. I'd do anything for him. But all I said was, "Let's go, armadillo."

17

JEDFIRE

"So, you met here three months ago and just...fell in love?"

"Walter, don't be rude." Grandma slapped Grandpa on the shoulder. I sent her an appreciative look which she returned with a soft smile. It looked like she might have been trying to purse them, but since her lip injections had veered into *almost overboard territory*, they didn't look anything other than full and plump.

While I was wallowing in an uneasy silence I seemed incapable of breaking out of, Conrad had been fielding the firing squad of questions my grandpa was aiming at us with nothing but graceful competence.

I couldn't have been more grateful to him.

First, he saved my chops and stepped up to be my fake husband. All of his own accord and with no prompting from me. Then he devised a decent plan to minimize the lying we'd have to do in front of my grandparents.

Conrad got me on that one. I hated lying with everything I had in me. The world was already screwed up enough as it was. Caking life with another layer of bullshit only complicated things even more. I might have been a fuckup in a lot of ways, but I wasn't a liar. At least, not a good one, given how quickly Conrad had picked up on how bad I was at it.

Wait, did that mean he knew about what I did at the wildlife center? Surely not...

And now, here he was, meeting my grandparents and not just returning the volleys Grandpa was lobbing at him, but doing it so sweetly and charmingly that I could tell they were falling under his spell.

Conrad had even managed to casually weave in a few husband-esque words into the conversation. Words like *business acumen* and *planning for the future* floated in the air. I was only half listening, but I could tell every time he'd say something he was proud of because he'd direct a beaming smile at me. When Conrad McCallister put on the charm, he really unleashed it. There was only one word for it: wow.

I could tell that Grandpa was loosening up a bit. The big lug came across as a serious tough guy, but he was a pure softie underneath. Spend five minutes with him around Grandma, and you'd see him thawing into the most loving and caring guy in the world. They were childhood sweethearts, married for almost fifty years, and the best bit? They were still going strong. Talk about couple goals.

"You're awfully quiet, Jed," Grandpa observed perceptively, shifting his eyes to me.

I shuffled in my chair. "Just a little thirsty, that's all." I craned my head. "Where is the server with our drinks?"

"Here. Have some water." Grandpa pushed the jug of water from the center of the table to my side.

Conrad swooped in with a smile. "Let me get that for you, honey-bee."

He added a wink and instantly, I felt some of the tension seep out of my shoulders. "What would you like to know, Grandpa?"

The man darted his gaze between the two of us as he rested his elbows on the table and interlaced his fingers. "I want you to be happy, Jed. That's the only thing I—we—want for you. For all three of you boys. Answer me this..."

Conrad had finished filling the glass, and as I reached for it, I noticed my fingers were trembling.

"...what do you love about Conrad?"

"Walter?" This time Grandma's slap was a lot more forceful. "Don't embarrass them like that."

Grandpa turned to Grandma and in that moment, he looked like a little boy. "What? Why is that an embarrassing thing to ask? If someone wanted to know what I loved about you, I'd be able to answer in a heartbeat."

Grandma's face softened as she slid her hand over Grandpa's cheek.

"And it would take me a very long time to answer because there's that many things I love about you."

"Oh, Walter," Grandma cooed, the love practically pouring out of her eyes.

Normally, this kind of thing would embarrass the shit out of me, but there was an undeniable sweetness to it that tugged at my heart. Besides, I was still getting over seeing my grandmother topless in public, so it would take at least a good decade or two for her to do anything to top that.

I glanced over at Conrad and I could have sworn I saw his eyes mist up. He returned my gaze and grabbed my hand under the table, giving me a firm squeeze.

"You want to know what I love about Conrad, Grandpa?" My words broke the spell between my grandparents and they both turned their heads to me.

"Fine. I'll tell you. He sees me like no one else ever has."

Grandpa interlaced his fingers. "Go on."

For a second, my mind went blank and I felt a wave of panic about to roll in. Oh god no, not the tongue twitch. But as I exhaled, I experienced a moment of clarity, and all the tension within me left me as I spoke. "He's the most generous and giving person I've ever met. He's kind, and he's cute. He hates karaoke, but that's okay. I'll work on that."

Grandma let out a loud laugh as Grandpa snickered.

"He believes in the importance of family. He'd do anything for someone he loves, even if it means sacrificing what he wants. He accepts me. All of me. Including my many, many, *many* imperfections. And"—I finally remembered to take a breath—"he's honest."

The server arrived with our drinks. It seemed that my impassioned, impromptu sermon satisfied Grandpa. At least, enough for the topic of conversation to turn to other matters.

"So," Grandma geared her head toward Conrad, "Jed mentioned something in passing to me the other day that you've been traveling the world?"

"That's right, Katie."

Grandma let out a cackle. "I love that you call me that, sweetie, but you can call me Catherine." She leaned forward and stuck her neck out. "Just quietly, of course, and just between the four of us."

"Got it." Conrad formed a pistol with his hand and winked at Grandma, who, if I didn't know any better, actually blushed. I flopped my head over to Conrad, my mouth agape. I'd never seen this charming, confident side to him before and damn, it suited him.

He regaled my grandparents with highlights from his five month around-the-world adventure. He loved London but had bad weather when he was there, so he didn't get to see as much as he'd wanted. He loved the canals and art in Amsterdam but thought the Red Light district was totally overrated and seedy. And he'd had an awesome time exploring remote villages in northern Thailand, where he did a farm stay with a local family for a week.

"So, yeah," Conrad wrapped up. "I've pretty much worked my way through my entire bucket list."

"Bucket list?" I sputtered into my wine. "Isn't that something old people do before they die?"

"Jedfire!" Now it was Grandma's turn to play bad cop,

proving, if nothing else, that you're never too old to be scolded by your grandmother. "That's a terrible thing to say. Don't be so rude."

"I'm not being rude, Grandma." I raised my hands. I really hadn't meant to insult anyone. "But Conrad's not old and he's not dying."

I turned to look over at Conrad, expecting to be met with a light smile. I thought he'd be getting a kick out of seeing Grandma handing me my ass on a platter. Instead, something heavy cast its shadow over his face. His eyes met mine and when they did, he shrugged off that weighty look with a smile that barely reached the corners of his mouth.

My forehead wrinkled in confusion and I felt an uneasiness settle over me. What was that about? Even Conrad's hand on my leg wasn't washing away the funny feeling that had settled in my belly.

Grandma directed another question at Conrad as I gave him a proper once over. Something had definitely shifted in him. I just had no clue what it was.

"Well." Conrad twisted the napkin around his fingers as he started to answer Grandma's question, which I hadn't heard. "I've been to pretty much everywhere I wanted to go, except for the Bungle Bungles."

"The what now?" I exclaimed, the funny sounding name snapping me out of my own head.

Conrad's smile didn't fully mask the nervous edge behind it, but I could tell he was trying to move on from whatever that was before. He went on to explain, "It's this amazing rock formation in Australia. I saw it in a documentary I watched with my dad and it fascinated me."

"Is it near Uluru?" Grandpa asked, his voice missing the trenchant quality contained in his initial line of questioning. He was back to being his big ol' teddy bear self. That made me smile as I listened to Conrad's answer, drifting from really hearing what he was saying to wondering why he'd reacted so strongly to my silly comment about the bucket list.

I might have had a secret or two up my sleeve, but something told me that Conrad was keeping something from me, too. And boy, was I determined to find out what that was.

18

CONRAD

I loved the feeling of warm sand between my toes. I dropped my shoes in an out-of-the-way spot near the entrance as I made a beeline for the water's edge. A nice long walk along the beach would be the perfect way to relax a little and reflect on a lunch that I thought went pretty darn well.

We'd been able to pull off a lie without it feeling like I'd sold my soul to the devil so that was, surprisingly, the easiest part. That, and just hanging out with Jed's grandparents. They were really good people: friendly, kind, and warm. The love they had for their grandson—and each other—was as clear as day, too. It made me happy knowing Jed had a good family like that around him.

Interestingly, not a word was mentioned about his parents, which again, made me think that something had happened to them. Something bad. But I wasn't about to spoil a perfectly pleasant lunch by bringing up a heavy topic like that. If Jed wanted to open up to me and tell me, he'd do it in his own time.

The water lapped at my feet. I turned my head, trying to decide which way to walk. Left was a little more scenic, as I'd have a view of a few tiny islands off the coast and a pretty lighthouse at the end of the beach, while the right option just had sky, water, and an empty shoreline. I swerved my head left and right a few times, before finally deciding to go right.

As I ambled off, making my way across the wet sand with the water reaching no higher than my ankles, my mind looped back to two things Jed had said during the meal.

The first was his little speech in response to his grandpa's question about why he liked me. I'd kept my eyes peeled on him as he answered, and he was looking both of his grandparents straight in the eye as he spoke. Which meant he was telling the truth and meant everything he was saying. That warmed my heart like crazy. Yes, it'd only been a few days, but there was something so real and true between us. I loved that he was feeling it as much as I was.

But then a seemingly innocent, didn't-mean-anything-more-by-it comment had flown out of Jed's mouth. The thing he'd said about the bucket list. I spotted a pinkish-gray stone the size of a golf ball and picked it up. I dipped it into the water to brush the sand off it.

As I continued my leisurely stroll, I was struck by how that comment had caused a mild panic within me. That, combined with my hypocrisy at cheering Jed on for not being able to lie well, felt like someone was wringing my chest out from the inside.

I wasn't outright lying to Jed, but I was holding something back. And not just a little something, but a gargantuan thing. Even though we'd only known each other a short while—despite it feeling like much longer—he had a right to know. And not because we were fake husbands, but because underneath that, real feelings were starting to form. For both of us.

Which meant only one thing: I had to tell him the truth.

I played with the pumice-like stone between my fingers as I took a pause. Despite walking at the pace of a snail, I was already out of breath. I winced as I thought back to the doctor telling me this would start happening more and more often.

I'd been lucky during my world travels. I'd felt fine the whole time. Sure, I took it easy, but the change in time zones and climates could've been a lot harder for my body to adapt to. Thankfully, I'd done okay.

But even during my hike with Jed, I'd needed to take a rest. And here I was again, out of breath and starting to wheeze, after covering a distance that couldn't have been any more than a few hundred feet.

I dropped down into the sand, resting my face on my knees. I still needed a few minutes to gather my thoughts and think about the best approach to take. I inhaled deeply and closed my eyes, surrendering to the salty scents and the sounds of the sea swirling around me.

When I opened them a few seconds—*minutes?*—later, it had become clear what I had to do. I'd known it all along, but there was a deceptiveness at the simplicity of it. I'd been overthinking it, combined with a little denial, splashed with a tiny helping of dread about having to do it. But what it boiled down to was this: just sit Jed down and tell him. No sugarcoating, no long-winded beat-around-the-bush stories. None of that. Just the cold, hard truth.

I lifted my arm and flung the stone I'd been carrying into the water. I had been going for that cool skimming-across-the-water's-surface effect. Instead, it got swallowed by a wave that was rolling in and, presumably, sank straight to the bottom. Maybe that was another thing I could add to my bucket list: learn how to skim rocks.

I got to my feet and dusted the sand off my backside, returning to the resort with a clear purpose. Find Jed, sit him down, and just tell him. Simple, right?

As I approached, a heavy feeling rolled in my gut, and no, it wasn't my reluctance to tell Jed the truth. It was something else. As bad as I felt about withholding something from him, there was something else I hated even more: pity. And that had been the reason why no one apart from my dad, a few relatives, and my closest friends back home knew—and why I hadn't told a single soul in all the time I'd been traveling.

Leo, the owner of the resort, was the only person who knew,

and he only found out because of the giveaway contest that had won me this five-day stay here. He was a perceptive guy and must've picked up on my dislike of pity, and instead, showed some brief compassion, before moving the conversation on.

Was I being stupid or naive to hope for a similar reaction from Jed? It would be a shock to him, that I was prepared for. But, since there was nothing that could be done about it, after he'd had time to process it, things would be able to go back to...normal?

I hoped so. The feelings I was developing for him were exciting and fun and just damn nice. I wanted that experience to continue. More importantly, I didn't want *this* to overshadow everything else. Especially if it was blanketed with pity and sorrow. I couldn't handle that.

All right. Time to get out of my own head and get this done. I'd reached the resort and was running my feet under some water to wipe the sand off, when I spotted Jed. Least, I thought it was Jed. He must've gotten changed after lunch. He was wearing jeans, boots, and a checkered button-up shirt. So he *did* have normal-looking clothes.

"Hey, Jed," I called out as I ran barefoot to catch up with him. "Jed!"

Finally, the six-foot-six frame in front of me turned around and yep, it was him, although his hair seemed a tint lighter than I remembered. Must've been the afternoon sun beaming down on him.

"Hey, can we talk?" I panted, a little out of breath once I reached him.

He opened his mouth to respond, but I grabbed him by the hand. "Please," I insisted. "This is really important, and I'm scared that if I don't say it now, I'll chicken out and never be able to tell you."

"Uh, okay." I could hear the uncertainty in his voice, but he let me lead him to a row of empty deck chairs by the pool. We sat down facing each other and our knees touched. It took me back to the bus ride to the hike and I smiled, quickly wiping it away when I reminded myself of what I had to tell him.

I bit down on my lower lip and started nodding my head in an attempt to work up the courage to say the words. "Look, Jed. I have to tell you something. It's not easy for me to say this, and it is kinda major—"

"Um, listen, can I just interrupt you for a sec—"

I raised my hand. "No, please, Jed. Let me finish." I counter-interrupted his interruption. "I'm sorry, I don't mean to be rude, I just—I just need to get this out of me."

My hands had gone all clammy and my heart was thundering in my ears. Jed gave a clipped nod.

Okay, this was it. Truth time.

I inclined my head to meet the wide, bronzed eyes in front of me. "Jed, I know we're doing this whole fake-married thing to help you deal with your grandparents, but there's something you need to know about me."

I gulped down some air, and with everything I had in me, said, "I only have six months to live. I'm—I'm dying."

Jed tried to cover his gasp, but his hand didn't reach his mouth in time. "Oh my God."

I lowered my eyes to the ground, let out the biggest breath I had ever taken, and let the words spill out of me. "I have primary myelofibrosis. It's a rare bone marrow disorder, which basically means that my body doesn't produce blood cells the way it should within the bone marrow. It causes weakness and fatigue. You might have noticed how I got tired pretty quickly on our hike and asked to sit down?"

I glanced up at him, but his eyes were as wide as saucers, and confusion was strewn across his entire face. I couldn't blame him for being in shock. I still remembered the wall of numbness that hit me when the doctor told me my diagnosis for the first time.

I avoided Jed's gaze and kept speaking. "I got the diagnosis six months ago. Before that, I'd gotten every single medical test under the sun. It turns out PMF—that's what they call it for short—is one hard motherfucker to diagnose."

I resisted the urge to look at Jed. I didn't need to. I could sense the pain radiating from him. "What's the prognosis?" His voice cracked with emotion.

"Not good." I clasped my knees and began gently rocking, the heaviness of both the conversation and Jed's reaction starting to crash into me. "On top of having PMF, the doctors also found that I have a mutated gene which makes treatment...impossible."

"Impossible?" It was barely more than a whisper.

I nodded. "Unless I get a bone marrow transplant from a suitable donor. But that's incredibly unlikely. There's a one in a million chance of a donor match, which means that in a country like America, with roughly three hundred and thirty million people, the donor match pool is—"

"Three hundred and thirty people." Jed finished the sentence for me.

"That's right." I kept my gaze away from him, but rested my palm on his knee.

A heartbreaking silence fell between us. I was trying my best to keep from losing it. I'd had six months to process this; Jed had had less than six minutes. My focus needed to be him right now.

With a clenched jaw, I lifted my head. "You can say something now," I offered as I took in his closed eyes and the thumb he was biting down on.

When his eyes opened and he looked at me, I couldn't tell what was going through his mind, at all. He just stared at me, blinking only occasionally.

"Jed, please. Say something. Anything."

He dropped his eyes to where my hand rested on his knee. When he looked back up, his eyes were filled with pain...and pity. When he finally spoke, his voice was oddly calm and, somehow, felt a little foreign.

"I'm so sorry, and I really don't know how to say this, but...I'm not Jed."

My body rocked backward and I almost fell off the deck chair. Okay, I hadn't been expecting *that*. I knew people reacted to bad news in a whole bunch of different ways, including denial, but I'd never heard of someone denying who *they* were.

"Come on, Jed. Stop kidding around." My eyes scanned his face, fervently. Was he trying to joke around, make me feel a bit better by being silly? If he was, he'd chosen a really weird time to be doing it.

Jed-slash-possibly-not-Jed sat up a little taller. "I'm sorry, but I'm really not joking. I'm not Jed," he repeated, and something about the seriousness in his voice made the hairs on my arms stiffen.

I shook my head, still in disbelief. "Are you—are you being serious right now?"

He looked down and tugged at the collar of his checkered shirt. "When have you ever known Jedfire Burns to wear something that's actually color-coordinated?"

I pinched the bridge of my nose as my head started to spin. I might've been on some heavy duty drugs, but what was actually happening here?

I stared again at the person in front of me, my eyes wide, my mouth gaping open. "Well, then"—I summoned my last remaining strength—"who the hell are you?"

19

JEDFIRE

"Your brother is arriving soon," Grandpa announced, taking off his thin, silver-rimmed reading glasses as he placed his cell phone down on the coffee table. The three of us had returned to the apartment after lunch, while Conrad had gone for a walk on the beach.

Grandma looked at the time. "In fact, he might already be here. His flight landed over an hour ago."

I settled into the sofa. "Which one?" When I was met with two blank faces, I clarified. "Which one of my brothers, Cooper or Mitchell?"

I was super close to both of my younger brothers, but I'd be lying if I'd said I wasn't a little more connected with Cooper. It had nothing at all to do with the fact that Mitchell was adopted. That shit didn't matter to anyone in my family, especially not me.

It's just that it was true what they said about twins—they did share an unspoken bond. And with Cooper and I being identical twins, it was as if that somehow only strengthened the ties between us even more.

"Cooper. Mitchell's staying back to hold down the fort," Grandpa explained.

"Wow. You think he's ready for that?" I heard the stupidity of that question as soon as it left my mouth. Of course Mitchell was ready to step up and run the plant. Grandpa wouldn't have entrusted that responsibility to him if he weren't. Me, on the other hand...

The steely, determined look in Grandpa's eyes mixed with his warm smile was all the answer I needed. "He might be a few years younger than you and Coop, but that boy has really found his feet since he met Cayman."

Grandpa stretched his feet out in front of him, while Grandma, seated next to him on the plush white leather sofa, brought her gin and tonic to her lips. "He's always been a good boy, but there's something about being in love that's ignited a fire under him. He's so much more outgoing, confident..." Her voice trailed off.

I smiled, my heart filled with happiness for my youngest brother. Then my thoughts quickly snapped back to my twin—and his impending visit. "So, why is Cooper here, then?"

My grandparents exchanged a look, like I'd seen them do countless times. Those times, funnily enough, always coincided with one of my adventures-gone-awry moments. I narrowed my eyes suspiciously, waiting for one of them to answer.

Grandpa finally filled the silence. "He's worried about you, Jed. What with Vegas, and the fact that you haven't spent more than a few days back home in lord knows how many months..."

"We all just want to make sure you're okay, honey," Grandma added, the ice cubes knocking in her tumbler as I considered her words.

Was I okay?

On the surface, it looked like my life was a continuing shitshow of fuckup after fuckup. That was to be expected. I wasn't the kinda guy who did things half-assed. No, when I screwed things up, I used my whole damn ass.

But maybe, after almost six years, it had gone on for too long. Enough was enough, and my behavior could no longer be excused or overlooked. I got that. I really did.

Maybe even a week ago, I would have fought back against that. But ever since a certain Cali-cute, surfboard-making, cute-catchphrase-saying someone had come into my life, my perspective on things was...changing.

I eyed my grandparents. Grandma was sipping on her drink, snugly nestled into Grandpa's side, while he stared out into the ocean. They had such a close familiarity with each other. Hardly surprising after practically an entire lifetime together, but something about seeing that so close up and personal right now unleashed a yearning in me that, up until recently, I didn't know existed.

Was it Conrad who had lit that spark? Yeah, it was.

I realized it was way too early to be thinking more than even a few days ahead, much less projecting forward a few decades, but my heart couldn't help but tug with a deep, almost desperate wanting.

Wouldn't it be amazing to find someone that you loved, who loved you back and that you could create a beautiful forever with?

I knew that wouldn't be the case here. We were practically strangers, entangled by the happenstance of a particularly sticky lie, on a vacation that would be over in a matter of days.

I settled back down on the sofa and rested my eyes for a moment. A warm feeling flooded the center of my chest as daydreams of a future with Conrad in it danced in my imagination.

Hey, a guy could still dream, right?

20

CONRAD

My mouth stayed open as I kept my eyes glued on the Jed...clone, apparition, alien...in front of me.

"I'm Cooper Burns. Jed's twin. We're—"

"Identical." I muttered the word with him.

Knowing there was a perfectly rational explanation for the figure sitting opposite me was comforting, but my head was still spinning out of control. "I, uh, just might need a moment."

Cooper smiled a straighter version of Jed's lopsided grin. That's when all the little clues started making sense. The clothes he had on that didn't look like he'd closed his eyes and raided a thrift shop. The lighter shade of his hair. The reason why he'd interrupted me before, trying to interject before I blurted out...

"Oh, god." I covered my mouth in shock. "I just told you..."

Shit. I'd not only told him about my condition, but I'd also revealed the fact that Jed and I were pulling the wool over his grandparent's eyes. *Double shit.*

Cooper's face tightened. "I am so, so sorry to hear about what you're going through. And this would have to be the worst time to ask you this, but...what's your name?"

I scrubbed my hands across my face. Oh god, I'd just told someone who didn't even know my name something no one outside of my closest circle knew. With a deep breath, I tried to pull my act together.

It wasn't his fault, I reminded myself as I stretched out my hand. "I'm Conrad. Conrad McCallister."

He shook my hand, but the pensiveness drawn across his Jed-esque features stayed in place. "Again, I'm so sorry to hear about your condition. If there's anything I, or my family can—"

"Stop. *Please*."

He snapped his mouth shut straight away. Pity was the last thing I wanted. It'd been the reason why I hadn't told Jed earlier, and now, witnessing his brother's—*his identical twin brother's*—reaction, maybe it had been a mistake to think that telling Jed was the right thing to do. I'd be met with pretty much the same response, wouldn't I?

Concern. Worry. And being coddled like a baby with my every move scrutinized while getting peppered with an incessant line of "Are you sure you're okay?" questioning. I knew it would come from a good place, like it did with Dad. After all, pity was always well-intentioned. I just didn't want that. I was not my disease; I was still Conrad. And in whatever time I had left on this planet, that's how I wanted to be treated.

I looked up and was met by familiar, yet now oddly faraway eyes. I shattered the silence between us with words I had a feeling he wouldn't like hearing. "You can't breathe a word of this to Jed."

Cooper's mouth flung open. "But you were about to tell him." He pinched his eyes shut. "I mean, you thought you were telling him. Why—why don't you want him to know?"

I bit down nervously on a fingernail and ignored his question. "Promise me, please, that you won't say anything."

Responding to the seriousness in my pleading, Cooper let out a reluctant nod. He repeated his earlier question, infused with a genuine softness and caring that I knew I wouldn't be able to successfully ignore again.

"I wanted to tell Jed because...something seems to be happening between us."

I had to choose my words carefully. Jed had told me he had two younger brothers—although he conveniently left out being an identical twin—but I still didn't know how much of *us* he'd be comfortable with me sharing with one of them.

"I like him," I continued, deciding to play it safe and talk about things from my perspective only. "I've never met anyone like him."

"Yeah, Jed is one of a kind, for sure."

"Well, one of two, as I've just learned."

A low chuckle emanated from Cooper. "He's still an original. I'm the normal, boring one."

It was my turn to grin. I couldn't help but wonder if being an identical twin was part of the reason why Jed had developed such a strong, independent identity.

I considered my next words very carefully. "When I said I liked Jed before, Cooper, I wasn't telling you the whole truth. The whole truth is that I'm feeling something for him that I've never felt before. That's why I wanted to tell him about my condition. I hated keeping something this big from him. He deserves to know the full story. As much as I like him, and I hope that he likes me, nothing can ever come of this because I don't"—a painful lump lodged in my throat which I did my best to swallow around—"because I don't have a future."

This time, Cooper almost managed to suppress his heavy wheeze. *Almost.*

"I thought I had to tell him, but I'm not going to lie, telling you was really hard."

Cooper's hand was covering the lower half of his face, his eyes overflowing with emotion. "I—I can't even begin to imagine."

"I was scared of how he'd react, you know?"

Cooper nodded, removed his hand, and gave smiling his best

shot. He only half succeeded. "That's why you have to tell him. Not that I'm telling you what to do. I don't even know you. But it sounds to me like your reasons for telling him are still valid. And I know my brother, Conrad. I know how he'll react. He will be so full of—"

"Pity?" I interjected.

Cooper swiveled to the side, letting his eyes drift aimlessly. "Yeah, maybe a little at first. But the one thing I know better than anyone else about Jedfire Burns is to never underestimate him. The only guarantee you have with him is that the guy will surprise you, over and over and over again. Usually in good ways."

I let out a low laugh, easing some of the tension in my body. "I've only known him a little while, but yeah, he's had me flabbergasted a few times already."

"Try living with him for almost twenty-five years," Cooper shot back with a knowing grin. Then his forehead crinkled again as he looked straight at me. "Tell him, Conrad. Please. Not just because I can tell you're a decent person who knows it's the right thing to do, but because Jed deserves to have the opportunity to surprise you."

My mind went blank, and I must have been gawking at Cooper for longer than I intended.

"Have I got something on my face?" His fingers flittered across his face.

"What? No. Sorry." I managed to stir myself back to life. Okay, poor word choice. "It's just still a little surreal to be looking at you and seeing Jed. You look like him, sound just like him, but you're different, too."

"Yeah, I'm the normal and boring one, remember?" he quipped.

I aimed a tight-lipped smile at him. "And I can tell you're a decent person, too, Cooper. Which is why I know you'll respect my wishes. Please don't tell Jed. I'm not ready yet. I thought I was, but I'm not."

I could tell he wanted to say something, challenge me on it. I recognized that defiant air. He might have called himself the *normal and boring one,* but that was definitely one trait he shared with Jed.

He gave a clipped nod, not unlike the one I'd seen from his grandfather the first time I'd so memorably introduced myself to the man. "Fine," he breathed out begrudgingly. "I won't tell Jed."

I pointed my finger at him shakily. "Do you promise?"

"I promise."

"Thank you."

I hated lying or keeping something this big from Jed, and on some level, I knew I'd tell him. Eventually. But I wasn't able to do it right now. I just needed a bit more time which was ironic, given that was the one thing I didn't have a whole lot of.

21

JEDFIRE

"What the fuck is the matter with you?"

My eyes shot up at Cooper. Grandpa and Grandma had only just left the living room to get dressed for dinner, leaving my younger brother and I alone for the first time. We'd been hanging out together in the apartment for the past few hours, ever since Cooper had returned from checking out the resort.

He'd seemed fine-ish. A little on the quiet side, but that was his thing. Besides, I made enough noise and caused enough commotion for the both of us.

I certainly hadn't picked up on any attitude or resentment from him, which was why the way he spat his question out struck me with such force.

"What the fuck is the matter with *you*?" I retorted, showering him with my most unimpressed look.

"Don't you play dumb with me, Jedfire."

Cooper stomped over from the stool he was perched on in the kitchen and plonked his pissed-off ass right next to me on the sofa, shoving my feet out of his path in the process before invading my personal space.

"Hey, I was comfortable," I complained.

"Your comfort is the least of my worries right now." His jaw was twitching wildly, a true sign he was angry at me. For what, though, I had no idea. I quickly filtered through my mental rolodex, trying to pinpoint any justifiable cause for his acrimony.

Sure, I had a tendency to do things that upset and irritated him. I was loud, messy, and believed that a towel's rightful place *was* on the bathroom floor. But I could, on occasion, be considerate, too. I always bought him coffee whenever I visited the plant before noon (which admittedly, wasn't all that often), I let him use me as a guinea pig to try on what he called fashion (khakis, seriously, bro?), and heck, I even stopped dicking Hayden, the local bartender, after Cooper developed feelings for him. It didn't work out between the two of them, but I still never went back there. Because that's the kind of older by two minutes brother I was—a damn good one.

"Care to fill me in?" I prodded, my displeasure ringing loud and clear in my voice.

Cooper scratched down the side of his arm. "I can't believe you didn't tell me."

"Tell you what, Cooper? I haven't got the faintest clue what's gotten you all pissy like this."

He tipped his head and side-eyed me. "I ran into your husband today. Or should I say, your fake husband."

I bolted upright. "You saw Conrad?"

"Uh, yeah, unless you have more than one fake husband. Which, given your history, I wouldn't rush to rule out polygamy entirely."

"Fuck you."

"No. Fuck you, Jed," Cooper growled as he pinned his index finger to my chest. "What the hell, man? I thought we told each other everything?"

"Yeah, well, this is kind of a recent development." I slanted my head back and scratched down the front of my neck. "A very recent development."

"Yeah, no shit, punk ass."

Silence followed and I had absolutely zero intention of breaking it. I could hold out for longer than Cooper, but my younger brother seemingly had a secret weapon up his sleeve. One which he wasn't afraid to use.

"He likes you."

That snapped my head back so hard and fast I was surprised I didn't sprain a tendon...whatever the hell a tendon was. "He said that?"

Cooper folded his arms across his chest and shot me his most patronizing smile as he poked his chin into the air sanctimoniously. "Apologize to me."

I gritted my teeth. He could be such a real shit sometimes. "I'm sorry," I muttered.

"*For?*"

"For not telling you that I met Conrad and fell—"

"In love?" he guessed as his eyes widened with each passing second I said nothing.

I mean, what could I say? It was so soon. *Too soon.* And also, maybe it'd be nicer to tell the person I was falling for my feelings before my annoying craptard of a twin brother.

"Maybe." I crumpled back into the sofa, a gust of emotions blowing inside of me. I hadn't seen Conrad since lunch and damn, if I wasn't missing him like crazy. And now I was finding out that Cooper had run into him—which I was guessing would've been a mild shock for Conrad—and somehow, Cooper had found out about our little plan.

"Hang on a minute," I said, my brain switching into a gear other than WTF-is-happening-here mode. "Okay, so you ran into Conrad, I get that. But why did he tell you about the fake marriage thing?"

Cooper's shoulders stiffened. He kept his gaze focused away from me as he said, "He thought he was talking to you obviously, and he, uh, wanted to go over some...stuff."

Yeah, okay, I saw it now. The Burns brothers were terrible liars.

"It's clear we have a lot to catch up on, Jed. But you have to grow up, man. You can't keep living like this. Flying head first into one shitshow after another, leaving a wake of destruction in your path. You're worse than a hurricane."

I scoffed. "How am I *worse* than a hurricane?"

Worry skated across his face as he turned to me. "Because hurricanes come to an end. They stop. Jed, you've been living like this since..."

He cleared his throat as a familiar lump settled in mine. "This isn't what Mom and Dad would have wanted for you. They knew how smart and talented and passionate you were—are," he hastily corrected himself. "You're throwing your life away by doing this."

"I don't want to run the business." I bolted to my feet. "I'd rather die, Cooper."

Something atramentous flashed across Cooper's face as he joined me, making my way to the giant glass windows overlooking the beach.

"*Don't* say that." Cooper's tone was sharp, his eyes blazing with something volatile.

"Why not? It's true. Running the plant is your dream. It's Mitch's dream. It's not mine. Mitch is back home right now, running the plant by himself. You guys don't even need me. "

His hand found my shoulder. "That's not true, Jed. We do need you. And if you bothered to spend more than a few weeks a year back home, you'd see that for yourself, rather than having to listen to me try and convince you of it."

Damn it, he'd cut off my next line, which would have basically accused him of spouting bullshit to make me feel better about myself. Okay, since that was a no-go, I defaulted to what came so easily to us Burns brothers: a change of topic.

"Hey, after dinner with Grandpa and Grandma, wanna come to karaoke? I can introduce you to Conrad properly then if you like?"

I bit inside my cheek, wondering whether Cooper would let the conversation get sidetracked so wildly. After a mini stare off, he conceded.

"Sure." He shrugged, turning to face the dimming day. "Conrad seems like a nice guy. Might be good to get to know my fake brother-in-law a smidge better. At least until, I'm assuming, your fake divorce?"

Cooper's questioning eyes only brought home the fact that Conrad and I really hadn't thought any of this out at all. But could you blame me? Whenever I spent time with him, my brain turned to mush, and all I wanted to do was to look at him, talk and laugh with him, and ideally, be held in his arms while I fell asleep.

Who had time for planning a fake relationship when something real was starting to happen?

22

CONRAD

What. A. Day!

Although, it felt more like a week than merely twelve hours since I'd woken up with my arms curled around Jed's body. That was followed by a pleasantly uneventful lunch—where I was pretty sure we managed to pull off the whole "we just got married" thing well—a nice stroll along the beach and then an *I still can't wrap my mind around it* encounter with Jed...'s identical twin brother, Cooper.

This was turning out to be quite the memorable vacation.

I finished off the seafood linguine I'd ordered to my old room. I couldn't believe running into Cooper like that. Much less what I'd divulged to him. Jed had sent me a text earlier to see if I'd like to join him and a surprise guest—*ha, little did he know*—for dinner. I declined. Not because I didn't want to spend more time with him and his family; I did. I just needed to rest up a little.

And while Jed had remained perfectly gentlemanly and gracious about my dinner refusal, he did good-naturedly warn me that he wouldn't take no for an answer for a round of karaoke afterward. So, I agreed.

After returning from the beach, I spoke to Dad. We were speaking more often now that I was back in the country. When I was traveling throughout Europe and Asia, we tended to text, given the time zone differences. Not a day went by in the five months I'd been gone that he hadn't touched base with me at least once a day.

I was starting to really miss him. But we had a deal. I got to spend six months doing something I'd always wanted to do: travel. And then we'd spend six months—my last six months—together.

After the call, I returned to my old suite. I'd kept the room card and thought it'd be a good idea to give Jed some more time with his family and me some alone time, too.

I ran a bath and whiled away a good hour or so luxuriating in the bubbly goodness of it all. This suite had everything, including beautifully scented candles and towels so soft it felt like they were made of silk. I'd never experienced anything this luxurious before, so I allowed myself to enjoy it.

That included staying in the super comfy white bathrobe and slippers for the rest of the day. I cracked open the sliding door to let the sounds and smells of the beach in, and I lay on the couch, staring out into the blueness before me.

I'd been doing a lot of reflecting over the last six months. I guessed that was to be expected when you received a diagnosis that gave you only one more year left to live. I could still vividly recall the numbness I felt at hearing the news. Everything faded to black and all I could hear was my heartbeat thrumming in my chest.

I didn't remember anything that the doctor had said to me after the words, "You have one year left to live." The car ride back home with Dad? Nope. Even the next few days were a little hazy.

And then one morning, three days later, I woke up in a panic. I'd had a nightmare about something. I couldn't remember what, but I woke up drenched in sweat. That did something to me—it opened a lock and unleashed everything I'd been keeping bottled up inside.

All of a sudden, I went from being an anesthetized zombie to a walking ball of hurt. I cried like I'd never cried before and spent the whole day in bed, sobbing like a baby. By dinnertime, my cheeks stung with pain and my throat was as coarse as sandpaper.

I felt it all. A fiery rage. Denial. Hopelessness at how unfair it was. The *why me-ness* of it all. It lasted a good three days.

Then, on the fourth day, after Dad and I had lunch, I went to pack the dishwasher, and just as suddenly as the emotions burst through, I had something else pierce my soul. I remembered staring out the window. It was a beautiful clear day and the sun was beaming down onto the steel roof of our surfboard-making shed in the backyard. A bit of light reflected off the roof and briefly blinded me. As I turned, covering my face, a quiet voice from deep inside spoke to me.

I knew it sounded weird and kooky as shit, but a feeling settled within me that, for whatever reason, made me feel a bit better for the first time since I'd received my diagnosis.

Yes, it sucked. It was beyond unfair. I, still, to this day, had moments where I curled my fists into balls of anger at the awfulness of it all.

But in that moment in the kitchen, as I straightened up and looked out the window again, I realized that, in a way, I'd received a gift. The condition was proving to be so hard to diagnose that I'd told Dad that was my last series of tests. I was done with hospital visits and being poked and prodded like some sort of science experiment.

Whatever I had, whatever was wrong with me, would have to go undiagnosed because I was over the testing. Had the last round of results shown nothing, I would have stuck to my guns. Which wouldn't have changed a thing. I'd still be dead in a year, but I wouldn't have had a clue that it was coming.

This way, I did.

And that gave Dad and I a chance to put our heads together and come up with this little plan of ours. My chance—my first and last opportunity—to travel and see a bit of the world.

In addition to funding this trip for me by taking on extra jobs and relegating sleep to the *nice but not needed* category, Dad entered me into a contest run by our local radio station, TBZ83.

It was a contest to give someone who had experienced something bad something good. Like an all-expenses-paid vacation at Elysian. Callers would dial in with their tales of bad luck and misfortune, and so that's what Dad did. And he won it for me.

That's how Leo, the owner of Elysian, knew who I was. It was the only reason I could even stay at a place like this. And it's how I came to meet one Mr. Jedfire Burns.

Which reminded me—I'd better start getting ready. What was appropriate attire for *I'm only going because I want to see your adorable face* karaoke?

Twenty minutes later, I was dressed in a pair of faded blue jeans and a white T-shirt and heading toward the very same bar I'd met Jedfire.

As I entered the packed place and began scanning for signs of Jed, I felt a pair of large and delectably warm hands wrap around my waist.

I twisted and instinctively rose onto my toes, my lips finding Jed's. His hands slid up my back, guiding me in place, while our lips stayed connected. I wanted more, but I held back. We were in public, and we were with his family. We had to convince them we were married, not tongue wrestling world champions. Although...maybe we could do both?

"Feels like I haven't seen you in forever," Jed murmured against my lips.

"You saw me at lunch." I smiled as I landed back on the balls of my feet.

"Too long. Much too long."

I studied his eyes and for a brief moment, wondered whether

Cooper had told him. But the mischievous twinkle he was doing a terrible job of hiding suggested he had no idea. No. The only thing on Jed's mind was having some fun tonight, which I had a sneaking suspicion involved trying to coerce me to do some karaoke. Ha, little did he know what I had planned in retaliation...

I didn't notice the outlandishness of Jed's outfit until Cooper stepped up beside us. His very normal and boring outfit of dark pants and a maroon polo contrasted sharply with Jed's fashion choice for the evening: a zipper front, V-neck flamingo-slash-floral print short-sleeved and short-shorted onesie. I didn't know if it was the lopsided curve of his smile or the fact that the skin he was showing on his arms and legs radiated with a sunny glow. All I knew was that only Jedfire Burns could pull off this ridiculous outfit.

Noticing his brother, Jed nodded and cleared his throat. "Conrad, I'd like you to formally meet my younger brother—and three-time consecutive winner of *Cowbell People's* Sexiest Man Alive, Cooper."

We shook hands, which felt a little strange, given the accidental insight I'd given him into my personal life, and also—

"Wait. You guys are identical. How did Cooper win the Sexiest Man Alive title and not you?" I asked, curling into Jed's warm body. "I mean, no offense, Cooper."

He threw back a laugh. "None taken."

"Yeah, beats me, too." Jed tightened his grip around my shoulder, and I never wanted his hand to leave me.

"We've got a booth in the corner," Cooper said. "I was just making my way to the bar to get Grandma and Grandpa another round. What can I get you guys?"

"Just my usual, thanks," Jed replied.

"Just a soda for me, please."

With that, Cooper sauntered off as Jed and I—his hand nestled into the crook of my shoulder—made our way through the crowded bar.

"Hey, listen. I hope I didn't blow our cover by telling Cooper about our fake relationship. I honestly thought I was talking to you."

Jed's fingers slid their way down my back, sending a warm rumble throughout my entire body. "It's all good. I should have told you he was coming, but I didn't find out myself until after lunch. We can trust him. He might irritate the life out of me sometimes, but he's a man of his word."

I blew out one very relieved breath. That meant that Cooper would keep our little secret and *my* big secret, too.

We joined his grandparents and the five of us enjoyed a wonderful evening talking and laughing together. There was something so special about getting to see a person with their family, particularly when their family was as nice and warm and loving as Jed's. They let their guard down and it gave you a deeper insight into who they were. That's what I was seeing with Jed.

In many ways, he was just as loud, outrageous, and downright Jed-like with them as he was all the time. That part didn't change. But I caught a glimpse of another side to him, too. A softer side.

Like when he would regale his grandpa with a story and looked at the man with nothing but love and devotion in his eyes. Or the way he'd tilt his head ever so slightly whenever his grandma spoke, deferring an unspoken respect to her. Or how his smile would reach his eyes—and stay there—whenever Cooper cracked a joke, the bond between them strong and unbreakable.

While we'd been having a great time, I couldn't help but notice that karaoke had started up on the stage at the front of the bar. I was seated between Jed's grandma and Cooper, so he'd glance in my direction every so often and waggle his eyebrows, being about as subtle as a freight train.

I knew it'd be his mission to get me up onto that stage. That was why I wanted to make sure I caught a good look of his face as I excused myself past Cooper, turned to the table, and announced, "I'm going to sing next."

The look of disbelief that shot across Jed's face was as priceless as I'd hoped it would be. With a cheeky wink, I turned on my heel and made a beeline for the stage. I didn't have the benefit of liquid courage since I couldn't drink. Just my father's words ringing in my ears. *Whatever life throws at you, go for it and have some fun.* And life had thrown Jedfire Burns at me, and I'd be damned if I wouldn't let myself have some fun with it.

As the applause from the previous singer died down and she exited the stage, I grabbed the mic and selected the song. I took a deep breath and stepped out into the spotlight. I had a terrible voice, so there was no doubt this was going to be one of those cringeworthy renditions. But it was late enough in the evening that most people should have been inebriated enough to be able to drown it out. I hoped.

What I hadn't expected when I looked out into the darkened crowd was to see, clear as day, an unexpected audience member in the front row. Jed's face was beaming up at me, his arms folded across his chest, and my heart caught in my throat.

The first notes began as I sent him a warm smile.

Here went nothing...

I brought the microphone to my lips, locked my gaze on Jed, and sang the opening line. Sure, *Chain Reaction* by Diana Ross might have been an unusual choice, but the lyrics really spoke to me.

I *was* there not dancing with anyone the night we first met.

He had taken a little and now he really was taking me over.

He did set his mark on stealing my heart away or, as he so eloquently put it, getting me into his bed by the end of my vacation.

When the song was over, thunderous applause filled the room, and as I made my way to the side of the stage, I could sense Jed following me. As he approached and we were about to meet at the bottom of the stairs, a pair of well-manicured hands pushed Jed out of the way.

Jed's grandma grabbed the mic out of my hands. "Great job,

kiddo," she exclaimed enthusiastically. Before I could react, she'd brushed past me and was making her way to center stage.

I curled into Jed's side as he wrapped an arm around me. The bar quieted, but before the song played, Jed's grandma stepped forward and she moved her arms wide of her body. With a beaming smile, she carved out four distinct letters. An *L*. Then an *O*. Followed by a *V*. And then with the help of her toned legs, lifting and jutting them out the side of her body, she managed an *E* as well.

Then, the song played. As I snuggled in even closer to Jed, the two of us smiled as we watched her perform the Frank Sinatra classic. Unlike my performance which played over the din of the bar, there wasn't a sight or sound coming from anyone but the stage. The woman had captivated everyone, just like her grandson had captivated my heart.

As the song reached its crescendo ending with a series of *Love was made for me and yous*, I tipped my head up, captured Jed's face in my hands, and crashed his lips into mine. I tasted his sweet tongue inside my mouth as cheers rang out all around us as the song ended.

When I pulled away, I found his lust-filled eyes again. I licked my lower lip and said, "We might not have cute names for each other, yet, but I think we just found our song."

23

JEDFIRE

Our song.

Our song!

The words ricocheted in my poor, overloaded head and my heart? Geez, how was the poor fella even managing to hold a steady beat? Oh, that's right, he wasn't. I couldn't believe that Conrad and I had a song—or the sheer exuberance that just the idea of sharing a song with him brought out in me.

I couldn't help it, I scooped him up in my arms and hugged him tighter than I'd ever hugged anyone in my life. We spun around at the front of the stage for god only knew how long. I felt Grandma's hand patting my back as she walked past us, but that could have been a year ago.

Minutes, days, sounds, words...everything was blurring and spinning, and I felt like I was plunging into the most heavenly kind of delirium.

All because of him.

My plan had been to spend an enjoyable evening with Conrad and my family. Okay, my *secret* plan involved getting him up to do a karaoke duet with me at some stage, too. What I hadn't expected was for Conrad to take charge and get up onto that stage himself without any prompting from me and belt the house down with his amazing rendition of that classic song.

They say that love is blind. They should add it's probably deaf, too, since every note he sang sounded like the sweetest tasting honey to me.

"Jed, I'm getting dizzy." The words buzzed around me and I knew it was time to let Conrad's feet touch the ground. Mine, on the other hand, I was perfectly happy for my feet to float on air for the rest of the night. Luckily for me, Conrad's next words were going to help me do just that.

His fingers hooked into my shoulders as he lifted his lips to my ear and whispered, "I want to be yours tonight, Jed."

I steadied myself, suddenly experiencing the delayed onset of my spinning. I was feeling giddy and overwhelmed and a million other kinds of emotions words hadn't even been invented for yet.

My brain managed to click into gear. "Are you sure, Conrad?"

His breath whistled across my cheeks as he uttered the *Yes* I'd been hoping for since I first laid eyes on him.

"Let's say our goodbyes to your family and then skedaddle."

I managed a nod but had zero brainpower to poke fun of his unique word choice.

Somewhere between letting my family know we were heading back and arriving at the door to my bedroom, I found my footing again. The first time we'd been together, I'd fallen into starfish mode, letting Conrad do all the work.

Not this time.

Tonight, I would worship and adore every square inch of Conrad's body, and if I was really lucky, I'd get a glimpse of his soul, too.

It's not easy to undress yourself and someone else while maintaining constant lip contact, but there was no way I was letting his sweet lips be anywhere else but on mine. Luckily, my uber-cool onesie was a breeze to undo, and Conrad's choice of a button-up shirt wasn't too much of a challenge for my fingers, either.

I finally broke away for one very important reason, but I kept his face cupped in my hands. "Is this really what you want, Conrad?"

I saw the instant his blue eyes turned a dark navy, overtaken by the depth of his desire. "I want you so much." His voice was guttural, barely more than a groan. I had needed that, more than I realized, because it unleashed something within me, too.

Our lips smashed together as we fell onto the bed. The same bed we'd made out on for hours and I marveled at how I was able to restrain myself. The time for gentleman-ness was well and truly over.

I was so fucking into Conrad, and for whatever reason, he was into me, and I just wanted to enjoy this night like it was our last night on earth.

Now that we were naked, I ran my hand down his smooth torso, enjoying the softness of his skin. I flicked my tongue against his bottom lip, and then my lips joined my fingers, kissing, licking, and nibbling down his neck, across his chest, and down his taut midsection.

I could see how excited he was. It was kinda hard to miss it. But I didn't want to touch him there. Not just yet. I kissed around his groin as I spread his legs apart, my tongue lacing its way around his inner thighs.

"Oh god." His fingers dug into my hair, scratching at my scalp. I let out an urgent breath as I gripped behind his knees and gently lifted him up. I reached for a pillow and placed it under him. "Is this comfortable for you?"

"Yes." It was barely more than a contented whisper, but it was all I needed. I brought my face closer to his body. The warmth radiating off him, mixed with the scent of him, it was almost too much.

I breathed in the sweetness before I buried my face in his ass, probing his hole with my tongue. "Oh, fuck." His voice had a raspiness that sounded so damn good, almost as good as he tasted. Almost.

I drove my tongue around his entrance, lapping at it with a hunger I didn't know I had in me. Once I'd gotten him nice and slick, I licked my finger and placed it against him. Gently, I pressed it inside.

Conrad's lower back lifted off the pillow as he inhaled. When he breathed out, he lowered, and his clenched muscles loosened, allowing me deeper inside. I took my time. I wanted to make this every bit as enjoyable for him as it was for me. Hey, I'd have no objections to fingering him all night long if that's what was needed.

But Conrad, it seemed, had other ideas. "More," he pleaded. "I want more."

I wiggled over on the bed and opened the top drawer of the nightstand, pulling out the necessary supplies. Spit was okay. Lube was a whole lot better. I drizzled the gooey substance in the crack of his ass. Conrad threw his head back and let out a little squeal. "It's cold."

"I'll warm you up."

Our eyes locked as he let out a moan. "Please."

After playing with his hole and getting it ready with two more fingers, it was time to take this to the next level.

I sheathed my cock in a condom and stroked it with my lubed-up hand. I was granite-hard, and my balls were full and heavy, but I had no concerns about my staying power. I wanted to fu—make love, to Conrad all night long.

And that's exactly what we did. I entered him slowly, falling down on top of him so that we could kiss and stay connected while I did it. Just as I was about to bottom out, I pulled away slightly so that I could take in his face. His forehead was lined with sweat and he was positively glowing.

Slow was the name of the game. Just being inside him was enough for me. Movement was an added bonus and one that I introduced gradually as we swapped positions, tried out different angles. I even scooped him up in my arms and we went under the shower and tried it in there. (Side note: that didn't work so great. No matter how fancy the resort, showers were never made with people who were six foot six in mind).

We made it back onto the bed, still a little wet from not having dried off properly. Conrad's blond locks framed his face so beautifully on the pillow and we both knew we were ready. I drove into him in long, sweeping strokes, holding his legs up in the air, breathing in the beauty that lay underneath me. Our bodies weren't just moving as one—it felt like we were moving *through* one another.

He reached for his cock and began fisting it, our eyes remaining locked on each other. I sped up, thrusting into him with all the urgency of a man approaching the edge of the most blissful cliff, ready to dive off and surrender.

"Oh, God," Conrad cried, closing his eyes and arching his neck in contortion as he began to come. I watched him rocking and writhing underneath me and the sight of it sent me over that cliff. My orgasm crashed into me with such intensity I dropped his legs and began to see black spots in my vision.

When I was finally done shaking and teetering on the brink of vision loss, I felt Conrad's hands on my shoulders as he gently guided me down onto the bed beside him. I wiped my forehead with the back of my hand, gulping for air. I felt him pulling the condom off my cock and wiping me down with something a little warm, maybe a towelette?

Turning my head to look down and see what he was doing required way too much effort. Thankfully, a few seconds later, he was nestled against my body, his face on my chest. I inhaled the slightly salty smell of his hair and closed my eyes. That scent would stay with me forever and remind me of this moment for as long as I lived.

"That was amazing," I heard him say.

"Yes," I gulped back, stroking my fingers through his hair. I could feel Conrad's cheeks lifting on my chest. He was probably smiling. He was definitely happy. I was as well.

He turned his head and gazed up at me, with nothing but warmth and affection in his eyes.

"Sleep?"

I nodded and right on cue, a yawn escaped me.

Conrad chuckled as I turned onto my side and he sidled up behind me. I lifted my arm and he threaded his through the space underneath, securing his hand right where I liked it: on my heart.

"Goodnight, Jed."

"Goodnight, Conrad."

I would have fallen asleep in under a minute, but before I did, one final thought drifted through my weary head.

For the first time since eight days after my nineteenth birthday, I had finally found happiness.

24

CONRAD

Jed was swaddled so tightly in my arms that when I first felt movement between us, I wasn't sure if it was coming from him or me.

But it was him, definitely him.

I gently peeked a half-eye open as I felt him carefully wriggling *away* from me. Under the blanket of the room's darkness, I stirred slightly as I spotted him tiptoeing out of the room.

As soon as his large frame disappeared behind the door and he carefully clicked it shut, I shuffled over to his warm side of the bed and glanced at the bedside clock. The red digits displayed that it was almost midnight.

Where on earth was he going?

My mind drifted back to the first night we'd met. He'd taken off before midnight, too. I thought it was a little strange at the time, but nothing more.

Now, having known Jed for even a millisecond meant that I knew he was up to something. Once, okay, that wasn't too unusual. But to be doing it again, it was too much of a freaky coincidence for it to be just nothing.

Diana Ross whirred in my brain... *You give me all the after midnight action...*

I was sure Jedfire Burns had a grift going on. And I was determined to uncover precisely what it was that had him sneaking out of our bed after the most amazing love making experience of my life.

My head bounced softly on the pillow and I smiled, remembering the tenderness of his touch, the deep soulfulness of his eyes as he burrowed his cock into me, and the earth-shuddering release we both reached.

So, yeah, whatever he was up to, it'd better be damn good. I wiped my eyes and got to my feet, shrugging on the nearest shorts I could find and a shirt, which happened to be the shirt he'd slept in last night. I inhaled his unique spicy scent before pulling it over my head. I slipped my feet into a pair of flip-flops and set after the six-foot-six troublemaker I was falling for. I was one hundred percent ready to get my sleuthing game on.

Outside the apartment, I caught a glimpse of him making his way past the pool. The resort was beautifully lit at night with colorful lights placed in the tropical bushes as well as along the pathways, giving the entire place a Survivor-esque feel.

I kept my distance, regretting my shoe choice almost immediately. Flip-flops were too noisy to allow me to get any closer and too impractical should I need to break out into a jog to keep up with wherever Jed was headed to.

The main lobby area of the resort was a beautiful, white, standalone building. It was also dimly lit given the time of night, but that didn't make it any less impressive. If anything, the subdued ambiance only added to its charm.

Jed ducked inside. I bit down on my lip. I couldn't follow him in because he'd surely see me, so instead, I scrambled my way over to a window on the other side of the building.

Once in a prime viewing position, I peered in. I could clearly make Jed out. Apart from a staff member behind the reception desk, the place was completely empty. Hardly surprising since it was almost midnight.

The interior was just as magnificent as the outside. Floor-to-ceiling windows lined one wall with the starry night sky streaming in. Elegant, ivy-filled furniture filled the space while a series of glittering chandelier columns gave the place a super polished, luxe vibe.

Jed loitered around the ATM in the far corner, flicking his wrist up every few seconds to look at the time. Then, suddenly, he jolted and lunged at the machine. With his whole body hunched over it, all I could see was his right hand furiously tapping away.

Why was he taking money out at this time? And why was he doing it with such fervor? None of it made any sense.

Before I could make any sense of it, Jed straightened up and headed back toward the entrance he'd come through. Shit. I needed to get back to the room before he did. I hightailed it outta there, cutting through a shortcut I'd found. Well, not so much a shortcut as a set of bushes that would get me ahead and back to the apartment before him.

As I raced up the stairs and into the room, I started panting and felt a little weak. I threw the clothes—as well as a few errant leaves —off me and threw myself into the bed. No sooner had I pulled the cover up over me, I heard the door crack open and the sound of Jed's light footsteps getting closer.

"Hey," I mumbled. "Where'd you go?"

"Nowhere. I just had to pee."

Even in the caliginosity of the night, I could hear the lie in his voice as he got into bed.

"Snuggles?" His voice skipped airily over his shoulder.

I pitched my body to his and threaded his body through my arms. "This feels nice," he said softly, while all I could feel was the drumming of his heart in his chest.

"Yeah, it does," I replied, sinking my chin into the crook of his neck.

"It feels like you've got me locked in."

As I felt him drifting off, my mind raced, frantically searching for an answer to the still-unanswered question that torpedoed around and around in my thoughts: what in the Sam Hill was Jedfire Burns up to?

TUESDAY

25

JEDFIRE

The next morning, everyone woke up at around the same time and the kitchen was a familial hive of activity.

Grandpa was flicking through *The New York Times* finance section, his glasses perched perilously close to the tip of his nose. Cooper was making everyone coffee, the sounds of the machine percolating through the air along with the enticing smell of caffeine.

But the best sight of all was the one right in front of me. I was perched on a bar stool, leaning on the cool island countertop as I watched Grandma and Conrad making pancakes.

"The secret to the fluffiest pancakes you will ever eat"— Grandma's eyes shifted left to right, as if she were checking to make sure the coast was clear to reveal her secret, while Conrad leaned in and giggled excitedly—"is...Sprite."

"Really?" Conrad practically shrieked the word out.

"It sure is. Cooper, darling, could you get me some Sprite out of the fridge, please?"

"On it," he replied brightly, handing me a freshly brewed cup of joe on his way. I pressed the mug to my mouth, but yeah, I didn't miss the *I know what you did last night with Conrad* look he aimed my way. But he was acting all light and happy, and I appreciated that he was cool with it.

We had each other's backs like that. Sure, we fought like cats and dogs, disagreed about a ton of stuff, and frustrated the life out of each other, but ultimately, we both wanted nothing but the best for each other. And that definitely included the one thing that had eluded both of us so far: romantic love.

Even though I hadn't had the chance to tell him how I *really* felt about Conrad yet, I knew that on some level, he already knew. Which made his coolness with it even more special.

As I sipped my coffee and took in the scene around me, something about the niceness of it all, the naturalness, made me stupidly happy inside. It was like Conrad was part of the family already.

And then just like that, something about the doorbell ringing out made all of those nice, yummy, early-morning feels come to a screeching halt and now, my stomach was churning.

Thanks, life. I couldn't have five damn minutes of peace, could I?

Cooper had brisked away to answer the door, which gave me what would become my last few moments of tranquility before everything came crashing down around me. I didn't know how I knew, but I just did. Whoever walked through that door would be the bearer of bad news.

"Walter, Catherine." Tommy's voice boomed as he strode into the kitchen, dressed in his usual three-piece suit. His hair, skin, everything was immaculate about the guy.

"Jedfire." He eyed me sharply. I knew that look. He'd been my own unofficial personal get-me-out-of-shit guy for so long, I not only knew that look, I knew it well. And yeah, it was never a good thing. So my intuition was right. Shit was about to go down.

With his eyes firmly planted on me, he tipped his head in Conrad's direction. I scrambled to my feet and walked over to my fake husband. As I crossed the floor and turned the corner of the island, that's when it hit me.

Tommy knew. I'd asked him to do some digging to find out who I had actually married in Vegas. And now my cover, our whole fake marriage story, was about to detonate.

I sidled up close to Conrad, whose expression was somewhere between early morning contentment and mild confusion, and introduced him to Tommy. "Tommy, this is Conrad." There, technically not a lie. Right? Just the guy's name.

"Conrad is Jed's latest husband." Cooper's comment was both unneeded and an obvious attempt at trying to get a rise out of me. I clenched my jaw, determined not to give him one, hoping that a dose of some newfound maturity would wipe that wide smirk off his lips soon enough.

"What brings you all the way out here?" Grandpa, never one to avoid getting straight to the point, asked as he put down the newspaper.

"Would you like something to drink, dear?" Grandma peered up at Tommy. "Cooper's a whiz on the coffee machine."

Tommy smiled and lifted his briefcase up. "I'm good, thanks, Catherine." The smile he gave Grandma thinned as he turned to face Grandpa. "We need to talk, Walter."

His eyes briefly darted across the room to meet my terror-filled ones. "You, Jedfire, and I need to talk. Preferably in private."

I guzzled the rest of my brew. "We can talk here. We're all family."

I felt Conrad's hand nuzzle into my lower back and something about the touch countered the rising panic gnawing in my gut.

"It's about work," Tommy whipped back, his tone making his intention for privacy clear.

I stood my ground, and just as I was about to dig my heels in even more, it happened. Starting like it always did, I felt a little jiggle at the back of my throat. It bubbled up to the roof of my mouth and then I did it. Completely helpless to stop it, my tongue *clacked* loudly against the top of my mouth.

I lost my train of thought, but instead of feeling self-conscious and ashamed about it like I usually did, all I felt was Conrad's hand sweeping up and down my back in long, firm strokes. Regaining some lost composure, I set my eyes on Tommy and repeated. "We can talk here. I'm assuming it's about me. I have nothing to hide."

"Are you sure about that, Jedfire?" Tommy's eyes softened an iota, before drifting over to Conrad.

Despite my relationship with Tommy being forged in often less than ideal circumstances—yes, due to my own stupid making—we'd reached a detente of sorts. Officially, I fell under the remit of 'risk mitigation,' or at least that's the line item his 'work' with me fell under on the company's profit and loss statements. But unofficially, over the past few years, I think the guy had developed a bit of a soft spot for me.

Enough of a soft spot for him to understand that my insistent silence meant what I said and that he would respect my wishes. He nodded his head, set his tan leather attaché case on the counter, and agreed. "Very well then. Let's talk."

"Is it about Vegas?" I guessed.

"No." His reply was as curt as it was surprising.

Tommy had been on it for a few days, so by now, I would've expected he'd have the name, social security number, even the shoe size and dietary preferences of the guy I had actually married. "I do have an update on that situation, but that's not why I flew all the way to Florida."

My family had stepped in closer to Tommy, encircling him. "So, why did you fly down here?" I could hear the irritation growing in Grandpa's voice. This conversation had gone on for way too long and we still weren't any closer to knowing what the reason for Tommy's surprise visit was.

Tommy clicked open the briefcase and pulled out a thick binder. Moving the case to the side, he proceeded to open the binder up, flicking through the pages, making a show of just how many pages there were.

"What is that?" Grandma squinted forward, trying to get a better glimpse.

"ATM transactions," Tommy replied with a steely crispness in his voice.

My tongue hit the roof of my mouth with such force it hurt. My pulse quickened and I had that feeling you saw in movies where people started to feel faint as the walls closed in on them. I steadied myself against the counter. Conrad wrapped his arm around my waist protectively, but I couldn't even bear to look at him.

There was no way he'd stick around after he learned *this* about me. Not that I could blame him. He was a good guy, and I was the very opposite of that, as Tommy's bombshell-in-the-making was about to reveal to everyone.

"What sort of ATM transactions?" Grandpa leaned forward as Tommy handed him the papers. He readjusted his glasses, but the expression on his scrunched face was one of utter confusion. "You'll have to explain what I'm looking at here, Tommy. None of this makes any sense to me."

"I was hoping Jedfire might be able to fill all of us in, Walter." Tommy interlaced his fingers as everyone's eyes landed on me.

My heart was thrumming in my throat. I was speechless and coming close to being airless, too. Breathing had become an afterthought as panic set in.

I pushed off the counter, away from Conrad's reassuring clutch, and I did the thing that I'd been doing like a coward for years now —I ran.

I sprinted outta there so fast everyone's voices converged into one giant holler behind me. I raced out of that apartment and legged it through the resort, my lungs burning and my head spinning out of control.

I didn't notice the looks people were throwing in my direction. I had no clue where I was headed. I reached the beach, and it was only the feeling of fingers on my shoulder that transported me back to reality.

I wheeled my body around, and standing there—gasping like he had run a marathon, his face flushed with sweat and his hair sticking out in every direction—was Conrad.

26

CONRAD

Ever chased a giraffe?

That's what it felt like I was doing as I bolted after Jed. Running like a madman, after a possible madman, was not something I should have been doing in my condition, especially a madman who had legs that reached half way up my chest.

If I'd had energy to spare, I would've yelled out for him to stop or at least slow down. But as it was, chasing him through the resort and onto the beach took up every last reserve of energy I had.

Thank god he'd stopped of his own accord. I didn't know how much longer I could have chased him for.

"Conrad." I couldn't tell if the surprise registering in his voice was because I'd followed him on his wild goose chase or the fact that I looked like I was on the verge of collapsing. "Oh my gosh, are you okay?"

I gulped in a few breaths and managed to nod my head. "Can we...sit?" I pointed to an empty bench up ahead.

"Of course." Jed's arms looped into mine as we walked the thirty or so feet to the bench.

By the time we sat down, my panting had slowed and the

burning feeling in my chest was subsiding a little. Eager to deflect any possible questions about my current physical state, I managed to get the first question in. "Do you want to tell me about what happened back there?"

Jed slumped against the back of the bench and folded his arms across his chest. "Short answer, no." Our eyes met. "Longer answer, I'm scared to."

I smiled wryly. "You have a thing for three-worded answers."

Jed's lips rounded slightly, and the momentary light reprieve helped my own heart rate slow some more, too. I was actually starting to feel like a human again.

He stared out into the calm, early-morning water as he blew out an unsettled breath. "You're going to hate me, leave me, divorce me, and then I'll never see you again."

Okay, that was a lot to take in.

Judging by the darkness shading his irises, I figured this wasn't the right time to point out we weren't actually legally married.

Something big had obviously gone down. All I knew right now was two things. One, whatever it was, it involved ATMs. And two, whatever it was, I wouldn't leave him. So that's what I decided to tell him.

"I'm not going anywhere, Jed."

He turned to look at me. Slowly. As if it was taking him a minute to process what I'd just said. When we were square on, I saw the pain splashed across his face. It was so real and raw that it made my heart clench tighter than ever.

"I've done something bad, Conrad. Like, really bad."

I cupped his massive hand in mine. "I figured as much."

"You did?"

I nodded. "You make a sound whenever you're uncomfortable."

"You noticed?"

Another nod. "Do you want to tell me about it?"

He dropped his gaze to the sandy ground. He started speaking, but his voice was so muffled I had to lean in to hear him. "I have a tic, a nervous twitch. I've had it since I was a kid."

I thumbed his knuckles, hoping the touch would maybe lessen a bit of his burden.

"It's just this thing that happens." He waved his other hand in front of his neck. "Whenever I freak out or get anxious or overwhelmed... I can feel it coming on, but I can't do anything to stop it. My throat tightens, and it travels up to my tongue, and then I make that fucking awful clicking sound. It's so embarrassing. I hate it. I've always hated it. I feel like such an idiot."

"Hey." I lifted my hand, stroking the side of his arm. "You have nothing to feel ashamed about, Jed. I actually like it."

"Huh?"

"I mean, not the part where you feel anxious and overwhelmed, of course. But it's something that's unique, and that's kinda your thing."

His cheeks rose a little. "Yeah, I guess it is. You don't think I'm a freak?"

"I do, but not in a bad way."

We both giggled and I scooted over to get closer to him, our shoulders nudging together.

"Very funny."

"It's nice to see you smile." I leaned over and nestled my head against the front of his shoulder. I stared out into the ocean. I loved the water. It was so soothing. It was calming Jed, too.

With our bodies close, I decided to try again. One last time. If he didn't want to tell me now, I'd drop it forever. "Hey, Jed?"

"Yeah..."

"Do you want to tell me what all of that was about before? It's okay if you don't. I won't bug you about it again if you don't want to talk about it."

He whistled out a warm breath.

"I meant what I said before. Whatever it is, Jed, I'm not leaving. I won't judge you, I promise."

"How can you say that, Conrad? Don't get me wrong, I appreciate it. But you have no idea what it is."

I mulled his words over as I watched two seagulls swooping around in circles in front of us. "You're absolutely right. I have no idea what you've been up to. But I do know one thing."

I gently pushed off him and positioned myself so that I was looking him in the eyes. "I know, deep down in here, that you're a good person." Jed's eyes traveled down to the fingers I'd placed across my chest. "And even good people make mistakes. And most mistakes can be fixed. Especially by good people."

Jed shook his head, his eyes dumbstruck. "You're such an amazing guy, Conrad. I can't believe how lucky I am to have met you."

I blushed at his words. "Thanks."

"All right. I'll tell you." Jed then flipped his head around madly, left to right, up and down, like he was desperately trying to find something he'd lost.

"What are you doing?" I asked with a smile, when it became clear he wasn't going to offer up an explanation on his own.

"Uh, I'm just...trying to find you...a seatbelt," he responded, still looking around all over the place.

"A seatbelt?"

Finally, he stilled, as he tossed me an audacious smile. "Yeah, 'cause you're gonna need to strap yourself in for this one. It's one wild ride."

"Is there any other kind with you?"

His laughter tickled my ears. As he calmed, he began rubbing down the fronts of his thighs. "So, it all started one stormy night just over a year ago."

I might not have had a seatbelt, but I settled myself in for what I assumed would be a long, yet incredibly interesting tale. "I was on my way to see a"—he averted my gaze—"a friend."

"A friend, huh?" I responded, picking up on the tell. He really was the worst liar ever.

His eyes flicked up at me. "Okay, I was on my way to a hookup. I wanted to get some cash from an ATM on the way. Anyway, I ran into Mrs. McClusky. She's Grandma's best friend, part of the family, really."

I nodded as he continued.

"Anyways, something was up with the machine. It was glitchy."

"Glitchy?"

"Yeah, it wouldn't let me withdraw my cash or even give me my balance. I tried a few times, and as I was doing that, Mrs. McClusky stepped out onto the road and into the path of an oncoming semi."

I covered my mouth. "Oh my God."

"It's okay, it's okay," Jed replied reassuringly. "She was fine. Nothing happened to her. I walked her back to her car and made sure she drove off safely."

My breathing returned to normal. "Good. I'm glad to hear that."

A smile peeked out of the corners of Jed's lips. "So, I went back to the machine and it was still uncooperative. I decided to leave it. I, uh, had to get going."

"To see your fuck buddy," I pointed out.

Jed looked down and blushed so cutely it took all the self-control I had not to pepper his face with kisses.

"Well, yeah... Sorry, this is a really long story. Am I boring you with this?"

"No way, you've got me intrigued. And I have literally zero idea where this is all going."

"Good, then. I like to keep you on your toes."

"Uh, you do that every time I reach up to kiss you," I pointed out lightly.

We both chuckled as Jed returned to his story. "When I checked my accounts the next day, it showed something weird on my balance."

"Oh?"

"It appeared that a transfer of $29,999 had been made."

"Were you transferring that much money?"

Jed shifted his shoulders. "No, I wasn't. But the numbers 2 and 9 are the first two digits of my pin number."

"All right, I am now officially confused."

"It took me a while to figure out what had happened, too. But when Mrs. McClusky almost got swiped by that semi, I was entering my pin number into the machine. I'd pressed 2, and then my finger caught on the 9 button as I turned to see what all the honking was about."

"Uh-huh."

"With whatever was going on with the ATM glitch, somehow, it registered that I had transferred $29,999 from my credit card to my savings account."

"Wow, okay."

"I know, it's weird. But it gets even weirder."

"Is that even possible at this point?"

"Hey, never underestimate the Jedfire."

"Hey"—I rubbed the back of my hand against his chest— "please never refer to yourself in third person or add a *The* in front of your name."

"Noted." Jed let out a slight snicker as he went on. "I wanted to see if lightning would strike twice. So a few days later, I went back to the same ATM at the same time—one minute to midnight—and I transferred the same amount, $29,999, from my credit card to my savings account."

"And what happened?"

"It worked. I was able to do it. Now, the really crazy part was that, for some reason, my credit card balance went back to zero. It was like it had made the transfer but then wiped it from existence, like it never happened. Which meant that, basically, I had access to free money."

"Wow." Yep, I was back to wow-ing my way through a conversation with Jed.

"Over the next few weeks, I experimented with it. I tried transferring different amounts at different times, but it never wiped the transaction like it did when I did the transfer at exactly 11:59pm for exactly $29,999. That was the magic combination for some reason."

Jed exhaled loudly. "I checked with the finance department at the plant. They confirmed it. There were no records of any transactions. I checked with Grandpa and he was none the wiser. So, in some weird *act of god* way, I'd stumbled upon this glitch—this *untraceable* glitch—that gave me access to thirty grand every day. It didn't matter which ATM I used. The issue was with my bank."

"Did you tell anyone? Cooper?"

"No, how could I? Everyone already thought I was an out-of-control fuckup, and now *this*."

I decided against correcting him. He wasn't a fuckup, but he also wasn't ready to hear that, either.

I drummed my fingers against my leg. So that explained why he had snuck off to the ATM just before midnight. I *knew* he had a grift. I had one more burning question I needed answered. "What do you do with all the money?"

His face tightened and a frown planted itself firmly across his forehead. "At first, nothing. The money just collected in my bank account. It took me about a month to realize that this was actually happening. I was in shock."

"I bet."

"I mean, after a month, I had almost a million dollars."

"Wow."

"Yeah, wow." Jed chewed down on his lip. "I was racked with nerves about the whole thing. I couldn't sleep. I felt this tightness in my chest that never left me for more than a few minutes. I was carrying this huge, diabolical secret around with me and my heart felt so heavy."

I was curious. "So what did you do?"

"I knew that it was wrong and that I should stop doing it and just return the money. But I'd withdrawn almost a million dollars. There was no way I could give it back without getting into some sort of trouble for it."

I could see his point. It sounded like a tough situation to be in.

"One day, I was bored so I decided to fly to London for the afternoon—"

"As you do," I interrupted with a laugh and a look of disbelief.

"As *I* do, yeah." Jed looked a little sheepish. "So, I'm in London and walking past a homeless charity. They had a sign in the window announcing a fundraising drive they were doing. They wanted to raise the equivalent of half a million US dollars. So, I went in there and donated all the money they needed."

"Wow. Just like that?"

"Yep, just like that. I did it to unburden myself from the oppressive guilt I was slowly choking under. I thought that it would somehow counter the wrongness of the whole situation. But, Conrad, when I walked out of there..."

His voice floated in the air as I leaned in closer to him.

"...I felt *alive*. Like I had done something important. Something that mattered. I'd finally found a way to feel like I was doing something meaningful, which, I know, is beyond ironic, considering what I was doing was so bad. But, hey, welcome to my life."

The peppiness Jed tried to infuse into his last words didn't work; the melancholy was too thick. I could see that the stress had been snowballing and was now threatening to drag him under.

"At first, I told myself if I got caught, I could pay the money back. But after a few months and once it had grown into the *millions*, it dawned on me that I could end up in jail."

"Why didn't you stop?"

He swung his gaze to meet mine. "I couldn't, Conrad. I became addicted to it. I loved being able to help. Seeing someone who has a problem that I can help them solve is like nothing else. It's the most amazing feeling in the world. Well"—heat swirled in his eyes and he peered up at me through his lashes—"the second most amazing feeling in the world."

Thrill bumps rippled up and down my spine as I leaned in closer, craving his touch more than ever. My words from earlier rattled in my head. I wasn't going to leave him or judge him. Yes, he'd done something wrong—*very wrong*—but it wasn't like he'd spent the money on himself. He was kinda like a modern day Robin Hood, although Robin Hood arguably had better fashion sense. What my heart had been telling me all along was true: Jed was a good person who had made some bad choices.

"I know I have to make this right, Conrad. I hired a lawyer a few months ago and confessed everything to him. He contacted a financial forensic detective to figure out what the fuck was going on. He's the one who discovered the bank's glitch and everything I'm sharing with you now."

"Are you going to stop?" My pulse was racing in my neck. This was it. Jed's answer to this question would either give final confirmation of what I knew about him, or expose him as someone who had successfully managed to pull the wool over my eyes—and my heart.

"Yes."

I released a breath I didn't realize I'd been holding as he kept talking. "I have to and I want to. I can't keep going on like this. The nerves are eating away at me. But the thought of going back home and running a cowbell plant just kills me, Conrad. I'm trapped. My life officially ends in less than a month."

I let his words settle over me. Well, not those last ones—*those* I tried to ignore. They hit way too close to home, but it was a nerve Jed had no way of knowing he'd even struck.

His ATM story was a lot to take in all on its own. So many pieces to a very complicated puzzle. "Ahhh, so that's why you donate anonymously." I snapped my fingers together, like I'd just put the final piece on said complicated puzzle into place.

Jed's eyebrow shot up.

"Sorry, I, uh, overheard you at the wildlife center after our hike. I was coming to get you to tell you we needed to get on the bus, but you were making a donation in the back office. I shouldn't have eavesdropped. I'm sorry, Jed."

Jed cupped his hand around mine. "Conrad, I think we can both agree that's the least bad thing going on at the moment."

I cleared my throat and turned away. Actually, despite how out-of-this-world crazy Jed's story had been, he was wrong. There was something going on with me that was even worse.

The question I had to ask myself was this: was I prepared to tell him?

And in that moment, as I stared into two whisky-brown eyes that had shared so much with me—something that had taken real courage—I knew I had my answer.

27

JEDFIRE

It was the last thing I'd expected to do when I ran out of the apartment, but confessing to Conrad felt oddly cathartic. It wasn't lost on me that the only person who knew about my shenanigans was someone I'd met only four days ago. Or that he was true to his word and hadn't left, nor judged me if the softness in his face was any indication of what was going on inside.

I reached down and placed my hand around his. "Thank you."

He tipped his head, intently boring his eyes into mine. "For what?"

"For not leaving. For not judging me. Just like you said you would."

A smile curved his lips. "I stand by what I've been saying all along. I don't mean to make you uncomfortable, Jed, but you *are* a good person."

His words settled over me like a blanket made of thorns. I squirmed, feeling beyond uncomfortable. "That's your takeaway from me committing financial fraud?"

"No." His body swayed into mine. "That's my takeaway from *why* you do what you did. I know you're already rich, but you could've spent that money on you. Bought more stuff for yourself. You could have done it all without a pang of guilt. And you could have kept going for as long as you wanted to. But none of that is true. And why?"

His eyebrows were perched halfway up his forehead and he was looking at me expectantly. Oh, right, he wanted *me* to say it.

"Because...I'm a good"—I suppressed a shudder—"person."

"You are, Jed. You really are. And one day, I hope you believe it as much as I do."

One day.

He'd said one day, which made it sound like we had a future. Did we? With all of my ATM-drama swirling around us, I'd lost track of the fact that Conrad was leaving tomorrow.

"Will you be there?"

Conrad's forehead wrinkled, so I continued. "Will you be there that *one day* when I discover that I really am a decent guy?" I found myself squeezing his hand, silently praying for the answer I so badly wanted to hear from him.

It came quietly. "No."

Fuck. Clearly not the answer I'd wanted, but, let's be real, what was I expecting here? We barely knew each other. We'd concocted a fake marriage, had amazing real sex, but at the end of the day, this was probably nothing more than a holiday fling with a dash of Jedfire crazy added to it for him.

"But not because I don't want to be with you."

My ears pricked up and I locked my eyes on his face. His tight, pained face with a bunched up jaw and a steely expression running through his features.

"I'm confused. What does that mean, Conrad?"

I didn't know what I was expecting, but it certainly wasn't the tears I saw welling in his eyes as he turned to face me. My chest clenched, suddenly realizing shit was about to get a whole lot realer. I braced myself and with a curt nod, asked, "What's going on?"

"I have something to tell you, too."

"Tell me. Please. Tell me. Whatever it is, Conrad, you can tell me." I exhaled sharply through my nose before adding some familiar words, "I won't leave you, and I won't judge you."

"How can you say that? You don't even know what I'm about to say." Conrad half smiled, doing a little echoing of his own.

"Uh, because if I'm a good person, then you're, like, the fucking Dalai Lama."

Conrad snorted. "I am definitely not like him at all."

"You're right." I nodded. "You have much nicer hair."

A silence settled between us. Conrad needed a moment, so I gave him that, taking in the waves crashing and foaming in front of us. Maybe later, after we'd put all this drama behind us, we could come back and spend some time in the water. My mind wandered, daydreaming up little scenarios Conrad and I could do on our last full day together until two little words tore into my chest and ripped out my heart.

"I'm dying."

I stared at Conrad and started blinking, rapid fire. Was he kidding? Were my ears playing tricks on me? But since he wasn't laughing and in fact, continued talking, and all I heard was, "I only have six months to live," I knew that this was no joke.

I was stunned. I couldn't move. I couldn't speak. I was in total and utter shock. The only thing I felt was Conrad's fingers rubbing against the back of my hand.

Conrad kept talking, his voice steady and deliberate, but only the occasional words filtered in. Something about a rare bone marrow disorder, how it made him tired and have no energy, how it had started getting worse over the course of the last few days, and about this idea he and his dad had come up with to travel the world and complete his bucket list.

Those words, those stupid words—*bucket list*—snapped me out of my shocked stupor and I sprang to my feet. That joke I'd cracked about a bucket list only being for people who were old...or dying. The way Conrad *would* get tired quite quickly, like on our hike or even after he'd chased me out here and was so out of breath. Oh god, I shouldn't have made him run like that. I wouldn't have if I had known.

"We can fix this, Conrad." I started pacing back and forth in front of the bench. "I have money. So much money. Whatever medical care you need. Any bills. All your expenses, I'll pay for it all. We can fix this. I can make you better."

Out of the corner of my eye, I saw Conrad stand up. He stepped in front of me, his hands landing on my shoulders, his sparkling baby blues steadying me on my feet. "I don't need money, Jed. But thank you."

"Then what? What do you need? Whatever it is, I'll get it for you." My voice was loud and scratchy and full of pleading.

No, don't let me lose him. Not like I lost...

"I don't need money, Jed, just a donor match. And so far, we haven't been able to find one, and in all honesty, we probably won't."

I lowered my gaze to the ground, I couldn't summon the strength to look at him. And that's when I noticed it. First one, then another, and then a fucking torrent of them. I was crying, no, wait, sobbing. A waterfall of tears unleashing from my eyes.

Conrad pulled me into his warm body, but it didn't stop the tears from falling. I leaned down and forward, over his shoulder slightly, and bawled like a baby. Everything faded to black. All I could hear and feel were the sounds of the waves lapping at the beach, me wailing and rocking against Conrad and two reassuring hands rubbing up and down my back.

After what felt like a long few minutes, I pulled away, wiping the back of my hand against my mouth which was covered in spit and tears. "Fuck," I spluttered. "I'm sorry. This isn't about me. I didn't mean to—"

He covered my lips with his fingers. "It's okay." Our eyes met and I could see his were misty, too. "It's a shock, and it's a lot to take in."

I nodded stupidly. I should have been the one reassuring him, not the other way around.

"Let's sit back down," he suggested gently as he guided me back to the bench.

I used the few seconds we had as we sat down to wipe the remaining traces of tears from my face. Blowing out a heavy breath, I turned to Conrad. "How are you okay with this?"

"Well"—he tipped his head up slightly to meet my line of sight —"I've had a bit of practice telling you."

"Huh?"

"Well, someone who looks just like you."

My mouth fell open. "You told Cooper?"

"In my defense, I thought I was telling you. And before you get angry, I made him swear that he wouldn't tell you."

I grumbled under my breath, but conceded. "He keeps his word. I'm not surprised he didn't tell me. But wait, I don't get it. Why did you tell him—"

"If I thought I was telling you?" Conrad finished my question for me.

"Yeah. That."

Conrad's teeth bit into his lower lip. "Honestly, it was his reaction. I don't want pity, Jed. His, yours, or anyone's. I don't want anyone to feel bad for me or treat me differently."

I straightened up and tried to adjust my face. Was my expression one of pity? If that was the last thing Conrad wanted, then I would do anything to make my face anything but.

Conrad quirked an eyebrow. "What are you doing?"

"Whaddya mean?" I said, putting on what I hoped was my most un-pitying voice.

"Your face looks weird, like you just swallowed a lemon and it surprised you, but you're trying not to look like it surprised you, so now you're putting on this weird wrinkly smile."

"You got all that from this?" I pointed at my face.

"Uh-huh." Conrad was trying his best not to smile.

"I'm sorry," I said, finally unclenching all the facial muscles I'd bunched up. "I was trying not to look like I was pitying you."

I didn't know what my words would be met with, so I was relieved when a laugh bubbled out of Conrad's throat. "You're incredible, Jed."

I cocked my head and waited.

"Meant in a good way," Conrad clarified quickly, picking up on my nonverbal cue. "I've never met anyone like you."

"And I've never met anyone like you, Conrad."

Our eyes met and I had no idea if it was the right moment or the right thing to do, but my gut told me to go for it, so I did. I wrapped my fingers around the back of Conrad's neck and pulled him in for a kiss.

At first, it was just lips. Then, when they parted, tongues got involved. Moments later, fingers were being swiped through my hair. I felt an urge to graze down the side of Conrad's throat, so I went for it.

Our mouths stayed entwined, probing and exploring with each movement, every flickering, but I was so lost in the moment that words escaped my brain, replaced by sensations. My skin prickling with heat, my throat murmuring with desire, and my eyes overflowing with so much wanting I felt like I was about to start shooting lasers out of them.

We broke the kiss—I didn't even know which one of us did it—but as I looked at Conrad with his puffy lips and beautiful blue eyes, I felt a shift. A deepening of something that stubbornly stayed welded to the edge of my tongue.

I gathered Conrad as close to me as I could, as we sat facing the ocean. Maybe it was good to break eye contact for a while. I was still only one look away from bursting into tears again, and I was determined not to succumb. I'd ugly-cried enough for one day.

"When I asked you before about how you're okay with all of

this, I wasn't talking about you breaking the news to me. I meant, how are you doing, dealing with your...diagnosis?"

I flicked a quick look his way, but when my bottom lip quivered, I yanked my head back and kept my gaze fixed firmly forward. That's where it would have to stay for the foreseeable future.

"I have good days and I have bad days." Conrad's voice remained so calm, so steady. I guess he'd had more time to process this, but still, what a fucking nightmare to find yourself in.

"Sometimes, I get angry about how unfair it all seems."

"So fucking unfair," I spat out angrily, before simmering down. "Sorry." I flashed an apologetic smile, but yep, back to eyes never leaving the ocean.

"But in a way, I'm lucky. I know what I'm dealing with, and I have time to prepare. That's...something."

Nowhere near fucking enough.

I bit down on the inside of my cheek to physically stop myself from uttering those words. I was scared that once I started, I wouldn't be able to hold back. And this wasn't about me. This was —one thousand percent—all about Conrad.

I shifted, sitting up a little taller. "You said something before about finding a donor match?"

"It's not going to happen." The steeliness in his voice faltered a little, and in that crack, I heard the faintest echo of disappointment.

"Why not?"

I heard a sigh. "Because there's a one-in-one-million chance of a donor match, so you don't need to be a Fermi genius to do the math on that one and know that it's not very likely."

Shit. I tapped my fingers against the bench. "And there's nothing else, nothing that we can do to help?"

Soft fingers hooked under my chin and my head moved involuntarily until I was blinking at the two most beautiful blue eyes I'd ever laid my eyes on. "There's nothing to do, Jed, but to accept it and try to make the most of the time I do have left."

"Okay." I nodded my head glumly. "Well in that case, let's do that. Let's make the most out of every single precious second we have together."

Conrad blinked heavily, tilting his head to the side. "Together?"

I clenched my jaw so tight I was surprised I didn't shatter any teeth. "Together, Conrad."

I felt a determination coursing through my veins, stirring me back to life after way too many fucking years asleep at the wheel. "I have no idea what the future holds, but you're stuck with me...if you'll have me."

28

CONRAD

I planned on writing a letter to the good folks who owned the Oxford English Dictionary, petitioning them to change the definition of *unexpected* to *Jedfire*.

Because that was exactly what Jedfire Burns epitomized. At every turn, from the moment we met and he tried to stump me with his whole 'how many waves do you think break around the world every day?' nonchalant coolness, to his ka-razy ATM adventures, to this—his beautiful, somewhat heart-wrenching reaction to my news.

Jed cried in much the same way that he laughed—with his whole body. As his warm tears soaked my shirt, I felt his entire being rumbling with shock and pain. I thought he'd be surprised—I mean, who wouldn't be?—but such ferocious tears? Followed by his *best yet totally horrible* attempt at not showering me with pity, followed by...the most amazing promise anyone had ever made for me.

Together.

Sure, we may not have had a lot of time left in that togetherness, but what we did have was going to be special. I felt it in my heart, right next to the space that told me Jedfire Burns was a decent, good-hearted, and loving person.

"Should we head back?" I asked, breaking about the third silence we'd fallen into on the bench. Jed was practically vibrating, still trying to take it all in, I guess. And I was giving him the time he needed to process.

I had a little processing of my own to do. The last thing I'd expected when I chased him as he ran out of the apartment was what had unfolded. Between his confession and my secret, it was a lot, even by our already kinda crazy, sorta elevated standards.

At least I had managed to keep it together. You couldn't go around telling people you didn't want their pity and then start throwing off the waterworks in front of them.

"Sure." He stood up and extended his arm. My fingers slipped into his palm and that's how we wandered back to the resort, hand in hand and in silence. I kept peering up at him, trying to get a read deeper than the crestfallen expression he was carrying. His eyes were flicking around, and I knew he was probably trying to figure out some way to help me.

I knew that look because the night before I'd left on my travels, I had what was my first and only panic attack. I'd gone into the bathroom to pack my toiletries, and as I clutched my toothbrush in one hand and toothpaste in the other, it hit me like a ton of bricks. The question I was sure that everyone in this situation asks themselves at some stage.

Why me?

Not that I ever would have wished it on somebody else. In my case, the *why me* question had a slight twist to it as it angled into more of a *why now?* I'd only turned twenty-two a few months earlier. Couldn't I have had a few more years at least? Even to thirty? There was so much I would never get a chance to do and so much that I could have done but didn't.

Dad walked in and found me in the fetal position on the floor, shivering and rambling something under my breath. I'd done everything I could, scraped the farthest recesses of my mind to come up with something—*anything*—to get myself out of this.

But as Dad lifted me onto my feet and blanketed me with his strong arms, his hand brushing the back of my hair, I knew deep down that there was nothing that could be done. And time became something that I didn't want to spend on things that led nowhere. It had always been too precious to waste. It was just a shame it took something like this to make me see that.

Stepping into the resort felt surreal, and I could tell Jed had a reaction to it, too, because he stopped dead in his tracks. We were back in the heart of vacation-land. People were walking all around us, laughing and chatting away. Music filled the air and sounds of water splashing came from the pool area.

Jed's grip on my hand tightened. "What do you feel like doing?"

"A swim might be nice," I replied.

A typical vacation conversation. All it was missing was, you know, the slightest sliver of actual enthusiasm.

"Might help us clear our heads a bit."

Jed nodded blankly at my words and we pressed on. To get to the apartment, we actually had to go past the pool. The area was starting to fill up. People were coming down to lay claims on deckchairs, and I could see the DJ making his way over to the booth in the far corner.

Maybe doing something normal and vacation-y *was* just what we needed. An antidote to the vortex we'd shot off to. A group of guys approached us, so I scooted in behind Jed as we passed each other, exchanging a round of friendly *hellos* and *what's ups?* I took a step forward. However, Jed didn't, meaning my face ended up imprinting into his back.

"Sorry, Conrad." He twisted around and gazed down at me. "Are you okay?"

I stepped back, rubbing my nose and nodded. I felt more embarrassed than anything else. "How come you stopped?"

Jed craned his neck over his shoulder before swooping down to my head height. "I just saw someone I know. Someone from back home."

"Oh, that's nice... Right?"

Jed ran a hand through his hair. "Uh, not exactly. It's my third grade teacher, Mr. Edmunds."

"What's wrong with that?" I tried to see past Jed but couldn't be sure who Mr. Edmunds was.

"Well, for one, he's not gay. And for two, he's here with his wife."

"Maybe they're bi? Or swingers," I offered with a shrug.

Right at that moment, a friendly male voice cried out, "Jedfire!"

Jed's eyes ballooned, then narrowed as he slapped a smile on his face and turned around to greet...

"Mr. and Mrs. Edmunds. What are—what are you doing here?"

Jed's palm was beyond clammy in my hand, it was positively soggy. Me? Truth be told, I was grateful for the distraction from more serious matters. And I loved that literally not a second could go by with Jed where something interesting didn't happen.

"We came as soon as we heard," Mrs. Edmunds said with a wide smile, but strangely serious eyes.

As I studied them closer, I was struck by their attire. Not very vacation-like, at all. No swimsuit, boardshorts, or flip-flops. No. They looked more like they were about to head off to run their Saturday morning errands than vacationing in Florida.

Jed's eyes narrowed. "Heard what?"

"Is this him—is this Conrad?" Mr. Edmunds didn't wait for an answer as he stuck his hand out. I pulled my fingers away from Jed and shook the man's hand, flashing Jed a confused look.

Okay, what was going on here?

"Hi, nice to meet you." I tried to flash what I hoped was a polite smile.

"Oh, honey—" Mrs. Edmunds stepped in closer, her sweet rose perfume wafting in the air. "I'm a hugger. Is it okay if I hug you?"

I glanced over at Jed who looked as stunned as I felt. "Uh, sure."

The lady pulled me in, and Jesus, did she have a grip or what. She held me close, and hard, and for way longer than the allowable maximum time limit for hugging a complete stranger. I blew a strand of her golden blonde hair out of my mouth and finally, she pushed back off me.

"What's going on here, you guys?"

Mr. Edmunds looked at Jed as he answered his question. "We were on our way back from a lovely lunch with Mrs. McClusky—"

"When Cooper came on the radio." Mrs. Edmunds overrode her husband excitedly. "I said to myself I know that voice. I know *that* voice."

"What was Cooper doing on the radio?" Jed asked, both brows raised in suspicion. We were still no closer to having the slightest clue of what was happening here.

Right then, two carrot-topped guys who looked to be in their mid-twenties approached and waved at Jed. "Hey, man."

"Who are they?" I muttered to Jed.

"What are the Finney boys doing here?" Jed directed his question at Mr. Edmunds.

"Half of Cowbell Creek is here, Jed," Mr. Edmunds announced, shaking his hands in front of him like he was an announcer at a rodeo.

"We came as soon as we heard." Mrs. Edmunds clutched her chest. "You've been in our thoughts and prayers, honey." She looked at me when she said that.

"I'm sorry. I don't understand what's happening," I offered meekly.

Why was half of Cowbell Creek at an all-male resort in Florida, and why was I getting the distinct impression that it was because of me?

We finally—at long last—managed to get a straight answer out of Mr. Edmunds. "Cooper called the radio station and told them about a wonderful young man called Conrad who needed to find a donor for a rare condition that he had."

"What!?" Jed and I barked at the same time.

"As soon as we heard, we jumped on the first flight we could and...here we are."

"We just got tested," Mrs. Edmunds waved her arm in the air, proudly displaying the small Band-Aid on her forearm.

Jed arched an eyebrow. "Where did you get tested?"

"At the other end of the resort," Mr. Edmunds said with a smile. "There's a staff bungalow there. The owner—lovely man, I think his name is Leo—he's set up a temporary medical center there. It was crowded, too. Seems like everyone's doing their part."

His eyes fell to me, while mine peered up to Jed.

"I'm—speechless."

"Well, I'll be," Mrs. Edmunds said with an affable smile curving her lips. "Jedfire Burns speechless. Now, come on, Henry. I hear this is a clothing-optional resort, and I'd like to see me some hot muscley men. Ooh, and we can get some margaritas, too."

With nothing more than a wave and a slightly terrified expression on Mr. Edmunds face, they were off. I turned to face Jed.

He raised his hands in the air. "I had no idea about any of this, I swear."

I chuckled. "I believe you. You look just as shocked as I feel."

"I guess you only told Cooper not to tell me, right? Never said anything about broadcasting it to the world?"

"Yeah, my bad," I replied sarcastically, and then we both giggled. "I might go and check out this medical center setup Leo had put together."

Jed nodded. "Cool. Well, I might go back to the apartment. I have a certain younger brother I need to have a few words with."

"Okay. Let's meet back here in, what, say an hour?" I suggested.

I nodded and was just about to leave when I felt a pair of

oversized hands cradle the small of my back. Seconds later, the softest set of lips landed on mine.

In all of the madness that was swirling around us, *this* felt so right.

Me and Jed.

Together.

29

JEDFIRE

"Cooper!"

I raced into the apartment, panting and out of breath, and called out again, "Coop—"

"I'm right here, man."

Cooper hopped up off the couch and strolled over to me. On my mad dash over here after Conrad and I had said—and kissed—goodbye, I couldn't make up my mind whether I wanted to strangle the guy or drop to my knees and kiss his stinking feet.

I still wasn't sure as I eyed him up and down. I guess he hadn't had the morning I just did. Before I realized I was doing it, I looped my arms around his neck and drew him in. "Thank you," I whispered into his ear.

We pulled apart. "He only said I couldn't tell *you*."

I messed up his hair and laughed. "I'm not angry. And neither is he, by the way."

"Where is Conrad?" Grandma's voice rang out as I spun around to see them observing us from the kitchen.

"He went to the medical center that Leo's set up."

"We've all been tested," Cooper chimed in brightly. I looked around at three raised, Band-Aid-covered forearms aimed at me.

I tried to smile and blink at the sight but couldn't. I always thought breaking the seal referred to taking your first piss when you were drinking. Now I was seeing it could just as easily be applied to crying, as more goddamn tears made their way down my cheeks.

Grandma scooped me into her arms. "Let's go upstairs and get you washed up, honey. Your face looks worse than mine before I got all the Botox. Okay?"

I nodded and let Grandma lead me up the stairs. After I splashed some water on my face, I patted my face dry and stared at my reflection in the mirror. God, I was really starting to lose my shit and looked the part, too. My skin was all blotchy, my eyes were puffy, and my hair...well, it was just as messy and all over the place as always. Least that didn't change.

When I composed myself and stepped out of the en suite bathroom, Grandma was lying on my bed, staring at the ceiling. I joined her, my hand finding hers. She'd turned the fan on, so we were both staring up at the spinning blades.

"I'm not really married," I confessed. "I mean, I am. I did get married in Vegas, just not to Conrad. I don't know to who, actually. Conrad just stepped in because he heard me and Grandpa arguing about it and he wanted to do something."

Grandma's smooth fingers rubbed against the back of my hand. "I know, honey."

"You do?"

She gave a slight nod, her perfectly botoxed face giving nothing away. "Tommy."

"Ah, of course," I mumbled.

I'd run out of the apartment like an idiot, so of course he would have filled them in on everything. I wasn't mad at the guy. He was just doing what he was being paid for.

"What about Grandpa?" I asked nervously.

"Jed, your grandfather is only hard on you because he loves

you. So very much. He just wants the best for you, and more than that, he wants *you* to want the best for you."

Something about the beautiful, fragile honesty of those words struck a chord with me and I choked up again. Seconds later, the tears returned. *Damn this stupid seal.*

"Oh, Grandma. There's so much going on. I've been doing something really bad. And Conrad's sick, and he's the first person that's made me feel something since..."

I sniffed, the memory of that day jolting through me. When I turned to Grandma, I could see tears rolling down her cheeks, too.

"What happened wasn't fair, Jed." She squeezed my hand as tears continued leaving both of us.

My mind went back to that day, eight days after my nineteenth birthday.

Mom and Dad were enjoying the County Fair. They always went, us boys avoided it like the plague. It was a typical Saturday with a crisp fall wind and a perfect sky and things were in full swing.

Until a deranged fucker decided to unleash a spray of bullets indiscriminately into the crowd. Despite almost everyone in town being there, somehow, he'd managed to kill *only* six people.

Tragically, a third of those fatally wounded were my parents, Mary-Anne and Peter Burns. They were in the prime of their lives, not even fifty, and it was all gone. Their lives over in seconds. So needless and random.

The assailant pulled the trigger on himself before the cops could arrest him. The investigation didn't turn anything up. No motive. No record. No out of the ordinary behavior. Just a guy who came to town the day before, picked up a semi-automatic rifle, and decided to add to America's gun fatality tally.

A monument was erected at the edge of Bayswater Road where the fair took place. But I'd never been. Too painful. Just being back in Cowbell Creek was hard enough. And until today, I hadn't shed a single tear since my parents' funeral.

And now, I was sobbing in bed with my grandma. I leaned over and asked her, "Will it ever get better?"

Mom was her and Grandpa's only child, so they'd both taken it hard, too. Grandpa doubled down, stepping into Dad-mode with us —even though Cooper and I were nineteen and Mitchell was seventeen—and CEO-mode at the plant, coming out of retirement to take the helm of the company he'd inherited from his father.

Grandma, much like me, went a little crazy...and a whole lot overboard with the plastic surgery, fancy trips overseas with girlfriends, wild shopping sprees, and let's not forget—as if that were even possible—the topless riding of cowboys.

"I don't know if *better* is the right word, honey." I could feel her fingers stroking up and down my arm as we continued staring at the ceiling fan spinning around and around. "But life does go on, and you can honor their memory by living the life you have to the fullest."

"That's what I've been trying to do. It's just—"

"No." Grandma turned to me, her eyes darker than I'd ever seen them. "You're not living your life, Jed. You're avoiding it."

The sharpness in her voice stung. So did the truth of what she was saying. So, of course, I scoffed and shot back with all of the maturity of an eight-year-old, "I'm only doing what you're doing, Grandma. Acting all crazy and going overboard with everything."

Grandma lifted herself up onto her elbows and then further up until she was fully upright. "That's where you're wrong, honey. I know it may look like we're doing the same thing on the surface, but we're not."

I wiggled myself upright, too. "We're not?"

She shook her head and smiled warmly as our hands met between us. "I spent thirty-five years working in that plant. Every single day. I raised a child. I supported my husband. I was the best, most doting grandmother I could possibly be." The smile died on her lips. "And while I don't regret any of it—not even for a second—I never got to do what *I* wanted to do. I fulfilled everyone else's obligations and expectations and never my own."

"So, that's what you're doing now?" I said as it dawned on me. "Living your life your way?"

"That's right, honey." She took a deep breath. "I only wish it didn't take a tragedy to make me do it. If I could go back, I'd only change two things in my life."

I had a feeling I knew what one of those things would be.

"I'd erase that horrible day and prevent it from ever happening..." Her voice trailed off.

"And the other thing, Grandma?" I gently nudged.

"The other thing, Jed"—she looked me right in the eyes as she spoke and lifted her chin—"is that I would have tried to find a way to have balance."

A sigh escaped her lips. "I've gone from one extreme to the other, and truthfully, I'm not happy with either. I wish I had found a way to do what was expected of me, while also taking the time I needed for the things I wanted to do."

She cupped my hand in hers. "I know how you feel about taking over the plant. But it doesn't have to be the horrible thing you're making it out to be in your mind. You can still have your own life, do the things you want to do, while fulfilling your obligations to your family."

I crashed back down on the bed. So many things were racing through my mind. My parents. Conrad. What I'd been doing with the ATMs. Taking over the plant. Getting married in Vegas. How I'd been living my life for the past few years. How I'd been avoiding spending time in Cowbell Creek.

Grandma was right, as always. I had tried to convince myself that I was living life to the fullest, but in reality, I'd become a tired cliché. I wasn't actually living—I was doing everything I possibly could to avoid anything real. A real emotion. A real connection. Because after my parents died, I equated *real* with *tragedy*. With the fucked up unfairness of the world.

But as the tears began to dry on my cheeks, I heard Grandma make the same cooing noise she made when she put Cooper and me to sleep. And suddenly, a little space opened up in my heart, and for the first time since it had happened, I felt like a tiny weight had been lifted from me.

30

CONRAD

I made my way past the *Staff Headquarters* sign at the far end of the pool. It led up a narrow cobblestone path, surrounded by lush green foliage and a bright assortment of sweet smelling flowers.

At the end of the path, the plants cleared and an old-style wooden bungalow emerged, perched right on the edge of the cliff, perfectly positioned overlooking the Gulf of Mexico. The sunlight reflected off the ripples on the water, making the view feel almost...heavenly.

As I stepped into the bungalow, the serenity of outside was replaced by a mass of people scurrying about. The kitchen area—which kinda looked like the set of an '80s sitcom with its gaudy neons alongside nauseating pastels—had been cordoned off by a railing and some drapes flung off them into four makeshift cubicles.

Elsewhere, a chunky TV set sat in the corner gathering dust, garish tiles lined the floor, and the walls were adorned with *tropical palm wallpaper*. Yes, three words that should have officially been banished forever from the English language. It was like stepping into a different era—one that good taste in interior design had overlooked.

A man wearing an aqua blue polo with the resort logo above the front pocket and a pair of black slacks approached. With a friendly smile he asked, "Can I help you?"

"Oh, hi." I slammed my hands into my pockets, suddenly feeling unsure of myself. "I'm—I'm Conrad."

The man's eyes lit up in recognition. "Oh my goodness," he gushed as he shook my hand. "It's so wonderful to meet you. I'm Miguel. Head of Housekeeping. Leo's told us all about you and your...story." His big brown eyes dipped as he said that last word.

I looked around. "Is Leo here?"

Miguel shook his head. "No. He's out trying to placate a bitchy old queen who seems to find fault with everything in his room. Last I heard, the thread count on his sheets was so low it made his skin itch."

"Oh dear," I replied, not sure what else to say.

"Just so you know"—Miguel lowered his voice as he moved closer to me—"every person who works here is going to get tested today. And Joel from marketing is working on flyers that we're going to put in every room, encouraging all guests to do the same."

I stepped back, hit by the force of Miguel's words. "Really?" I clutched at my chest. "Oh, wow. I don't know what to say."

Miguel tossed me a smile. "This isn't just any resort, Conrad. Leo wanted this place to be something special, where everyone belongs. We're like family here, so when one of us gets sick, we all band together. I'm lined up to go in next."

"But you don't even know me. No one here does. I can't believe you'd do all of this for...me." I was holding back tears, overcome with emotion. I'd never experienced kindness on this scale before.

Leo was truly an amazing man. Not only did he understand my aversion to pity, he then went ahead and did this for me, with Cooper's prompting, no doubt. I owed them both the biggest *thank yous* in the world.

"People are generally good and decent. They like helping

RUNAWAY: AN ESCAPE NOVEL

others when they can." Miguel pursed his lips. "My reasons are slightly less altruistic."

"Oh?"

He waved his hand dismissively. "It's a long story. Let's just say I've done some bad things in my past. This could be my chance to do something good for someone's future."

And with that, his name got called out by one of the attendants dressed in blue scrubs.

"I gotta go," he said before leaving. "I really hope we can find you a donor match, Conrad."

"Thanks." I swallowed hard. "I hope so, too."

I figured I'd only be in the way if I stayed, and the last thing I wanted to do was to get under the medical team's feet, so I turned on my heel to leave.

My head was spinning with so many emotions: Disbelief. Amazement. Gratitude. My faith in humanity had never been higher.

I knew I shouldn't be getting my hopes up, but a small part of me couldn't help it. Maybe, just maybe, a staff member, or a guest, or even one of the folks from Cowbell Creek could be a perfect match.

And as I reached for the handle, the door swung open and standing there in front of me was none other than Jedfire Burns.

31

JEDFIRE

"What are you doing here?"

"I could ask you the same question," I whipped back with a cheeky grin as my heart ticked up a notch, the way it did whenever Conrad was around. "Last I heard, you can't be a donor match for yourself."

"Ha, very funny."

"Yes, humor is one of my many fine attributes." I adjusted the collar on my vintage brown-and-red-striped polo as I casually strolled through the door, pecked a kiss onto his cheek, and looked around the pop-up medical center. "Sign me up!" I balled my fingers into a fist and raised my arm into the air.

Conrad hesitated for a moment before bursting out into the sweetest sounding laughter. The sound of it rippled delightfully through my chest. Ah, mission accomplished.

Conrad had mentioned a few times that he thought I was unique, but the truth was he was the one who was truly one of a kind. No one had ever been able to glide through my walls—undetected, I might add—and make me lose my balance in the best way possible. I didn't know if it was his smile, the way he served it back to me, how he saw past my put-on bravado to the real me underneath, or just how fucking sexy he was that whenever I was around him I just wanted to smother him with kisses...and snuggles.

In all honesty, I knew the answer: it was all of the above.

Which was why I needed to step up my game for him. This might have made me sound like the biggest loser in the world (and I was okay with that), but I needed to cry like a baby with my grandma. Like, *really* needed it. More than I could have known until I finally had exhausted myself and had no tears left to cry.

All this time, I thought I was being super cool and living this awesome lifestyle that most people couldn't even conjure up in their wildest dreams, when in reality, I was bouncing around a place called Rock Bottom. (Not to be confused with Little Rock, Arkansas... Rock Bottom had way better pizzas and more scandals that would even make a former president blush.)

But that was then and this was now. And right now, my only focus was on the most beautiful guy I had ever seen, whose crystal blue eyes were staring at me...expectantly...as if he'd just been talking and I totally vagued out and had missed it all.

What I was guessing was his unanswered question lingered in the air between us.

"You haven't been listening to a word I've been saying, have you?" He placed a hand on his hips, but it was more of a pose than a menacing gesture.

"Missed it all," I said, grabbing him by the hooks of his shorts and tugging him into me.

"Hey, don't think you can get away with it with your cute smile and eyebrows waggling at me like that."

"Hey, my eyebrows move on their own accord. It's got nothing to do with me. *And*...did you just say I have a cute smile?"

I didn't give him a chance to respond, my lips finding his and melding together. I kissed into the sigh that escaped his throat and brought him in even closer to me. I needed to feel the warmth of his body, just like I needed to feel it at night, when he locked me up and we slept in a snuggle-like dream state.

"I was thinking about something while you were talking," I admitted when we pulled slightly apart. Our noses were almost touching and I could have stared into that face forever. Damn...that stupid word.

In the cruelest of twists, fate hadn't given us forever. But whatever time it did give us, I was determined to squeeze every single last drop of juicy goodness out of it. And that started with me stepping up and *manning up* for Conrad. This was some seriously heavy-duty shit he was going through—and there was no way in hell I'd let him go through it alone.

As Conrad peeked at me through his sun-kissed lashes, suddenly, the words were a little hard to find. Thinking it was one thing. Saying it was another. Oh, well, fuck it. Here goes nothing.

"I meant what I said earlier, Conrad. We *are* in this together. If you want me, I will do everything I can in my power to step up and be whatever you need me to be. I know it's too early to say this and not exactly the ideal environment"—we both looked around the weird-looking bungalow, which looked like someone had smashed up the sets of *M.A.S.H.* and *The Golden Girls,* seen what he'd done, and then jumped off the cliff into the Gulf of Mexico—"but...I'm falling for you, Conrad."

Conrad's lips parted, but before anything could come out, we were interrupted by a male voice from behind us. "Sir? Are you here to see if you're a match?"

We both stayed frozen, staring at each other, until I finally turned around and nodded. "Uh, yeah."

"Great, we can see you now."

Conrad lifted up on his toes to give me a peck on the cheek.

"I should go," I said reluctantly, wishing Conrad had gotten a chance to respond.

He inclined his head and nodded. "Listen, I want to go and find Leo to thank him for doing all of this. Meet you on the bench by the beach in, say, thirty?"

"I'll be there with clothes on."

"No need for clothes," Conrad shot back, pulling me in for one more kiss and making me giggle like a schoolkid. "See you in a bit."

"I should probably let you know I have a super low tolerance for pain. Like, really super fucking low." I covered my mouth. "Sorry, I shouldn't have sworn in front of a doctor. Wait, you are a doctor, right?"

Whoever he was, he clearly wasn't thrilled with my rambling.

"I'm a nurse. My name is Alex," he replied, looking up only briefly before returning to prep the tray positioned beside the high chair I was sitting on.

"Hey, Alex. I'm Jedfire..." I should have clamped my mouth shut there and then, but did I? Spoiler: No fucking way. "...and I'm a painaholic."

Silence. That eerie, uncomfortable silence when two strangers find themselves confined in a small space and one of them had just let out the verbal equivalent of a post-curry fart.

"Seriously, though"—I reached out and grabbed his arm, which, judging by how his eyes darkened, I quickly pulled back— "I can't handle any pain. Like, a papercut is my version of childbirth. No joke. And I have no shame, either. I *will* cry. And I will make sure everyone around me knows the sheer agony I am—"

"All done," Alex announced, smiling for the first time since I'd stepped into the makeshift cubicle.

"Oh. That was it?"

"Sure was," he said, carefully placing my blood into a clear plastic Ziplock.

"So, what happens next? When will you find out if I'm a match?"

"We have preliminary results back within half an hour usually."

"Oh, wow. That's fast."

Holy shit, I'd know within thirty minutes whether I could help save Conrad's life.

"It's mainly a process of elimination at this early stage," Alex continued. "We can pretty much rule out ninety-nine percent of results immediately. Due to the large volume of tests we're doing, if you don't hear from us within an hour, it means you didn't pass the prelim stage."

My heart sank. I thought back to Mr. and Mrs. Edmunds and my family, too, all proudly raising their arms and showing off the sign that they'd been tested. None of them had heard back from the medical team, which meant that none of them were a match.

Determined to fight away the heavy feeling that had arrived in my gut like an unwelcome visitor, I asked, "And what about the remaining one percent?"

"We call back and run more tests. I should point out that even at that stage, the match isn't guaranteed. That's why we need to do more testing, and the odds of a match are still...very low."

"Oh." I lowered my gaze to the nightmarish fuchsia and lavender tiles.

"We're all done." Alex's gentle reminder got me to my feet.

Before I pulled open the curtain, I turned around to face Alex. "Do you think it would be a sign?"

He scrunched his nose. "A sign?"

"Yeah. Like if I'm a match, do you think that's a sign that Conrad and I are destined to be together?"

Alex, unsurprisingly, looked a little shocked. Straightening up his shoulders, he flashed me a warm smile. "I think that would be very romantic, but Jedfire, please don't get your hopes up. There is a very, very slim chance that you're a match."

I smiled and left. Hey, a teeny tiny bit of hope was better than no hope at all, right? And Alex was right—it would be romantic.

Hmm...speaking of romance. I fished out my cell phone and called just the guy for the job...

32

CONRAD

I walked up to the front desk at the resort lobby to find a receptionist on the phone and Leo standing a few feet away, pinching the bridge of his nose. I stepped over toward him and tipped my head. "Bitchy queens getting you down?"

Leo's mouth gaped as he came over to me, leaned in, and spoke in a hushed tone, "Actually, yes. How did you know?"

I shrugged. "Telepathy is one of the most common side effects of the condition I have."

His mouth dropped even more. "Really?"

"No, I'm kidding. Geez..."

After Leo recovered, he joined my laughter.

"Not funny, mister." He playfully waved a finger at me.

"Have you got a moment to talk, Leo?"

"Sure." He looked toward a door behind the reception desk and scratched the back of his neck. "My office is a little untidy. How about we grab those seats over there?"

I nodded and followed him over to a table with two chairs in the corner of the lobby. It was a bit away from everything so it gave us a chance to talk privately.

"What can I do for you, Conrad?" he asked as we sat down.

"See, that's the thing, Leo. You've done so much for me"—I fought back the tears I could feel forming behind my eyes—"first with the giveaway to let me stay at a place like this. Then helping me put together the picnic basket—"

"I trust you boys had a good evening that night?"

I must have lit up like a Christmas tree because Leo let out a hearty chuckle. "That good, hey?"

"Yeah. It was amazing." I smiled at the memory of that evening. "So, you've done all of these wonderful things for me, and now...the medical center." I clapped my hands in front of me. "Leo, *thank you* doesn't even begin to cover it. I can't tell you how grateful I am to you."

I glanced over at Leo and he seemed genuinely moved by my words. He cleared his throat subtly. "It's my pleasure, Conrad."

Then his eyes met mine. "Just be sure you leave me a good review on TripAdvisor, okay?"

I let out a giggle. "I will. I promise."

"I really hope we find you a match, Conrad."

There was that word again—hope. "I do, too, Leo. I'm trying not to get too excited about it, though. The odds are still against me."

His lips pursed into a thin line. "Which reminds me," he said, getting to his feet. "There's something I have to do that I really don't want to do."

And with that cryptic comment, Leo gave me a curt wave and took off, and I headed back to the bench by the beach.

33

JEDFIRE

"Hey, are you okay?"

Conrad's skin was pale and his eyes looked diluted. He waved his hand between us. "I'm fine."

I wasn't buying it. I pulled him in closer to me, scanning his face, but not saying a word. Finally, he crumpled under the weight of my stare.

"Okay, fine." He pushed back from me and sat down on the bench. I joined him a moment later, never peeling my eyes off him for a second. "I threw up before I got here."

I threaded my fingers through his. "What happened?"

"I went to see Leo in the lobby. We'd finished up and as I was walking down here, I felt nauseous. It came on suddenly and without any warning. I'd been feeling fine all day. Luckily, I was near some bushes and no people, thank god, so I was sick in privacy, at least."

"How do you feel now? Do you need anything?" Sitting here, he seemed to be getting some color back to his face—and his eyes.

He turned to face me, his eyes softening around the edges. "I'm starting to feel better now. But there is one thing I need."

"What? What is it? Anything." I was literally on the edge of my seat.

"You."

I shook my head and blew out a shaky breath. "You can have me whenever you want me. Whether you're sick or not."

"I know." I felt his fingers grazing my knuckles. "But I am feeling better, so let's just put it behind us, okay?"

I eyed him carefully, doing my best to remember exactly what he looked like in this moment, so that I'd notice any change in his demeanor. I got the feeling that I couldn't rely on real-time medical updates from Conrad, so I needed to observe the guy like a hawk.

Not waiting for my response, Conrad sat up straighter, turned to me and blurted out, "I'm falling for you, too."

"Excuse me?"

He looked lost in his head as he shook it from left to right. "Sorry. Context. Before, in the medical center, you told me that..." He blushed as his words left him.

"I was falling for you?" I filled in the blank.

"Yeah, that." We smiled at each other. "And we got interrupted before I could say it back."

"I didn't say it so that you'd say it, too." But oh god, oh god, oh god, now that he was saying it, it felt so damn good.

"I know that." His grip on my hand firmed. "But I mean it... Jed, I'm falling in love with you."

He got teary, which made me teary, and the last thing I wanted was to spend any more of this day crying.

"I fought against it at first," he continued. "I didn't think it would be fair to get involved with someone with all of the stuff I have going on."

"Oh, Conrad—"

"Wait. Let me finish. Please."

I settled against the back of the bench, my eyes not leaving Conrad for a second. It was hard to miss his Adam's apple thrashing around in his throat. He looked out into the ocean, as if to try and steady himself.

"A part of me fell in love the first night I met you, Jed. And then, it's like every time I'm around you, more and more parts of me fall more and more in love with you."

I clenched my jaw so fucking tight, praying with everything I had in me I could keep it together. I squeezed his fingers. "I feel the same way."

A sudden gust of wind ruffled his hair and with the way the sun lit up his face, I knew then that I'd never see anyone more beautiful in my life. He turned to me with a small smile on his lips. "I wish I could kiss you right now."

I flung my eyes open. "Wish granted."

Conrad looked sheepish. "I just threw up and still feel kinda gross in the whole mouthal region."

I nodded sympathetically. "I get it."

Did I like it? No. Did I want to dash back up to the apartment and bring him a toothbrush, toothpaste, and half a pound of gum? Hell yeah.

But I also didn't want to get up and leave this moment. The longer we sat here together looking out at the beach, talking like this, holding hands—connecting—the more I became aware of how special it was. I never wanted it to end.

"All right, in the spirit of putting that behind us, have you got any ideas of what you'd like to do this evening?" I glanced down at the sun, lowering in the sky. "It is your last night here, after all."

"I still can't believe I'm leaving tomorrow." Conrad muttered the words so quietly I could barely hear them. "What—what do you want to do?"

The softness in his voice melted me. Luckily, I had come prepared. "I'm so glad you asked. I've organized what I hope will be a very memorable night."

Conrad rubbed his hands together excitedly and practically squealed, "Oooh, do tell!"

"Well, I won't reveal everything. But I got my man Tommy onto it, and let's just say there'll be fireworks, helicopter rides and"—I twisted to face Conrad and bit down on my lower lip—"were you a Backstreet Boys or NSYNC fan?"

"NSYNC, obviously," he replied without missing a beat as if he were stating the most obvious thing in the world.

"Phew." I pretended to wipe away sweat from my forehead.

Conrad's eyes narrowed at me. "Why?"

"Look, I'm not going to say that I'm trying to organize a mini-reunion for us over dinner at one of Key West's finest restaurants, but I'm also not saying I'm not doing that."

His lips parted so sweetly it made me want to reach out and kiss him, until I remembered why that wasn't such a crash hot idea.

"Wait. Even Justin?"

"Hey, I'm not a miracle worker. But that is why we pay Tommy the big bucks."

"I just want this to be the bestest of bestest nights ever, Conrad. I'm even trying to fly venison in from, I don't know, wherever the fuck venison comes from."

The sound of his honeyed giggles erupted between us. "I have to tell you something, Jed. I don't even know what venison is."

I nudged my shoulder into his. "Guess what? Neither do I!"

We both burst out laughing and there were literally no words for what seeing Conrad happy did to my insides. I felt so good and light, like I was floating on air at the sight of his beaming face.

I interlaced my fingers behind my head and closed my eyes for a minute. "Not a bad plan, now, is it?" Yeah, I was a little cocky, but give me some credit here. This was going to be the most epic, most unforgettable night ever.

I heard a weird, strangle-like sound gurgle from Conrad's direction.

"Conrad?" I angled my head over just in time to see him heaving over the side of the bench. The poor guy was throwing up again. "It's okay, it's okay," I repeated reassuringly while gently stroking his back up and down.

"I'm so sorry. I'm ruining everything," Conrad gulped out in between fits of doing—well, you know what.

"Hey, don't worry about that. Just...do what you have to do."

After a few very long minutes, Conrad sat upright again, wiping his mouth with the back of his hand. "I am beyond mortified and embarrassed."

"Oh, please. Don't be." I teamed up with my eyebrows and did that cute waggly thing I knew he liked so much. "I've thrown up in planes, on a bus in Nepal. One time, I was so wasted I threw up right in the middle of that famous Shibuya Crossing intersection in Tokyo. It's on YouTube if you search for 'stupid American giant disgracing himself publicly.'"

That managed to draw a slight chuckle out of Conrad. But the paleness had returned to his face, so I knew that despite all my best laid plans, we weren't doing any of them tonight. I had to pivot, which was fine.

Good thing I had a pretty wicked *Plan B* up my sleeve.

34

CONRAD

"I am so, *so* sorry."

Yes, that was probably the eighty-seventh thousandth time I'd apologized during the walk from the beach back to the apartment, but I couldn't help it.

I felt bad. And not just nausea-sick bad, but bad that I'd hurled my guts up in front of the guy, bad that he had to hold my arm as we walked back through the resort like I was some sort of invalid, and bad that I'd ruined our last night here together. Especially after hearing about how much trouble Jed had gotten Tommy to go through for me.

"Forget about it." That had been Jed's response every time I'd said sorry.

We reached the top of the stairs in the apartment, and even though we'd taken them at a snail's pace, I was puffed and out of breath. Thankfully, no one from his family appeared to be in, so at least I didn't have any more witnesses to this embarrassing display.

"We're almost there," Jed said, encouraging me as he guided me toward his bedroom door at the end of the hallway.

Once inside, he helped me lie down on the bed, fretting over me like I was made of porcelain china. It should have bugged me, but it didn't. I liked seeing the way he stuck his tongue out in concentration as he focused on making sure I was just right. It felt...nice.

"What about all of your plans for tonight?" I asked as he fluffed the pillow before gently sliding it under my head. I was propped up against the headboard, in a half-lying, half-seated position, which, despite looking uncomfortable, actually felt good.

"Forget about it," he repeated without the slightest hint of irritation in his voice. He took hold of my shoulders and our eyes met. "Nothing in the world is better than just hanging out. You and me. Okay?"

I shook my head. I believed him. I really did. But... "And Justin?"

Jed flung his head back and laughed. "I'm afraid there's bad news on the Timberlake front."

I shook my head, smiling. "You sound like you're a weatherman."

"Tommy said Justin was a no-go. Actually, all the NSYNC-ers declined. But apparently we can have one of the secondary Backstreet Boys do a Cameo for us?"

"I have no idea what any of that means," I replied.

"Good. Neither do I. Now, are you comfortable?" Jed eyed the setup of pillows, sheets, and blankets he had carefully constructed around me. "Would you like anything to drink? Water? Juice?"

"Actually, some apple juice would be nice. My throat's a little dry."

"I'm not surprised," Jed said over his shoulder as he headed to the door. "You threw up more than I do whenever Cooper makes me watch an episode of *Botched*."

"What's *Botched*?" I asked, sitting up a little taller against the headboard.

Jed covered his mouth. "Can't even talk about it without feeling it come on. I'll be right back with your juice."

35

JEDFIRE

As soon as I closed the door, I pressed my back against the wall and released a breath I'd been holding for close to longer than humanly possible.

I was doing okay. Conrad was safe. And comfortable. And looking way too many kinds of cute propped up in my bed.

I could do this. I could be strong for him. He needed me, and I needed to step up for him.

Starting with some juice. I mean, how hard could that be...?

Fifteen fucking minutes later, I pushed through the bedroom door and trudged over to Conrad, sitting right where I'd left him.

"Geez Louise, Jed. Are you okay? What happened?"

Yeah, exactly. What happened? Trust me to screw up something as simple as getting the guy a drink. I handed Conrad the cup and took a moment to wipe the sweat off my forehead, which didn't really work considering the back of my hand was equally sweaty.

"Sorry," I puffed as I tried to sit down as elegantly as I could on the bed and not fling myself onto it like I would have preferred.

Conrad took a sip as I commenced Operation: Talk-slash-Ramble. "There was no juice downstairs. So I ordered room service. They apologized and said that they were short-staffed, so there'd be a half hour wait on it."

"Yikes."

"Exactly. So I ran down to the poolside bar. They were out of it. Turns out, every other café and restaurant on site was also out of it."

"What did you do?" Conrad's eyes peered up at me over the rim of the cup. He was taking his time, drinking it slowly.

"I ran down the block to some Italian joint. Turns out, they don't do takeout. I mean, who doesn't do takeout in this day and age?"

"Agreed," Conrad carefully placed the cup on the nightstand. "That is weird. Almost as weird as using the phrase *day and age*."

"Hey."

He shot me a lively smile which instantly made me feel better knowing that he was coming back to himself.

"Anyway, I finally found a place that had orange juice, ran back to the resort, crashed into an idiot who was too busy looking at his cell phone instead of where he was going, managed to avoid punching said idiot in the face after exchanging a few unpleasantries with him, ran back to the place that had the juice, got you another one, and now, here I am."

I looked up and my breath caught in my throat. I didn't know what I was expecting, but it sure wasn't the single tear that was rolling down Conrad's cheek. He reached his arm toward me and I instinctively scooted down the bed to be closer to him.

"I can't believe you did all that for me."

"Yeah, well," I tossed him a cheeky smile. "I am pretty unbelievable."

"That you are, Jed. Even if you did get me the wrong juice," he threw in just for good measure.

I bolted upright. "Shit. Seriously?"

He nodded, but reached for it again and brought it to his lips. "It's fine, though. I like OJ, too."

I got up. "I can go back and get you—"

"No. Stay." That was the strictest I'd ever heard Conrad sounding and man, was it all sorts of sexy. "Besides, I don't want you bowling over any more innocent guests."

"But *he* was the one not looking—"

"Kiss me." The last syllable hadn't even left his lips and I was already in mid-air, lunging myself at the guy. "The only good thing about you taking forever to come back is that I brushed my teeth. I'm all minty fresh for you."

And with that, our lips connected and I savored the delicious, minty-orangey taste of Conrad's mouth.

WEDNESDAY

36

CONRAD

Despite feeling waves of nausea and tiredness sweep over me at random times throughout the evening, I was having the best night of my life with Jed. And yes, while my inner teen was slightly disappointed at not getting the chance to meet JT, this was a million times better.

Somehow, a bed, a half-drunk glass of OJ, and the windows open to capture the beautiful sea breeze was all Jed and I needed. We'd whiled away the hours happily chatting and laughing away.

Admittedly, talking wasn't my favorite thing to do on a bed, especially a bed that was draped with Jed's gorgeous six-foot-six frame inches away from me, but as much as I hated throwing up in front of him, the thought of throwing up with him *inside* of me was even less appealing.

"I'm sorry we didn't get to have sex on our last night here," I said wistfully, playing with the hairs on his forearm.

Two dark eyes met mine. "You should be." The words rumbled out of his mouth. "Not having sex with you is a criminal offense in my book."

Then, his face softened and I didn't have to wait too long for the eruption of laughter to follow. I'd seen a lot of the world lately—the Eiffel Tower, the London Bridge, fields of tulips in Holland, beautiful castles in Eastern Europe—but there wasn't a sight more breathtaking to me than that of Jedfire Burns in full-on laughing mode.

"Hey, look at that." Jed followed my stare to the red digits flashing at us from the nightstand. "It's after one. Nice to not have you run out on me before midnight," I teased.

"You'll have to kick me outta here because I ain't leaving you. Not even for a second."

He wiggled his way up my body, peppering my jawline with a tsunami of light kisses.

"Jed, what are you going to do about your whole...ATM situation?"

Jed flipped himself over, rolling off to sit beside me, our feet touching. Out of the corner of my eye, I could see the square set of his jaw hardening. "Tommy's filled Grandpa in on all the details of what I've been doing, so I'm assuming I'm grounded for life, and my punishment is taking over the plant for the next twenty-five years."

"Hey, you're too old to be grounded," I pointed out affectionately.

"Hey, I still get an allowance. Well, trust fund, technically."

I bit down on my lip. It struck me that there were still so many details—big and important ones—that we didn't know about each other. I worried for a second about that, but then my heart exploded as Jed picked my hand up, raised it to his mouth, and kissed it so softly.

Speaking of details... "I Google mapped how far it is from San Clemente to Cowbell Creek."

Jed snapped his head back. "I did, too."

"No way." I giggled like a school kid. "So, apparently it's a three and a half hour drive between the two places."

"Pffft." Jed gave me a little shove. "Drive? What is this? The '90s? It's under an hour by helicopter."

I arched an eyebrow. "Helicopter? And I suppose you've just got one of those lying around somewhere?"

Jed shot me the cutest naughty smile I'd ever seen. "I don't, but I can arrange for one."

I wasn't giving up so easily. "Won't you be grounded, though?" I reminded him.

Jed tilted his head, pinning me with a look of playful mischief mixed with desire. "I'm used to being grounded, Conrad. Which means, I'm also used to sneaking out."

I tossed my head back and laughed. "I can *soooo* picture you sneaking out and getting into a helicopter. Scary. Isn't it?"

"Why scary?" Jed flicked a loose strand of hair off my forehead.

"Because I feel like I know you so well, but the truth is, we don't know everything about each other. We've really only just met."

"Agreed." Jed mulled my words while his tongue darted across his top lip. "But like you said, you felt something straight away. And I did, too. And I don't think that there are any rules when it comes to love other than following the feeling."

I pressed further into the headboard. "Following the feeling...I like that."

Jed leaned over and kissed my smile. "I don't love you because of the details. Your address. Your middle name. Your favorite color. I just love you—"

Our gazes collided. Holy shit, did he just say...

"Do you mean—"

"I mean it." Jed swallowed so hard I could feel it in my own throat. "I totally mean it. I—I love you, Conrad."

The words whistled in my ears as air vacuumed from my lungs. I closed my eyes and when I opened them, I knew beyond a shadow of a doubt that I meant every word I uttered back to him. "I love you, too, Jed."

He grabbed my head in his hands and we kissed. Hard. Roughly. Like it was the last kiss I'd ever get to enjoy. I devoured his lips, tongue, mouth, but I wanted more. My hands ran up and down his broad chest. I pulled him on top of me, his weight like a protective blanket.

"Hey." He flipped us around so that I was on top of him, and in that moment, the nausea hit again. I felt giddy and lightheaded, and it had nothing to do with the words we'd just exchanged.

I reached for the headboard as Jed gently guided me back to my starting position.

"How are you feeling?" The seriousness in his voice was unmissable.

"Ummm." It was all I could manage to get out of me, the room still spinning like a theme park ride that just wouldn't stop.

"You need a drink."

"I'm fine." It wasn't until I tried to smile that I realized how dry my lips had become. "Okay, maybe some water."

Jed bounced off the bed and raced out of the room. He returned a few moments later and I downed the water in one go. "Do you want some more?" he asked when I finished.

"I'm okay." I shook my head, feeling the tears that were threatening to break through. "I've done it again."

"Done what?" Now his eyebrows pinched together.

"Ruined the moment." I sighed despondently. "I hate that I'm ruining our last night"—I looked across at the time—"actually, technically, our last morning together."

"You're not ruining anything, Conrad." He slid his lengthy fingers across my cheek. "This has been the most amazing few days I've ever had in my life. I wouldn't change a thing."

"Not even the whole 'I'm dying' thing?" I joked meekly.

"Oh, yeah, that part can totally fuck right off."

We smiled and I could see how strong he was being. "It's getting late, or early," I said as I shuffled down the bed and drew the covers over us. "Let's get some rest."

A pensiveness filled the air. "Do you...?"

When he didn't continue, I prodded. "Do I what?"

He rolled over and craned his head over his shoulder. "Do you wanna snuggle me?"

"Do I ever!" And with that, Jed nestled against my body, I did the same with his, and when we were closer than we could possibly be, I raised my arm, looped it under his, and he locked it into place.

"Got ya," he said, letting out a big yawn.

"No," I replied, starting to get drowsy myself. "I've got *you*."

With my chin lodged against his shoulder, I felt Jed's whole body relax as he drifted off to sleep. I wasn't too far behind him, until a gentle vibration stirred me awake.

I looked over him and saw my phone light up. As carefully as I could, I extended my arm out over Jed and grabbed the phone. Snuggling back into his fiery warmth, my heart jumped into my throat and started beating madly in there as I read the text message that was about to change my life forever.

37

JEDFIRE

"Morning, Conrad."

I rolled over and felt nothing but cold sheets. Something about the iciness on my back pierced through my usual ten-minute morning procrastination routine of *should I get out of bed or shouldn't I?* It also stubbed my morning wood out instantly, too.

The hairs on my neck were up and alert. Something was definitely up. I could feel it. Sitting upright while rubbing the sleep out of my eyes, I stole a glance toward the closed en suite door.

Maybe Conrad was in there having a shower? A silent shower in the dark, since no noise or light was coming through underneath the door. "Conrad?" I yelled out into the silent room.

I shot up out of bed and strode across the room to tap on the en suite door. When that didn't elicit a response, I knocked a little louder this time. Okay, he definitely wasn't in there. I swung the door open and yep, no sign of the guy.

I dragged my fingers through my messy hair and flicked on the light switch as I surveyed the room. For what, I had no idea. Nothing seemed out of place. As I was about to let my mind drift to memories of last night and how wonderful it had been, I saw it. Or rather, I didn't see it.

Conrad's phone. It'd been on the nightstand and now it was gone. Somehow, that small fact confirmed a larger one: that he was definitely gone, too.

My insides were filling with panic and...something else. A feeling I couldn't figure out, which I didn't like. Normally, my emotions were pretty black and white. Even when I was doing something wrong, I *knew* that what I was doing was wrong. I felt it. I couldn't lie to save myself. I liked holding doors open for people and remembering my *P's* and *Q's*. All things that neatly fit into a good or bad column.

But not being able to decipher what a feeling that was bubbling inside of me was...that was something new and disconcerting.

I shrugged on whatever clothes I could find lying about and was about to head out the door when Cooper came rushing through it.

"Hey." I jumped back defensively. The guy had scared the living daylights out of me. "I know we're meant to be on vacation, but ever heard of knocking? I could've been naked."

Cooper looked a little out of breath, like he'd just run up the stairs way too fast. "If I wanted to see you naked, Jed, I could just look in a mirror."

It wasn't until he finished his quip that I noticed a piece of paper in his hand. "What's that?"

"A note." He stretched his arm out to pass it to me. "From Conrad."

I swallowed. "Don't worry," he continued, picking up on my vibes. "It's not bad. In fact, it's totally awesome."

I scanned it for myself and practically jumped for joy. "Oh my god, this is wonderful!"

They'd found a donor! Someone from the resort—Conrad's note didn't say who—had been a match.

"It is," Cooper agreed, his eyes sparkling. "He's at the Lower Keys Medical Center. Come on, let's go!"

He didn't have to tell me twice. "Grab your phone and wallet," Cooper reminded me as we bolted toward the door, knowing I'd leave without taking my head if it wasn't permanently attached to me. My brain was totally checked out of my body.

Conrad had been saved! This was the best news ever. My whole body flooded with an endorphin rush like I'd never experienced before.

Conrad was going to be all right.

He was going to live!

The tires screeched into the driveway of the Lower Keys Medical Center and before Cooper had even pulled up, I jumped out of the car and raced through the automatic doors. The hospital was tiny, only three floors, so I was able to find Conrad's room easily.

What I hadn't expected to find was a man sitting out the front, with his face cupped in his hands. He wore all black—boots, denim, shirt, and leather jacket. Despite me coming down the corridor like the Pamplona running of the bulls, the man didn't move or give any recognition of my presence.

"Uh, hello?"

His fingers that were dug into his medium length brown hair with threads of gray through it shifted slightly. A few moments later, he whipped his head up in one sudden movement, revealing a weathered face and bloodshot eyes.

He looked at me. Actually, he looked through me. The guy didn't seem to register that I was there.

"I'm Jedfire Burns." I took a step closer to him.

He cocked his head the second he heard my name.

"The cowbell kid?" His voice was barely more than a rumble.

"Uh, yeah, I guess." Who was this guy? My mind was still not fully with it.

The man got up and to my surprise, he pretty much matched my height.

"Wade McCallister."

Oh, shit. This was Conrad's dad.

"Sir." I returned his finger-crushing handshake as best I could. I didn't even have time to process how unlike Conrad he looked when I blurted out, "How's Conrad?"

The man let go of my hand and scratched the side of his face. "Recovering. And doing well so far. The team is just in there checking up on him, but I think"—his face twisted and he turned away from me—"I think he'll pull through it."

"When did you get here...sir?"

"I flew in yesterday. Had a client, a very rich client, break his surfboard, so he flew me out to Florida to fix it." He smiled as if he couldn't believe the lengths people with money would go to. "It all happened so fast. I didn't even get a chance to tell Conrad I was here. But thank god I was because when I got his voicemail..."

He brought his fist in front of his mouth, trying to control himself. Mr. McCallister may have had a policy of not crying in front of strangers, but I sure as shit didn't. "Conrad's going to live," I exclaimed as my tear banks came crashing down.

And of course, nothing made a better addition to public humiliation than even more public humiliation because that had to be the moment that Cooper, Grandma, and Grandpa all showed up.

"Honey." Grandma wrapped me up in her arms.

"What's going on?" Grandpa's authoritative voice rang out as the door opened and the doctor and two nurses stepped out.

"Good news, I'm happy to report," the doctor said, sporting a wide smile that instantly cut off my waterworks. "Conrad is recovering well. All his vitals are where we want them to be. And if he remains stable and doing this well for the rest of the day, then it looks like a full recovery is on the cards."

It was like air had been let out of a balloon. The relief was palpable. Mr. McCallister's eyes prickled with tears, and Cooper gave Grandpa a big hug, raising the old man off the ground.

"The thing to remember is"—we all twisted to face the doctor as he continued speaking—"Conrad is going to be weak. Very weak. And for a while. We're talking at least four weeks, maybe even up to two months, for him to get back to full strength. And while he does have age on his side, there is no way to rush this healing process. He's had major surgery and he needs rest."

A round of "Absolutelys" and "Got its" filled the air as the medical team left. That was followed by a round of introductions, as my family introduced themselves to Mr. McCallister, who insisted we call him Wade.

"Walter, Cooper honey, how about we go get some food from the cafeteria? It's almost lunch time."

I glanced over and spotted Grandma shooting them both her best let's *leave these two alone* looks.

Cooper draped his arm around Grandma as they left. "Do you think they'll have anything gluten-free here?"

"Oh, honey, please. I was just doing gluten-free because it was trending on Instagram. I need carbs and lots of 'em."

Grandma looked over her shoulder and winked at me. I smiled and waved back at her.

The oh-so-subtle departure of my family wasn't lost on Mr. Mc —Wade.

"You have a nice family." His voice remained deep, but the grumbling was replaced by a smooth, dulcet tone.

"Yeah, they're all right."

I smiled and he tipped his head at me. Sitting beside the man gave me a chance to inspect him a little closer. He really looked nothing like Conrad. He was so manly with a square set jaw, weathered features, and a ruggedness that Conrad just didn't have.

I guessed I must have been examining him a little too closely because Wade turned to me, his lips curved, and said, "He gets his looks from his mother. Her parents were Swedish."

"Ah, got it. Sorry. I didn't mean to stare. It's just—"

His thick hand landed on my knee. "It's okay." Then his jaw bunched up and he pinned me with a serious look. "Conrad's crazy about you."

Even though my mouth was closed, I must have somehow swallowed a fly or something because it became hard to swallow all of a sudden. "He—he told you about me?"

He nodded as a smile stretched his lips. "He did."

I slid back further into the seat, a warm fuzzy feeling vibrating in my chest. Something about Conrad telling his dad about us made me really happy. It's like it solidified what we had, made it even realer.

It dawned on me that I hadn't really spoken to Cooper as much as I would have liked to about my rapidly developing feelings for Conrad. But, in my defense, I had a whole *multiple bombshells I'm trying to defuse* situation going on.

I turned to face Conrad's father and cleared my throat. Nothing like diving into the deep end, right? "I know Conrad and I have only just met. But we both feel something real and deep. And I want to look after him. I told him we're in this together. I meant it then, and I mean it even more now. I want to do everything in my power to help him get better so that we can—"

Somehow I managed to catch myself there, not entirely sure how I planned on finishing that sentence.

The man's heavy hand found my shoulder as he said words that he couldn't have had any clue as to how eerily they echoed his son's. "You're a good kid, Jed."

And just like that, tears cascaded down my cheeks as my head collapsed into my hands. Two wide arms flung around me and *great*, now I was sobbing into the man's chest. Talk about making a memorable first impression. What must the guy have been thinking about me?

As we pulled apart, I didn't see judgment or pity or anything even remotely mean-hearted in his eyes. Instead, I was met with an anguished expression.

"I'm sorry," I blubbered, manically scrubbing away at the tears that had fallen. "I'm not usually like this. I've just been so worried about Conrad."

"I know the feeling." His rich timbre was oddly soothing.

And then the most unexpected thing happened. *He* started crying. So now, not only had my own tear-seal broken, somehow I'd transferred that dubious ability onto him as well.

"Fuck," he growled, angrily wiping away the tears.

"It's okay. We're both stressed out," I said in my best but probably-not-very-good attempt at comforting him.

Taking a few deep breaths, he managed to compose himself. But when he turned to face me, tears still threatened the corners of his eyes. "He's saved me. So many times. And this whole time he's been going through this, I've been powerless to save him in return."

I noticed his hands were trembling, and I thought back to what Conrad had told me about the man's PTSD, the ugly divorce from his Mom, his drinking, and now, his successful sobriety. I took a guess that the regret and shame of it had only been compounded by Conrad's condition. But thankfully, and by some massive miracle, that was something that was behind him now.

"You're here now. And Conrad is going to be okay."

TWO DAYS LATER

38

CONRAD

The first thing I felt was a relentless throbbing at the side of my head. Wait, at the front of my head. Actually, no, my *whole* head was pounding.

Then I felt my eyelids fluttering. But they weren't my normal eyelids. It was as if someone had attached weights onto them because they felt heavy. It was hard to peel them open, but finally, I did.

And when I did, and the initial blurry fuzz sharpened, I saw a rainbow. A moving rainbow. Until my sight honed in better on the shapes and colors lined up against the pale blue wall.

Faces started to come into view.

"Dad," I croaked.

The man leaped to my side, and I felt his familiar hand brushing against my face. "Conrad. You're awake! How are you feeling?"

Wow. That was a lot of words to take in. I managed a nod but nothing else.

"You have to take it easy. Doctor's orders."

I looked up at him, my gaze continuing to pull into better focus.

He looked worried. Actually, he tried to look like he wasn't worried, which was even more concerning.

That's right. I'd had an operation. I was in the hospital. Thoughts were beginning to sift their way through the fogginess in my mind.

"How did it go?"

"Very well. You've been out of it for two days. It's Friday today, and we're still in Florida."

I nodded as I noticed movement behind Dad. Then a face appeared over his shoulder. A face that instantly made me smile and want to reach up and grab it with both hands.

"Jed."

"That's me," he replied as he stood next to my father.

"You're here." I didn't know what made me say that.

"Of course I am." He didn't sound hurt at all. In fact, he sounded...happy.

"He's been here the whole time, Conrad," Dad chipped in. "Hasn't left the room other than to go to the bathroom."

"So, yeah, if you're wondering what that lovely fragrance wafting in the air is..."

I laughed at Jed's joke, and immediately, it felt like my entire torso was being prodded by a thousand razors.

"Whoa, there." Dad's hands reached around me, steadying my movement. "You have to take it easy, son," he repeated.

Okay. So I'd need to work my way up to laughing. Good to know.

With both men directing looks of joy and relief at me, a question popped through the final balloons of haze that lingered in my head. "Who?"

"You mean, the donor?" Jed clarified, and I nodded.

"He's right here," Dad said, and as both he and Jed separated, a figure approached to step in between them.

I let out a strangled cry of disbelief. "Leo!"

"Hey, Conrad. Good to see you."

He was dressed in a white hospital gown and attached to a walking IV drip. "*You* were the match?"

He nodded and replied softly, "Yeah, I was."

A memory came back to me. "Wait. Last time when I saw you to thank you for everything, you said you had to leave and do something you didn't want to do..."

He picked up where I left off. "I suffer from trypanophobia."

"Try-pano-what?" I heard Jed cry out from behind Leo's frame.

I smiled. No pain. Okay, smiling was allowed. Noted.

"What's try-pano-whatever-you-said?"

He simpered. "Fear of needles. I can't"—his face distorted—"I can't even think about them without feeling all gross and disgusting."

I felt a warm tear falling down my face. "And despite that, you still did what you did for me."

"What can I say?" He brushed down my arm affectionately. "I really want that five star review on TripAdvisor."

That made me laugh, and again, the fierce pain returned.

"Shit, I'm sorry." Worry skated across Leo's face as I straightened myself out.

"It's my fault," I replied, grinning as the pain subsided a bit. "I need to have fewer funny people in my life."

"I should probably go back to my room. I'm checking out later today. I'll leave you with your family."

I smiled as he waved, and I remarked to myself that he'd only said family and not friends.

As he left, guided by a nurse who had been waiting in the corner, I noticed three other people lined against the wall. Cooper and Jed's grandparents.

"Hey, you," Cooper said, walking up to the bed and flashing a brilliant smile. It was still a little surreal seeing him right next to Jed. The double sight of them made the lightheadedness that was starting to leave me return again.

"We're going to go now, honey." Jed's grandma smiled, leaning over the bed as she grazed my forearm with her soft fingers. "We just want you to know that you've been in our prayers and we are overjoyed for you."

"Thank you."

What else was there to say? I couldn't believe that we'd found a donor and that I would actually...live.

"I might go grab a coffee," Dad announced as he gave my hand a tight squeeze. "I'll leave you two alone."

Once the room had emptied, Jed pulled a chair toward the bed, sat down, and melted his fingers into mine. Before either one of us could say or do anything, I burst out into tears.

"Oh my gosh, Conrad. What's wrong?" He got to his feet so fast the chair fell to the ground behind him with a noisy bang. "Are you hurt? Or sore? Should I go get help?"

The flood of emotions that had burst through and overwhelmed me started to subside a bit. "These are happy tears," I managed to get out in between sobs.

Relief washed over his features as he gathered the chair and sat back down again. I wiped the tears away and turned my attention to the gorgeous, wild, crazy creature gazing up at me, with nothing but what looked like love in his eyes.

But was it...? My memory wasn't entirely all back. Had we just had those five days at Elysian or had I imagined the whole thing?

"Just before I came to," I started saying. "I had a dream."

"Oh." He sidled up even closer to me.

"I was dreaming about you, about us, and when I woke up, I thought—I thought that I'd dreamt you. But you're real."

"I am, Conrad." He leaned down and peppered the back of my hand with a thousand sweet kisses. "I am so real."

"So it wasn't a dream when you told me you loved me?"

Two of the most sincere eyes I'd ever looked into held my gaze. "No, it wasn't."

"I, uh, might need to hear it again."

He jumped to his feet, a little more carefully this time. "I'll jump up onto the roof of this fucking building and scream it so the whole world knows," he declared proudly, before turning to me, clutching his heart and saying the most magical sounding words, "I love you, Conrad McCallister."

A delicious heat infused every cell of my body, and it had nothing to do with what was coming out of the machines I was hooked up to. "I love you, too, Jedfire Burns."

EPILOGUE 1 - JEDFIRE

SIX MONTHS LATER...

I peered through the heavy navy blue drapes and grimaced. Yikes, there were a lot of people here at the Cowbell Creek Convention and Cow-Mating Center. (Don't worry. First dates only. The actual mating took place twenty miles north on a field under a full moon. Cowbell Creek's bovine-mating rituals went way back and were a very long and intricate story.)

My tension eased considerably when a pair of soft hands and a sigh of warm breath hit the back of my neck. Turning around, I was met with what I was strongly petitioning to be made the eighth wonder of the natural world: a healthy, beaming Conrad McCallister smiling right at me.

He flung both arms over my shoulders and looked up at me with glitter in his eyes. "I am so proud of you." He was beaming, which made me uncomfortable, but I knew better than to ask a question in return.

This whole *learning to accept a compliment thing* was still new to me, but I was learning.

"I'm kinda freaking out," I admitted to him as I craned my head back around. "Everyone's here, the entire *who's who* of the cowbell media industry. *Cowbell Living*, *Cowbell Digest*, *Cowbell Housekeeping*, *Cowbell Weekly*. Even *Cowbell People* sent a reporter."

Conrad cupped my face and drew my attention back to him. "Hey. Relax. You got this." Then his eyes dropped to the ground, before returning to me. "I made sure *Cowbell People* were invited. If this doesn't put you into contention for Sexiest Man Alive, then I don't know what will."

"My ears are burning," Cooper announced, walking up behind us with a smug grin on his face.

I tried to level a sneer at him, but how could I? How could I ever be mad at my baby twin brother after what he'd done to—literally—save Conrad's life?

Conrad loosened his grip around me and faced Cooper. "Hey, a random thought popped into my head this morning as I was brushing my teeth."

"Ooh, do tell," Cooper practically squealed as his eyes lit up. I loved that he got on so well with Conrad. And my grandparents adored him. And everyone in Cowbell Creek instantly fell under his spell as they got to know him, ever since he moved in with us at the family ranch after we flew back from Florida. Not that anyone else's approval was needed, but man, it felt so damn good that it was unfolding how it was.

"Well," Conrad began, grabbing Cooper's forearm excitedly, before his expression turned serious. "I realized I never thanked you."

Cooper's eyebrows waggled, but it wasn't anywhere near as adorable as when I did it. According to Conrad, that was.

"Thanked me for what?"

"You know," Conrad said, looking almost a little sheepish. "If you hadn't told all of Cowbell Creek about my condition and worked with Leo to set up the medical center at Elysian, I wouldn't—"

Cooper pulled him into a tight embrace before he could finish that ugly sentence. "You don't have to thank me for anything, Conrad," Cooper said with a wide smile, hugging Conrad but staring right at me. "You brought Jed back home. And every day I get to spend running the family plant with my big bro is all the thanks I need."

"Oh, Cooper." I wrapped my arms around both my brother and my boyfriend. Yeah, I never got tired of that word. Although, I had been making some plans for a slight, er, upgrade.

Cooper's sentiment hit me right in the middle of my chest. I'd always thought that coming back home and fulfilling my familial obligations would be a death sentence. A kind of hellish torture that I had no way of escaping.

But the crazy thing was—I felt happier than ever being back home and running the latest division of the plant we were unveiling today.

Grandma's advice as I bawled on the bed with her at Elysian had stuck in my mind. I hadn't been living my life by getting into crazy adventures and jet setting all over the world. Partying like crazy. Doing every extreme activity ever invented. Getting married in Vegas...twice.

That wasn't living life. That was running away from it. I'd been a soul without a purpose, drifting aimlessly. But not anymore.

There was a beauty in simplicity, in living a life that meant something. I saw that now. It's what Conrad and I had been doing and talking about while I helped nurse him back to health and full strength.

It was something I was determined to continue for the rest of our lives together.

(Side note #1—Tommy tracked down the unlucky groom I'd married in Vegas. Luckily for me, he had close to zero recollection of our time together either. He only vaguely remembered that our night together involved lots of coconut tequila shots, an Uber ride that somehow detoured into an Elvis chapel drive-through, and thankfully, no sex when we got back to his place and crashed. The marriage was annulled without a hitch.)

(Side note #2—I 'fessed up to my family about my ATM shenanigans. At my request, Tommy arranged a meeting with the chief financial officer of my bank. I told them everything I'd been doing. It wasn't an easy decision. I knew that there was a very good chance they'd call the cops and my ass would land in jail. But I also wanted to do the right thing, and like that morning when I woke up in Florida and Conrad wasn't in bed with me, I carried this weird, unknowable feeling around with me leading up to the meeting with the bank.

As it turned out, they had no idea about the glitch. Their response didn't surprise me. What did surprise me was their reaction and their decision not to press charges. Turned out, if this ever got out, it would severely harm their reputation, severely compromise their *judiciary insurance risk profile,* and expose them to litigation by the Federal Deposit Insurance Corporation. Yeah, I had no idea what any of that meant either. I'd stopped listening after they said they weren't taking the matter any further.

They were so desperate to have nothing to do with me that they were even happy for me to keep the money I'd already taken out. So, while Conrad recovered from his surgery, the two of us would read about charities that needed help. (Something about dispersing just under seven million dollars proved to be the best kind of healing...for both of us.)

"Jed. Jedfire, hey!" Cooper snapped his fingers in front of my face.

"What?" I shot back.

"You're on." He tipped his head toward the stage. Fuck. I was.

"You'll be great, Jed. I am so proud of you," Conrad whispered into my ear as he pulled me in for a quick last-minute hug before gently, yet firmly, pushing me toward the stage.

I stole one quick glance over my shoulder, watching as Conrad and Cooper scurried around to get to their seats in the audience for the grand announcement. It wasn't hard at all to set my face to beaming. All I had to do was think about how wonderful my life had become ever since the night Conrad came into it.

As the applause grew louder in my ears, I confidently strode across the stage, shook my grandfather's hand, adjusted the mic height on the podium, and took a deep breath in, ready to address the crowd.

EPILOGUE 2 - CONRAD

Cooper and I managed to shuffle into our front row seats while the applause for Jed continued. I slipped into the chair right next to my dad, who shot me a warm yet relieved smile.

He leaned my way. "I was starting to think you were going to miss it."

"I wouldn't miss this for the world."

My heart was so happy it felt like it would burst out of my chest. I couldn't believe how awesome this day would be and what Jed was going to announce, but even if it was raining and cold and miserable—heck, even if Trump was still the goddamn president—I would have been the happiest person on the planet.

Why?

Because I was *ALIVE!*

Nothing wakes you up to the beauty and sacredness of each and every moment of each and every day like a *you only have one year left to live* diagnosis. Take my word on that one.

The first thing I did every morning when I opened my eyes was think to myself, *Thank God I'm alive.*

The second thing I did was kiss Jed's shoulder and thank God for him.

Every moment we had spent together in Florida was special and something I wanted to capture and store in a time machine, so that the memories would never fade. From his opening line on the terrace of the bar, to our hike, to meeting his wonderful family— Cooper, thinking it was actually Jed, and the image of his grandmother in the pool (well, that was seared into the time machine memory vault whether I liked it or not)—to waking up at the hospital and hearing that he'd been by my side the whole time.

I knew that the five days we'd spent together there wasn't a whole heap of time in the scheme of things. We didn't know a lot about each other, but the feelings we had developed were so strong and so intense that we both just *knew* on a deeper level that we had found something special. And over the last six months, that bond, the connection, and that one-in-a-billion love that we shared only deepened with each passing day.

I knew Dad was a little disappointed that I hadn't moved back in with him. But he also trusted that Jed was a good person and would look after me like he'd promised. Dad and I would always be close. He was such an important part of my life.

We still got to see each other every second weekend. Dad would drive up to Cowbell Creek once a month, and then we'd helicopter down to him in San Clemente two weeks later. Dad had even made Jed a custom-sized surfboard, and I had started giving Jed surfing lessons. For someone of his height, he was picking it up remarkably well. He even managed to stand up on the board after only a few tries. The smile on his face when he did was priceless.

More than anything though, Dad wanted me to actually live my life. I didn't regret giving up the things I had for him. I would do it all again in a heartbeat. I loved my father with all of my heart and we would always be there for each other, through thick and thin.

But the diagnosis had shown me the truth to some words that

got flung around a lot but were rarely considered as deeply as they deserved to be.

Life was short, time precious. You had to get involved, do stuff. It didn't matter what, just get out there and live life. We couldn't sit life out on the sidelines and let it pass us by.

Good thing then, that I was dating someone who grabbed life by both of his massive hands and squeezed every last juicy drop of goodness out of it.

I settled into my seat as Jed began speaking, starting off with a round of the usual thank yous and acknowledgements. After a short while, he got to the heart of the matter, why we had all gathered here.

I'd heard him rehearse this speech all week as he paced up and down the bedroom before bed, but the words still brought tears to my eyes. The speech was one hundred percent Jedfire Burns: honest, raw, and magnificently unforgettable.

As many of you know, over six years ago, my parents were murdered in an act of senseless gun violence. I honestly don't know if my family or I will ever truly recover from the pain and heartache of losing them in such a horrific way.

One thing I do know my parents wanted is for their children, Cooper, Mitchell, and me, to continue their work through a plant that has been in our family for seven generations.

To be honest with you, that thought didn't exactly thrill me.

A polite hushed laughter rang out through the audience.

As some of you know, I may have gone through a few rebellious years.

"A few?" Cooper shouted, and this time, the crowd laughed a whole lot louder.

Okay, it's been a wild ride.

I giggled, loving the way he blushed when he said that and the fiery look he sent my way while saying it.

But I'm here. I'm back in my hometown and running the plant with my brother, Cooper. He has the title of Managing Director, and his responsibilities include oversight of all as-is functions. Our manufacturing division, supply chain logistics, finance, HR, as well as the R&B and hip-hop departments.

My younger brother Mitchell is continuing his great work looking after daily operations and supporting Cooper and me tremendously. You might not see or hear much from him, but he is the secret ingredient of our success sauce.

Which may leave you wondering just what it is that I'll be doing. And that's why we have asked you here today.

My parents may have wanted us to continue their work, but I wanted to go further than that. Do more. Make them even prouder of us than what I know they would be if they were sitting with us here today. That's why I will be spearheading not just a body of work, but what I hope will be a long, lasting and fruitful legacy in their honor.

Ladies and gentlemen, it is my great honor to announce the launch of our brand new R&D Division.

With that, Jed's grandpa and Cooper pulled the strings to reveal a stone and glass plaque. Sounds of cameras snapping and applause filled the air.

He announced a few of the initial focus areas for the division—fighting climate change thorough developing leading-edge bovine methane capturing technology, addressing animal welfare concerns by increasing research into aural and vibrational impacts on cattle, and starting an online awareness campaign for the use of authentic cowbell sounds in the music industry—and then it was over.

He fielded a few questions, before exiting the stage, flashing me a not so subtle look—yes, one that involved the borderline criminally cute waggling of eyebrows—as he tapped at his watch.

I blew out a deep breath and gave Dad a hug. He did that thing where he was clearly worried but trying to act like he wasn't. It never worked and I could always see right through it, but I appreciated the effort anyway.

"It'll be fine," I said reassuring him. "It's just a routine six month checkup."

"Everything with your recovery is going perfectly," Dr. Weissman said, taking off his thin-rimmed silver glasses. "All your blood work is showing us exactly what we want to be seeing, your vital signs are strong, and from what you've been telling us, your energy levels have returned to peak condition."

"So...?" Jed leaned forward, not needing to finish the question he'd asked at every one of my monthly checkups. Dr. Weissman shot him a knowing smile.

"Yes, Jedfire. You have my all-clear to travel."

Jed bellowed out a *woo-hoo* that I was sure half the ward heard, followed by some fist pumps, and then he planted a few sloppy kisses all over my face.

I cleared my throat and angled my head at the amused doctor sitting across the table from us.

"Just make sure to be on the lookout for anything out of the ordinary, okay? And if anything does come up, please let us know.

Otherwise, we'll see you back here in six months, Conrad, and then we can swap it out to annual visits."

We both hugged Dr. Weissman before leaving and I felt like I was walking on air. The nightmare was over, and we were finally on the other side of it.

We had our whole lives ahead of us, and it didn't take an Einstein to see that Jed had some travel plans in our future. What they were, though, I still had no idea.

And he stayed stubbornly quiet the whole car ride back to the ranch. In fact, he didn't say a word until he walked me to his grandpa's library. He sat me down at one end of the tan Chesterfield, walked over to the mantle above the fireplace, and returned holding a vintage brass antique armillary globe.

"So, let me guess, you're just gonna spin that thing and wherever your finger lands, that's where we're gonna go?" I offered.

A smirk curled the corners of his lips. "Sure. Let's go with that."

Before I could say anything else, Jed scooted over to me so that our legs touched. Carefully—and in a way overexaggerated motion —he raised his arm as if it was taking all of his strength to spin the globe. It spun like crazy, but then Jed stopped it with his index and middle fingers, before walking them across Asia, over the Indian Ocean, and landing in what looked like the middle of nowhere in the northwestern part of Australia.

"Oh, would you look at that?" He clutched at his chest in mock surprise as he stared at where his fingers had landed. "Where on earth have my fingers landed without me doing it on purpose at all?" His voice was in an octave range that would have made Mariah Carey proud.

I peered down closer, then snapped my head back. "Oh my god. You mean it?"

He nodded as his whole face lit up. "Yep. The trip is all booked for next month. We're going Down Under, baby!"

∾

ONE MONTH LATER...

Clop!

"Father fuck!"

"Jed!"

"Sorry, sorry, sorry," Jed apologized for swearing to the pilot sitting in front of us while rubbing the side of his head he'd bumped against the roof of the helicopter as he got in.

"She'll be right, mate," the pilot, Steve, hollered over his shoulder. "You can swear your arse off for all I care."

"Thank you, Steve." I shot the man a nervous smile before turning my attention to Jed. "You okay?"

"I'll be fine," Jed replied, still massaging the top left side of his head.

He didn't seem fine. In fact, all morning he'd been acting jittery and out of sorts.

We'd arrived in Australia four days ago. We'd spent the first two days taking in the sights and hitting up all the tourist hotspots in Sydney—the Opera House, the bridge, the zoo, and the beaches. Then we hopped on a three and a half hour flight to the middle of the country, landing in Uluru yesterday afternoon.

By the early evening, we were having the most romantic dinner with an incredible backdrop of a rock. That's right, a rock.

Oh, sorry, I should've mentioned it wasn't just any rock. It had formed over five hundred and fifty million years ago and it just so happened to be the largest rock in the world. Or at least, that's what I thought until the server informed us that Uluru wasn't the largest rock in the world. It wasn't even the largest rock in Australia.

(That honor went to Mount Augustus in Western Australia, which was apparently over double the size of the rock that served as our unofficial dining companion.)

That morning, we jumped on a chartered flight and made our way northwest to...the Bungle Bungles!

I had to skip Australia during my five month world travels mainly for financial reasons. I'd already stretched my tiny budget to the max, and when I looked into it, coming to Australia and seeing some of the sights like the Great Barrier Reef, even Uluru, wasn't exactly in the budget travel realm.

So, of course, this was the number one place Jed wanted to bring me as soon as I had gotten the all-clear to travel. He'd been practically bursting out of his skin all month leading up to the trip. Then, in Sydney and again last night, he'd been...subdued. That was an alarm bell. Jedfire Burns was a lot of words, but subdued was not one of them.

And ever since we got off the chartered flight at Purnululu Airport and boarded the chartered helicopter we were now seated in, he'd been practically shaking with...nerves? No. That didn't make any sense.

"Ready to take off, fellas?"

"Sure thing, Steve," Jed answered, mustering a smile as I snuggled into him. I eyed his face, and he didn't seem to be bruising, so that was a good thing.

Only a few moments after lifting off, we were gazing down at one of the world's most fascinating geological landmarks. The Bungle Bungles were beehive-shaped rock formations that had a distinct orange-and-black-ringed pattern running all down their surface.

"It looks like something from another planet," Jed observed, his eyes gleaming at the wonder underneath us.

It did. It looked so otherworldly, so distinct. It was so much better than I ever could have imagined.

"Thank you for this trip," I said, shuffling as close as I could to him.

He reached out his hand and I grabbed onto...a clammy palm and a whole bunch of dewy fingers. I tore my eyes away from the view for a moment and studied his face. Beads of sweat had formed across his forehead. Even his messy hair looked kinda damp. Sure, Australia was hot, but this was something else entirely.

"Don't tell me you're afraid of being in a helicopter, Jedfire Burns," I teased. "You base-jumped off mountains in Japan and I think you hold the world record for skydiving, right?"

My goal had been to lighten the mood. It didn't work.

Jed kept staring down. Yes, the view was amazing, but I got the distinct impression that he was deliberately avoiding looking at me for some reason.

"What can I say?" he muttered, eyes transfixed out the window. "Helicopters freak me out."

Jed was still a terrible liar and I wasn't buying it. We flew down to see my dad in one of these every month. But whatever it was that was bugging him, I'd take it up with him later. Right now, I had some of the most amazing natural scenery in the world to take in.

At least, that's what I tried to do.

Jed had been tapping his foot since we got into the chopper. But the more time we were up in the air, the more he shook. And since feeling every vibration of his foot was more than just a little distracting, I twisted in my seat to face him and was just about to say something when...

Jed turned his head to the side, his eyes meeting mine, and he gave me his best James Dean look. "*L is for the way you look at me...*"

Huh? His voice was low and calm-ish, but those words. They sounded familiar—where were they from? Just as I was about to answer my own question, remembering Jed's grandma's rendition of the Frank Sinatra classic, Jed unbuckled his belt and stood up.

"*O,*" he said as he straightened up, but as he did, he smacked his head against the roof of the chopper. Frank's *O* now became Jed's "Oh fuck!" as he lost his balance and whatever he'd been holding in his hand—I didn't get a good look at it, but it looked small and black—slipped out of his fingers and out the window.

"Oh my god, Jed, what was that?"

Jed angled his body, twisted around, and slumped back into his seat, his eyes wider than I'd ever seen them in a very long time.

"An engagement ring."

Okay, now I was starting to feel dizzy and like I was about to lose *my* balance. Turning away from him, I pressed my forehead against the window and looked down. Shit. The chances of finding it were...

"You're a smart guy, Conrad." Jed's voice sounded all sorts of shocked, dazed, and confused. "Can you apply a Fermi problem to our chances of finding the ring?"

My mind scrambled. I knew there was an answer. There had to be. It would have involved figuring out our speed and altitude, location, and the size and weight of...the ring.

That's when all problem-solving thoughts screeched to a complete halt and my heart fell over itself in my chest.

Wait. An engagement ring. *Jed was going to propose!*

Steve had been quiet all this time, but he hadn't missed any of the action going on back here.

"There's a clearing down the way there, fellas. I can drop you down. You can have a look for it and have a picnic that came as part of the package you've booked, while I go back to base to refuel."

"That sounds good," Jed muttered, his whole face still suspended in disbelief.

I slid my fingers into Jed's now even clammier hand. "So...engagement ring."

He sat up taller, his eyes registering signs of life as he smiled sheepishly at me. "Yeah. Thought tying it into our song would be kinda cool. Guess I blew it, huh?"

"Not at all," I said a little too eagerly.

Hey, I wanted to spend the rest of my life with this incredible guy, not parade about some piece of gold on my finger.

He held my stare "What? You—you still want me to ask you?"

"Hell yeah, I do," I retorted as I folded my arms across my chest and lifted my chin. "Beyonce was wrong. You don't have to put a ring on it, but you gotta ask the damn question."

Tears welled in his eyes as he went to unbuckle his seatbelt again.

"Just stay strapped in please." I placed my hand protectively across his chest. "It's bad enough we lost an engagement ring. I don't want you falling out of this thing, too."

With a low chuckle, he gathered me in close. And as we circled the clear blue Aussie sky around the Bungle Bungles, Jed pressed a kiss to my hand, and with glossy whiskey eyes, asked me, "Conrad McCallister, will you do me the honor of marrying me?"

Let's just say you didn't need to be a Fermi-solving genius to figure out my immediate answer.

THE END

~

What's next for Casey Cox?
Get the latest buzz, a FREE prequel novella to the ESCAPE series, and exclusive behind-the-scenes author sneak peeks.

CLICK HERE to get the goodies!

MESSAGE FROM CASEY

Thank you so much for reading *Runaway: An Escape Novel*.

This has to be my wildest story yet. But I can't let my overactive imagination take all the credit. The ATM hack? That really happened. And of course, it was a fellow Aussie who did it. So there you go!

Can I ask a small favor? If you enjoyed the book, would you mind leaving a short review on Amazon? It really helps me out because reviews help other readers decide whether the book is right for them.

Happy reading!
Casey, xo

ABOUT CASEY COX

Casey Cox is devoted to delighting readers with contemporary MM romance stories that are unique, thoughtful and funny. Casey's books are great to read if you're looking for something sweet and smart, with a side of sass, and a small helping of sexy!

Casey lives on the east coast of Australia, loves the beach and is a proud fur-parent to two utterly adorable, perfectly-perfect French Bulldogs named Ralphie and Lilly.

For more information, please visit
www.caseycoxbooks.com